I0748290

Louise's Christmas Champion

THE BOOKSHOP BELLES
BOOK THREE

CATHERINE BILSON

EBONY OATEN

Content Advisory

- Emotional abuse from relatives
- Arson
- Battle scenes, minor character death and broken bones
- Rampant unfairness and sexism because women were considered second-class citizens
- Cats breeding uncontrollably as desexing pets had not been invented

We also advise people not to take any of the herbal remedies mentioned in these books. While some might work, they are not always reliable and indeed the quantities and efficacies would vary from person to person. Please do not constitute anything in these books as medical advice.

CHAPTER 1
Louise In Charge

Hertfordshire, 1814

L ouise Baxter, second-to-youngest but indisputably the tallest—and certainly the most capable, at least in her own opinion—of the four Baxter sisters, stood at the edge of the muddy roadway. She waved a brisk farewell as the post-coach carrying her sister Marie rattled away, its wheels kicking up dirty clumps of earth that speckled her boots and hem. The coach was bound for the north, and with each lurch and sway, it carried Marie further along the first leg of her long journey to Cumbria. Louise kept her posture erect, her shoulders squared, and her chin tilted high, determined to appear resolute until the coach disappeared entirely from sight. She owed her sister that much, at least.

Only when the coach vanished around a bend in the road did Louise allow her shoulders to slump. A sigh, long and heavy, escaped her lips as though it had been bottled up there for hours.

"What a lot of work this is going to be," she muttered,

1

turning towards her youngest sister, Bernadette, who stood at her side. The two of them were ankle-deep in the muck of the roadway, the cold damp seeping through their sturdy boots.

"She had to go," Bernadette pointed out practically. Her tone was light, even if her expression was not. Together, they trudged back toward Baxter's Fine Books, the family business that had consumed nearly every moment of their lives since they were old enough to dust shelves and arrange displays. Before stepping inside, they paused at the bootscraper outside the Red Lion Inn next door, scraping away the worst of the mud with practiced efficiency.

"The Earl of Demanding ordered nearly a hundred and fifty pounds' worth of books," Bernadette continued, shaking her skirts free of mud droplets. "But, we had to deliver them personally."

"He thought he was writing to our father!" Louise's voice took on a sharp, frustrated edge, her words clipped as though she were biting them off before they could escape entirely. "I hope he still pays up when it's Marie who turns up on his doorstep!"

"Oh, don't be such a worrywart," Bernadette chided. "He's getting his books, isn't he? It's not as though we've shortchanged him. Marie will charm him, no doubt, and she'll be back in time for Christmas—with her pockets jingling full of coin."

Louise gave an exasperated snort. "And in the meantime, we're left to do all the work!" Her boots thudded against the floorboards as they stepped inside the shop and closed the door, shutting the cold and damp outside.

It wasn't just Marie's absence that weighed on her. They were already one sister down, with their eldest, Estelle, having married Mr Yates and gone off to Ireland to visit his mother. Estelle wouldn't return until spring at the earliest.

Still, as Louise glanced around the bookshop, her irritation softened into something warmer. The shop felt like home, as it always had. It smelled of musty paper and old leather, a scent she thought might linger in her memory forever, underpinned with the sharp, tangy notes of fresh glue. The light filtering in through the windows was scant, most of the panes long since covered over with bookshelves crammed to bursting. Instead, the shop's many corners and nooks were illuminated by carefully shielded oil lamps hanging from beams and mounted in strategic locations. Their golden glow brought the shelves and stacks to life, casting shadows that danced across the walls.

Ruth Millings, their young assistant, was busily sweeping the floor when Louise and Bernadette entered. Her father, the fiery Reverend Silas Millings—known privately among the Baxter sisters as "Old Brimstone"—had made it abundantly clear that Ruth was to behave with the utmost propriety. Ruth had only been permitted to take the job on the condition that her wages went directly into the church's collection plate each Sunday.

"I didn't go behind the counter yet," Ruth said tentatively as Louise and Bernadette peeled off their coats. Her voice was soft, almost apologetic, and her hands tightened nervously around the broom handle.

"That's all right," Louise replied with a reassuring smile. "I'll take care of it."

She fetched the small dustpan, scraper, and rags they kept specifically for this task and stepped behind the counter. There, waiting as always, was the morning's 'gift' from Crafty, the bookshop's resident cat.

Crafty, whose full name was Wollstonecraft when she was in serious trouble, had been a vital member of the shop's operations for years. She was a skilled huntress, keeping the mice that threatened to nibble at the book paper firmly in check. However, her habit of leaving partially eviscerated 'presents' for her mistresses behind the counter was less than endearing. Recently, her son Pie—a young cat with his mother's talent for hunting but none of her discretion—had joined in the habit, doubling the number of unpleasant surprises Louise had to clean up each day.

"Ugh, Crafty," Louise muttered, wrinkling her nose as she scraped up the offending mess and took it outside to bury in the midden. "And Pie, too! Between the two of you, I'm not even sure the mice are worth it."

Once the floor behind the counter was clean, Louise washed her hands, dried them briskly on her apron, and returned to her post. This had once been Estelle's regular domain, then Marie's. Now, with both of them gone, Louise and Bernadette took turns managing the counter.

The bell above the door jingled, and Louise glanced up, expecting a customer. Instead, it was Rosie, the young maid Mr. Yates had hired for them before taking Estelle away to Ireland. Rosie helped Mrs. Poole, the housekeeper, with the cooking, cleaning, and laundry, which freed the sisters from the household chores they had previously split amongst themselves.

"Good morning, Rosie," Louise said warmly. "Mrs. Poole will be glad to see you when you go on upstairs."

Rosie bobbed a quick curtsey, her cheeks pink, before scurrying off toward the staircase. Louise's gaze lingered on her for a moment, and she felt a pang of envy. How nice it would be to escape upstairs herself, to the quiet sanctum of her bookbinding workshop! There were several projects waiting for her attention —books with cracked spines and fragile pages that needed careful rebinding. It was work she enjoyed, work that required focus and precision, and she longed to lose herself in it.

But someone had to keep an eye on the customers, and Bernadette was busy this morning, out visiting women who needed her herbal expertise. So Louise stayed put behind the counter, ready to greet the steady trickle of patrons who would inevitably wander in.

A steady flow of customers came into the shop, and then young Brutus Baxter arrived. The middle son of their cousins, he was a nice boy afflicted with a terrible name courtesy of his awful parents. He spent time in the bookshop to escape his home, where he was neglected by his parents and bullied by his dreadful older brother.

"Any books to bind today, Cousin Louise?" Brutus asked eagerly. He was showing an interest in book-binding, and Louise was happy to teach him the craft.

"Indeed." Louise thought about it. There were quite a few tasks they might be able to do at the counter, especially with Brutus to be an extra pair of hands. "Mind the counter for a moment. I'll go and fetch down some things."

Mrs Poole came down the stairs, bubbling over with excitement. "You'll not believe what I've just heard from Rosie, Louise!"

"I probably would not, no," Louise agreed dryly. The maid barely ever said a word in Louise's hearing but seemed to be full of Hatfield gossip for Mrs Poole.

"There's been a fire!"

"A blocked chimney or something?" Louise asked,

without much interest. Fires weren't exactly uncommon in the winter; everyone needed fires for heat!

"No, deliberately lit!"

Now that *was* newsworthy. Louise gave Mrs Poole her full attention. "Where? Did they catch the culprit?"

"You know that little cottage on the St Albans road, the one just out of town, with the roof falling in?"

Louise did not, in fact, know the cottage. Bernadette was the one who went tramping all over the place visiting people with her herbs; Louise preferred to stay closer to home. But she nodded, because otherwise Mrs Poole would spend all day trying to make her think she did know it.

"Well, nobody lives there now of course, it's not fit, but some of the returned soldiers were sleeping rough there." Mrs Poole made a bit of a face.

They were very grateful to the brave soldiers who had defeated Napoleon and thwarted the looming threat of the French, of course, but there did seem to be somehow more of them hanging around Hatfield than had ever left to go off to war. Certainly more of them than were jobs for men during the winter. Louise didn't quite understand why they didn't go back to wherever it was they'd originally come from, or to towns who'd lost a lot of their men in the fighting.

"Was it one of the soldiers who set the fire?" she asked, though she wasn't sure who'd be silly enough to set fire to a building they were trying to live in.

"No! They woke up in the night to someone throwing a lamp in at them! It smashed and lit fire to the straw they were sleeping on, so they had to get out in a hurry. Lucky nobody was burned!" Mrs Poole nodded wisely.

"It seems like perhaps the culprit is someone who didn't

6

want the soldiers here," Louise suggested. "That seems the most obvious motive."

"Listen to you, talking about culprits and motives! Have you been reading novels about murderers again?"

Louise pretended she hadn't heard the question. She did have rather a penchant for novels, the more thrilling the better, and she had a particular weakness for a novel with a good murder to solve. "I hope the returned soldiers find somewhere better to sleep," she said.

Unable to excite her to further speculation over the fire, Mrs Poole left to find someone better to gossip with, and Louise returned to work.

"What are we doing, Cousin Louise?" Brutus asked excitedly as she put down her supplies on the counter.

"Yet another set of Shakespeare folios, I'm afraid," she said. "If I never see another set, it will be too soon. Every aspiring gentleman seems to think it an essential addition to his library."

"The colour's nice," Brutus said, running gentle fingers over the green-dyed calfskin.

"Yes, and being calfskin, it's not cheap, so we need to do a good job with it, with as little waste as possible. Let's get measuring and cutting…"

"Measure twice and cut once," Brutus said in a sing-song fashion, making Louise smile.

"An excellent motto, I'm glad you've been listening to my instructions!"

They busied themselves with the work, Ruth handling the customers who came in unless they wanted something out of the ordinary or required recommendations.

Bernadette returned in the early afternoon with a basket full of food items folk had given her in trade for her herbs, so they sat down and feasted on fresh crusty bread with butter and honey.

"Would you mind very much if I went back out this afternoon instead of working the counter?" Bernadette asked hopefully, eyeing the neat piles of cut green calfskin on the desk. "I still have some people I'd like to see…"

Louise nodded. "Go on, so long as you're back by closing to help me add up the accounts. You know they make my head hurt. Brutus and I are going to start sewing the sections to the bands this afternoon."

Brutus looked quite excited that she was going to let him help with this specific task, which could be quite tricky and required accuracy. Louise smiled fondly at him as Bernadette scooped her basket up and took it back upstairs to refill.

Soon after Bernadette left again, Benjamin Baxter barged in with the air of someone who believed the world owed him deference, immediately setting his sights on Brutus.

Louise had been in the middle of clamping one of the folios behind the counter when she overheard Benjamin's jeering tone. She looked up to see Brutus shrinking back, his face pale, while Ruth stood frozen nearby, her expression caught somewhere between embarrassment and dread. With a few sharp words, Benjamin had managed to turn the air in the shop sour, his insults aimed at his brother before pivoting to Ruth with a sly tone.

Louise wasn't even entirely sure what some of the words Benjamin said next even meant—though the suggestive tone made their nature clear enough—but she knew they were entirely inappropriate. Without a second thought, she seized the broom leaning against the counter and marched toward him.

"Out," she barked, holding the broom like a soldier

might hold a bayonet. "This is a bookshop, Benjamin, not a tavern—and certainly not a place for such foul language."

Benjamin's retort was cut short as Louise raised the broom an inch higher, her expression leaving no room for argument. "Would you like me to tell your father what you said to Ruth? Or should I let Reverend Millings hear it first?" she asked, her voice cold and clipped. She gave the broom a small, purposeful jab forward. "Out."

Benjamin's bravado crumbled in the face of her sternness. With a muttered curse, he backed toward the door.

"You'll regret this," he said, but his attempt at menace fell flat as Louise advanced another step.

"I sincerely doubt that," she replied.

As the door swung shut behind him, Louise gave it an extra push for good measure. "And stay out!" she called after him, before turning back to Ruth and Brutus. She sighed, setting the broom aside. "Dreadful behaviour," she muttered, shaking her head.

Ruth, still standing near the shelves, wiped away a silent tear.

"Are you all right?" Louise asked, her voice softening.

The girl nodded quickly, though her hands twisted nervously in her apron. "Yes, thank you, Miss Baxter. You were jolly brave, standing up to him like that!"

"Spiffing," Brutus chimed in, his wide-eyed admiration making Louise chuckle despite herself.

"Most bullies will back down if you stand up to them," Louise said, her tone firm but encouraging. She glanced at Ruth, appraising her carefully. The girl was sweet-natured, but far too timid. "And a firmly wielded broom—or a correctly applied knee—can make even the more stubborn ones reconsider."

9

Several days later, the weather had turned utterly foul, heavy rain intermixed with sleet. It was so wet that the fire in the small stove in the centre of the shop - safely set far away from any bookshelves - went out in the middle of the afternoon.

"I'll clean the grate," Brutus volunteered, "and we can lay a new fire with fresh wood."

"I don't suppose we have much choice." Louise shivered, picking up her winter coat and shrugging into it. Bernadette was upstairs in the kitchen mixing herbal teas, no doubt enjoying the warmth from the kitchen stove. "We need the shop to be warm, or nobody will browse books long enough to buy anything!"

Brutus set to with a will, scooping out half-burned, damp sticks of wood and ash into the ash pan before taking them out and dumping them in the midden in the back yard. He laid the fire quite expertly and soon had it going again.

"A good job, Brutus," Louise praised. "Best keep an eye on it, though. Use as much extra wood as you need to keep it hot enough so it won't go out again, but don't forget to keep the fireguard in front of it."

"Can I sit here by it and read a book?" Brutus asked hopefully.

"Of course you can. Choose any book you want." She ruffled his hair fondly on her way back to the front counter. Brutus' father, Joshua, was too pinch-penny even to buy a subscription to the circulating library they maintained; he certainly wasn't about to spend money on books for his disregarded middle son. Louise was happy for Brutus to read all the books he pleased in the bookshop; his help was well worth it.

"Wash your hands first," she warned, seeing his ashy fingers. The boy gave her a grin before rushing off to take care of that business.

Settling down again at the counter, Louise picked up the day's correspondence and began working through it. A few orders in response to their last advertisement in The Times, a note from the printer to please collect the next batch of Shakespeares to bind… Louise groaned. More Shakespeare! The green calfskin batch were still drying in the book presses! Well, she'd send Brutus over in the morning.

The doorbell jangled, and she glanced up with a frown as a damp, chilly draught blasted across her, ruffling the papers on the desk. It was only Mrs Poole coming in, though, and Louise nodded to her and returned her attention to the correspondence.

It was a quiet afternoon, not too many folk straying far from their homes on such a miserable day. The post-coach roared past in a great clatter of hooves and rattle of wheels before turning into the inn-yard, the driver shouting for fresh horses.

It must be almost four, then. Louise sighed, reaching for the sales ledger. Time to add up the day's takings. Although the afternoon had been quiet, they had made a lot of small sales that morning, she noticed, and laboriously began to add them up, hoping her sister would come down and check her workings.

The church clock struck four, and Louise was about to call out to Ruth to lock the door and turn the little sign to say CLOSED, when the shop door opened again. Words of

11

welcome died in her throat as she saw a tall man almost wholly blocking the door with his sheer size.

From the corner of her eye she spotted a black shape darting for the open door, and cried out "Crafty, no!"

The huge man in the doorway lifted a massive boot, neatly fended off the would-be escapee, and shut the door behind him, before coming to stand in front of the counter. Louise stared up at him, quite mesmerised. There were few men in the district who could even meet her eye-to-eye, but this man was a near-giant; he would be a full head taller than she if not even more.

"Where should I put this?" he rumbled, and it was then that Louise noticed he had a crate balanced on one broad shoulder.

CHAPTER 2

An Unscheduled Stop

The coach rattled into the bustling yard of a sizeable inn, the driver shouting impatiently for a fresh team of horses. Rain dripped steadily from the brim of Shaun's hat, and despite the good quality of his many-caped greatcoat, water had begun to trickle down his neck. He hunched his shoulders against the chill, feeling the dampness pooling between his shoulder blades.

He regretted, for the third or fourth time, his impulsive decision to surrender his inside seat to the fragile-looking older gentleman who had climbed aboard at the last stop. Yet even as he grimaced, Shaun knew he'd do the same again if presented with the choice. Really, he could be too soft-hearted for his own good sometimes.

"Hatfield!" someone shouted, and Shaun perked up slightly. Not far now to London. If his memory served, this would be the last change—or perhaps one more before the final push into the city. He could make it by tonight, if he wanted to.

But then what?

The thought tugged at him, heavy and unwelcome. London, cold and dark in the middle of December, would hardly offer a warm welcome. He'd find himself in an over-crowded inn, eating some dubious excuse for food, and likely still damp by the time he went to bed. There was no one waiting for him in the capital, no fireside with his name on it, no family or friends eager to greet him.

He glanced out at the inn, its windows glowing yellow through the rain with a promise of warmth. The yard bustled with activity—the burly post-boys, the stamping hooves of restless horses, and the smell of wet hay mingling with the promise of a hearty meal.

Shaun made his decision. He leaned out and called to the driver above the noise. "I'm getting down!"

The driver shrugged, indifferent, but Shaun wasted no time. Grabbing his bag, he descended into the muddy inn-yard, boots squelching slightly as they met the ground.

As Shaun stepped clear of the coach, he watched a burly man climb up and unstrap two heavy wooden crates from the roof. They looked sturdy and well-made, the kind of containers that might hold something valuable—or simply very heavy.

"For the bookshop," the burly man said, shouting down to a spindly boy, "take one over, Ned, and I'll be there in a moment."

The boy did his best, but the crate was too much for his arms to get off the ground. If it was for the bookshop, it was probably packed with books. Stepping over, Shaun held out a penny.

"I'll take the crate if you'll mind my bag for me, lad."

"Right good of you, sir! Bookshop's just next door thataway." The coin disappeared in a flash and the lad grabbed Shaun's bag, hugging it tight to his chest.

"Thank you, sir," the burly man called over, climbing back down and going to assist with the horses. "Please tell the Misses Baxters I'll be there with the other crate in a moment."

"Misses Baxter?" Shaun repeated to himself as he made his way toward the indicated shop. He hadn't expected to be delivering books to ladies, but the notion intrigued him.

The crate was heavy, but well within Shaun's capacity. Hefting it to his shoulder, he headed through the archway and turned to the right, in the direction the lad had indicated, immediately seeing the hand-painted sign announcing *Baxter's Fine Books* hanging above the door of the neighbouring building.

A bell above the door tinkled softly as Shaun shouldered it open, stepping into the welcoming warmth. He paused just inside to let his eyes adjust to the dim, cozy interior. The scent of old paper and fresh glue filled his lungs, strangely comforting, and the crackle of a fire in a distant hearth added to the sense of quiet industry.

He caught a blur of motion near his feet and looked down just in time to see a sleek black cat attempting to dart past him. He gently blocked the animal's escape with his boot.

A woman's voice called out from somewhere nearby, sharp and urgent, though Shaun didn't quite catch the words. He assumed it was a warning not to let the cat out. The animal glared at him for a moment, then turned tail and slinked back into the shop, clearly displeased at being thwarted.

Closing the door firmly behind him, Shaun took a

moment to soak in the atmosphere. Like every bookshop he'd ever visited, it was a haven of wooden shelves crammed with bound volumes, illuminated by glass oil lamps hanging strategically throughout the space.

And then he saw her.

She was seated behind the counter, her dark hair swept up into a neat bun at the back of her neck, with long ringlets framing her pale face. Wide hazel eyes looked up at him, and for a brief moment, she seemed utterly startled.

Shaun was fairly used to people looking at him like that - standing six feet six in his bare feet made most folks stare when he crossed their paths - so he simply said, "Where should I put this?"

She blinked at him, still looking rather startled, so he used his free hand to gesture to the crate on his shoulder. "There's another one coming. Where do you want them?"

The door opened again, letting a fresh blast of icy air in, and then closed, and the burly man from the inn said; "Good afternoon, Miss Louise."

"Good afternoon, Mr Thomas." She seemed to recover from her shock and stood up. Now it was Shaun's turn to be surprised. She was quite the tallest young lady he'd ever met. He glanced down to see if she was perhaps standing on a platform behind the counter, but no, she walked past him and the top of her head very nearly reached his chin.

"Over here, please." She pointed to a clear section of floor just beyond the counter. "Thank you, gentlemen."

Shaun put his crate down, and Mr Thomas did too. "Yer welcome, Miss Louise!" Mr. Thomas touched his cap and headed off again, leaving Shaun to linger. He couldn't quite decide what had drawn him to stay—the welcome warmth of the bookshop, the comforting smell of paper and ink, or the striking young woman. Perhaps it was all three.

"Can I help you get those open?" he offered, nodding toward the crates, which were both nailed shut.

"I'm sure I shall manage, thank you," Miss Louise replied politely. She reached behind the counter and retrieved an iron crowbar, handling it with a weightless ease that caught Shaun slightly off guard.

He watched, intrigued, as she deftly positioned the flat tip of the crowbar beneath the lid of one crate. With a practiced movement, she leaned her weight onto the other end, eliciting a satisfying groan of protest from the wood as the nails began to pop free. Shaun raised an eyebrow, impressed.

It wasn't just the casual competence of her movements and her handling of the tool, though that was remarkable enough. It was the contrast—the elegance of her dark hair coiled neatly at the back of her neck, the graceful line of her posture, paired with the sheer practicality of what she was doing. He had never seen a woman wield a crowbar before, and he would have been lying if he said it wasn't rather fascinating.

Miss Louise continued her work methodically, prying up each nail with quiet determination until the lid finally came free. She tilted it upward just enough to glimpse the contents, nodded to herself as though satisfied, and then replaced the lid. Without so much as pausing, she moved on to open the second crate with the same quiet efficiency.

Shaun caught himself staring and cleared his throat, glancing away. He wasn't fool enough to voice his admiration, though. A comment like "I've never seen a woman do that before" would likely earn him a sharp retort and a look of disdain—and rightly so.

"Can I help you, sir?"

The soft voice startled him, and he turned to find a much smaller figure standing at his elbow. It was another girl - this one barely more than a child - with fair hair and wide, nervous eyes that seemed to take up most of her face. She clutched her hands in front of her apron as she looked up at him, her gaze darting briefly to Miss Louise before returning to him.

"Are… are you looking for something in particular?" she stuttered, her voice trembling slightly.

"Just browsing," Shaun said, realising with embarrassment that he'd actually been standing there staring in admiration at Miss Louise. *Browsing indeed!*

"Very good, sir!" The little blonde skittered nervously off among the shelves, reminding him rather of the black cat who'd done the same.

"Do you have a preference?" Miss Louise asked, replacing the top of the second crate and standing up.

Tall, competent women. He bit his lower lip to keep from saying the words, but it took him a moment to realise she was asking what kind of books he preferred to read.

"Novels, I confess," he said. "Though at the moment, I'm travelling, and don't have a home to keep them, so I'm afraid I can't make any significant purchases. Something to read on my travels would be nice, though."

"Novels are those two shelves behind you." She gestured toward the far wall, then paused, looking him up and down with an appraising eye. A wide, bright smile lit her face. "*Gulliver's Travels?* You must feel rather as though you're living in the land of Lilliput most of the time."

Shaun gave a low chuckle, appreciating her quick wit. "I have read it," he replied.

She tilted her head slightly, as though considering his words, but said nothing more. Instead, she returned to her seat behind the counter, leaving him to linger where he was. It was hard to tear his attention away from her, though. He was far more interested in the tall, capable young lady than in any of the books on the shelves.

He should go to the shelves and look at books, but instead he leaned casually against the counter. He was very out of practice at speaking with pretty young ladies—especially ones who smiled like that—and silently prayed he wouldn't come across as too awkward. At least she didn't seem intimidated by his height, which was a refreshing novelty.

"I noticed when I came in," he ventured, "that your shingle from the fire company is crooked."

"Is it?" she replied, not looking up. "I'm sure it won't matter if we actually have a fire."

Her tone was so dry that it caught him slightly off guard. He smiled, leaning a little closer, but she was already preoccupied, a quill in hand as she began adding numbers in what appeared to be a sales ledger. Shaun noticed her fingers flexing slightly, as though helping her keep track of the sums. Her focus was admirable, but as his eyes skimmed the page, he couldn't help but notice something off.

"That's not right," he said instinctively. "You didn't carry the two."

She froze, her quill hovering mid-stroke. Slowly, she looked up at him, her hazel eyes wide with surprise. "I beg your pardon?" she said, sounding quite astonished. "How can you possibly see that *upside down*?"

"I like numbers," he said with a small shrug. "Always have. My father taught me when I was a boy, and I've had plenty of practice since. In the Army, it was part of my job to review ledgers—usually in poor light and at awkward angles." He gave a faint smile. "It's the fastest way to know if someone's skimming the treasury."

The astonishment in her expression softened, giving way to something closer to curiosity. "I see," she said slowly, though she still seemed sceptical.

"I'd be happy to help?" he offered, stepping around the counter before she could protest.

But as he made his way to her side, something on the floor caught his eye. He stopped abruptly, glancing down to see the remains of half a rodent lying there.

Shaun grimaced. How the lady hadn't stepped on it already was a miracle, given her recent flurry of activity. He took a step back, carefully returning to his original position on the opposite side of the counter. "You have a talented mouser," he said dryly, gesturing toward the grisly evidence.

Her eyes followed his, and she sighed, making a rueful smile. "Very much so. Unfortunately, she's also talented at leaving us… reminders."

Louise turned the ledger around and pushed it toward him, clearly unbothered by the interruption. "If you insist on being helpful, you may as well make yourself useful," she said, though her tone had softened considerably.

Shaun accepted the ledger and quill, unable to suppress a small smile. She really was a very unusual young lady. He glanced over the page, starting from the top to ensure he didn't miss anything in his overconfidence. The numbers were straightforward, and it took little effort to correct the miscalculation—but he felt oddly compelled to take his time, if only to prolong the interaction.

When he was done, the numbers balanced perfectly.

Shaun set the quill down and slid the ledger back to her side of the counter.

"There," he said. "All sorted."

Louise examined his work, her expression unreadable at first. Then she looked up at him, and for a moment, he was caught off guard by the sparkle in her hazel eyes.

"I thank you," she said softly.

Shaun suppressed the urge to grin like a fool. "My pleasure."

CHAPTER 3
What a View

Never in her life had Louise been tongue-tied, but she was now. When it came to qualities she wanted in a man, this man was perhaps the first she had ever met who fulfilled all of them. He was distractingly good looking, making her heart stammer and her muscles twitch, as if she needed to suddenly run the length of High Street to burn off energy. Another quality was how smart he was. He'd quickly seen her mistake in the numbers whilst looking at it upside down in dim light. And now she watched him complete the sums, with an audience, as if it was no bother. That was swoon-worthy in Louise's opinion.

He'd also noticed their fire insurance shingle was awry. She made a mental note to see to that. The coup de grace though, was spotting Crafty's entrails - how she hadn't stepped in it and slipped over was utterly baffling. This was a very observant man.

They'd checked and cleaned this morning as part of the routine, but for some reason Crafty had deposited another one. Was this a new development in her habits? Louise hoped not. Then again, Pie was picking up his mother's skills; it was probably the younger cat who'd left the mess.

But the most outstanding part of this man was how large he was. Louise had become so used to being at eye-level with men, or often being taller. She'd inherited her father's tall and stocky build, rather than her mother's slighter frame. Which was never really a problem, except that compared to most men, she was considered ungainly. A giantess. This lovely man before her was at least a head taller than she, and for the first time in her life, she felt delicate.

"I thank you," she said, looking up at him with what she hoped might be a *delicate* look. There weren't any mirrors immediately nearby to know whether she'd achieved that or not.

"My pleasure," he said, giving her a nod. He didn't exactly give her a smile, but the corner of his mouth quirked so attractively it had the same power as one. If he gave her a real smile, she might even faint.

That would be a new experience.

"Where are you from?" she asked indelicately. "I haven't seen you in Hatfield before. Are you moving to town?"

"I'm passing through," he said with a shrug.

Her heart dropped as her flirting failed. "A man of few words."

"Force of habit. From my time in the army."

Louise looked up at him more directly as he volunteered the information, enjoying this new sensation of tilting her head up to see eye to eye. "You're a returned soldier?"

"Aye," he said. "And to answer your earlier question, I'm not really from anywhere, not any more. My family came from Yorkshire originally, up Halifax way, but they're all gone now. I was away with the army for the last few years but I sold my commision and now I need to … figure out what to do next."

It was the longest sentence she'd heard from him, and it explained so much. She'd wanted to get him talking so she could discern his accent, and there it was, a hint of northern burr that revealed itself every now and then. He had the speech of a gentleman, though, and the clothes to match, her experienced eye assessed. Not flashy or fashionable, but of quality make, even if his coat was quite wet through at the moment.

"So you're coming back from Yorkshire and heading to London? Lets see about getting you some novels to help pass the time. Come right this way," she said, carefully stepping over the entrails as she came around the counter and led him to the novels. "We have a good selection of titles. My father is in France at the moment, sending us occasional crates of books. That was one of his you brought in, most kind of you."

"Don't mention it," he said, as they reached the shelves of novels featuring bold adventures at sea or discoveries in far-off lands.

"This is an amusing read," Louise said, grabbing a copy of *The Diverting History of John Gilpin*. "It's popular in our lending section, so we always have copies to purchase for travellers as well."

She handed it to him, and he measured it against his coat pocket. It fit, and he nodded with satisfaction.

"I'll keep an eye out for you, for more like this, if you give me your forwarding address I can let you know when similar titles come in."

"Well," he scratched his head. "Not quite sure what that

address will be. Not even sure where I'll be staying tonight for that matter."

Instantly she said, "I highly recommend the Red Lion next door, you should get a room before they're out. I do not recommend The Swan, which is a few streets away. The last person who stayed there caught bed bugs."

An expression of horror crossed his face, and he nodded thanks for the recommendation. "I've slept in ditches while in the army, but now that I'm out, a little comfort is always welcome. Let me pay you for the book and I'll head to the Red Lion and seek a room."

They completed the transaction and he headed out the door. Bernadette returned at the same time and easily ducked under his elbow.

He lightly stepped back, scanning the room. Louise immediately realised he was checking for the cat before he turned and left. Louise imagined there was a hint of longing or some form of regret in the look he gave her as he left.

"Who," Bernadette's voice startled Louise from her wistful stare at the door, "was *that*? He was a veritable giant!"

"Just a traveller passing through. Watch out!" Louise exclaimed, almost too late as Bernadette caught her toe on the edge of one of the crates.

"Ow, ow." Bernadette hopped on one foot around the counter, and Louise hastily grabbed her shoulders and stopped her before she landed in the mouse entrails.

"What the… Crafty!"

"I think it might have been Pie, actually." Louise guided Bernadette to sit down on the stool while she gathered the mouse-cleaning equipment. "Is your toe all right?"

"I think so." Bernadette wiggled her foot around. "A

good thing I was still wearing my boots. What's in the crates?"

"One of them's from Pa." Louise smiled to see her sister's eyes light up with this good news. "I didn't have time to search it for a letter yet."

"Just one of them? There are two…"

"The other one is the latest delivery of novels from Minerva Press." It was the larger of the two, the one the burly former soldier had carried in. A slight blush stained Louise's cheeks at the thought of him carrying a crate of romance novels; she'd hastily closed the lid again before he could see the contents.

"Well, we'd better unpack them before anyone else comes in and falls over them. Brutus and Ruth, are you still here?" Bernadette called out.

Ruth appeared like a ghost from behind the shelves, nodding shyly. Brutus was right behind her, a book in his hands.

Louise smiled indulgently. Neither of the youngsters had a chance to read much at home; they were often found singly or together in some quiet corner of the shop with their noses in a book. She didn't mind in the slightest, because they completed their work quickly and were always ready to assist when needed. The rest of their time they could be at leisure.

"We need to get these crates unpacked and out of here. Can you help? And then I'll walk you both home." This late in the year, it was already dark outside, and she didn't think either of the youngsters should be out on their own at night.

With four pairs of hands, they made quick work of unpacking the crates, stacking all the books on the counter in neat piles ready to sort through further on the morrow.

There were no letters to be found in the crate of books from their father, and Louise and Bernadette shared a frustrated glance. Would it really be so difficult for their father to pen a brief note?

The church clock struck five, and Ruth straightened up. "I need to get home, Miss Baxter," she said apologetically.

"Of course you do, let's be off." Louise would not for a moment have Ruth be late, knowing the girl would likely bear the brunt of her father's wrath if she was. "Get your coat. And you, Brutus."

"I could stay and help," Brutus offered.

"Thank you for the offer, but I shall walk you home too. I also need to call at the printer before they go home for the evening, so let's go." Louise chivvied him towards the door.

"Can I come tomorrow?" Brutus begged.

"It's Saturday, we will be closed." Louise relented as he gave her a pleading look. "If your parents have no need of you, yes. You can help me sort some more books and carry out the empty crates."

It was a short walk to the vicarage where Ruth hurried inside, and only another two streets to the rather grand house where Brutus' parents Joshua and Phoebe Baxter lived. Joshua was her father's first cousin, but being the son of the older brother he had inherited the bulk of their mutual grandfather's estate and was consequently much wealthier than Louise's branch of the family. Not that it seemed to deter Joshua from wanting even more, Louise thought grimly as she walked Brutus to the door.

"Good night, Cousin Louise," Brutus said, before shaking his head. "I'm sure this is all backwards, I'm sure it's me who should be walking you home."

She resisted the urge to ruffle his hair; he was growing

up and would not thank her for the gesture. "When you're taller than me, you can walk me home."

"But that might be never!" Brutus protested, and she grinned at him.

"Then you'll never need to walk me home. Good night!"

Walk her home, indeed. Louise laughed quietly to herself as she turned and walked back up the street. Turn one corner and she'd be at the printer, two more and she'd be home at the bookshop. There were plenty of folk about, hurrying home, but even if the streets had been quiet, she wasn't afraid. She knew everyone in Hatfield and everyone knew her; knew she was quite capable of knocking heads together if someone was silly enough to misbehave.

A door slammed behind her somewhere, but Louise paid it no mind, marching briskly onwards through the chilly evening.

Arriving at the printer, she tapped lightly on the locked door and was granted entrance by Mr Horace Black, one of the middle-aged brothers who ran Black and Sons.

"Evenin', Miss Louise," Horace said amiably. "Mite chilly out, eh?"

He led her deeper into the shop, with its mingled scents of ink, paper and oil. One of the other brothers was setting print, the typeset rattling under fast fingers, while yet another was aligning stacks of papers under the biggest printing press. Black and Sons was the largest printing press in Hertfordshire, almost as big as some in London or Oxford, and always busy, preparing to print the local newspaper, innumerable pamphlets every month, books and more.

"Ten sets of full folios, as you requested," Horace said, guiding Louise over to some paper stacks on a bench. "Unbound, of course."

"Of course." Louise considered the heavy stacks. "I'll take three tonight and stop by for the rest tomorrow, if that's all right?"

"I'll have one of the boys run the rest around in the morning." Horace smiled at her warmly and helped her load three stacks carefully into a box.

There had been a time, fairly recently, when the printers hadn't been quite so obliging, but that was when Baxter's Fine Books hadn't had quite such an ability to pay their bills on time. Of late, thanks to some very rare and expensive books their father had sent back from his travels in France, that had eased, and Estelle's marrying Mr Yates had put paid to their biggest money worries. Mr Yates had even paid several months' worth of their loan from the bank in advance, as well as Mrs Poole's and Rosie's wages, just in case he and Estelle might be delayed returning from Ireland.

"Thank you, and good night!" Louise called as Horace Black let her back out of the print shop. It was getting even colder outside and she shivered, picking up her brisk pace again. She didn't think it would snow again tonight, but more bad weather was surely not far off. Best to be home tucked up warm in front of the fire.

Footsteps thumped on the cobbles behind her, and it didn't take long for Louise to realise they were keeping pace with her. They turned the corner onto Market Street ten paces behind her, and were the same ten paces as she made the turn onto the High Street.

Louise wasn't the kind of girl to look over her shoulder or panic about being followed. Her eyes narrowed, however, and she deliberately slowed her pace, as though perhaps she was tired from carrying the heavy box. The footsteps behind her slowed too, and Louise measured the distance between herself and the bookshop's door with her eyes. She had to pass through a darkened spot of shadows just before the bookshop where no lit windows poured light, and it was on the edge of that spot that she stopped dead and whirled around, putting herself in the shadow but leaving whoever was following her exposed, right in front of a bright window in the building next door.

"Benjamin Baxter!" She recognised her young cousin immediately. Joshua's eldest son was one of the few men in Hatfield who was as tall as Louise, though he was only sixteen and still had a boy's lanky frame. "What are you doing following me?"

He froze, then scowled at her. "Mind your business," he said.

"It is my business, young man. You're loitering about outside my family's shop, not to mention that you're my cousin. Do your parents know you're skulking about in the dark following ladies home?"

His scowl only deepened.

"Go home, and stop bothering me," Louise snapped, far more angry than afraid. This was Joshua's fault. His disrespect and continuous harassment of the Baxter sisters had led to this; to his son starting to bother them as well. And since Joshua was the local magistrate, Benjamin was no doubt quite unafraid of any possible reprisals for his terrible behaviour.

Confronted, and given a direct order, Benjamin scuffed at the cobbles with his toe for a moment and then turned around, slouching away. Louise watched him go, all the way along the street until he was out of sight. He didn't make the turn that would have led him home, she noted, and shook her head. A boy of his age shouldn't be wandering about after dark alone. Up to no good, indeed.

Her arms were beginning to ache from the weight of the box, so she turned and made for the bookshop door, confident that even running at a full sprint Benjamin couldn't possibly catch her before she got inside. Once there, she checked the fire shingle and it was indeed crooked. She'd best fix that in the morning. She locked and bolted the door firmly behind her and left the folios on the counter to deal with tomorrow before making her way upstairs.

The kitchen was an oasis of light and warmth after the cold, dark December night outside and Louise sighed with pleasure, making her way over to the stove to warm her hands before removing her coat.

"Dinner's ready, Louise, do sit down," the housekeeper Mrs Poole urged. A motherly widow, Mrs Poole had come to live with the Baxters when their mother had died and the girls all looked on her as family.

"Smells good," Louise said with an appreciative sniff as Mrs Poole ladled a bowl of stew for her and placed it on the table beside sliced crusty bread already spread with fresh butter. "What's in it?"

"Rabbit." Bernadette smiled at Louise from her own place at the table. "Mr Warrener dropped them off earlier. As thanks for helping his wife."

It was quite normal for their table to be supplemented by such offerings. Bernadette's knowledge of herbs, learned at their mother's knee, was second to none in the area, and the poorer local folk regularly came to her instead of the doctor or apothecary, both of whom required payment in cash. Louise wasn't sure what ailment Mr Warrener's wife had suffered, but she had no doubt Bernadette would have

CATHERINE BILSON & EBONY OATEN

helped even if the man hadn't had so much as a potato to give them in exchange.

"It tastes wonderful," Louise said after one bite of the deliciously savoury stew. So good, in fact, that she had to restrain herself from gulping it down. She settled for the slightly unladylike action of wiping the crust of her bread around the bowl to soak up the delicious gravy, and finally sat back, replete.

"If you need to go out at night, Bernadette," she said, choosing her words carefully so as not to frighten her sister, "would you let me know so I can go with you?"

Bernadette set down her own spoon and fixed Louise with a perceptive stare. "Why?" she asked.

"Well, the fires, my love!" Mrs Poole answered before Louise could. "There was another one just last night."

Louise hadn't heard about this latest fire, and looked at Mrs Poole with interest. "Another fire?"

"Yes, indeed!" Mrs Poole nodded sagely. "A hay barn, belongs to Lord Ferndale, it does. Not a stick could be saved!"

Louise was aghast. "And nobody knows who did it?"

"Bitterly cold last night, nobody was about. The barn was well ablaze before anyone saw the glow. I'm sure Lord Ferndale is furious, he'll have to buy more hay for his cattle for the winter now."

"What a waste," Louise murmured, while also calmed by the fact the fire had to be a good distance from Ferndale Hall if nobody saw it until it was well alight.

"I don't see what that has to do with me not going out alone after dark," Bernadette pushed, and Louise sighed.

"I wasn't talking about the fires, actually. Benjamin

followed me home from the printer, and I don't think it was because he wanted to see me safely to my door."

"What do you think he was about?" Bernadette asked after a moment, surprise warring with curiosity on her face.

"I don't know, but he's a silly young thing full of boyish fearlessness, and Joshua's attempts to abuse us might make him think he can do the same. He might try to do something to impress his father." Louise shrugged. In truth, she didn't think Benjamin was really capable of doing anything serious, but she did know that she wouldn't want it to be Bernadette who discovered the hard way that Louise was wrong in that assessment.

"All right," Bernadette acquiesced, looking thoughtful. "I really don't go out much at night anyway. The ailments I attend to aren't usually urgent, I leave those to the doctor and the midwives."

Louise nodded, pleased with Bernadette's answer, and sipped at her tea. Her sister's next remark made her shoot straight upright in her chair, almost spilling the tea in her lap.

"Now, Lou, you really must tell Mrs Poole all about that gigantic man who was in the bookshop this afternoon. I could have sworn he was flirting with you when I came back!"

Sensing gossip, Mrs Poole put down her own cup, eyes alight. "What's all this then, Louise? A giant of a man?"

Louise shot a glance full of daggers at Bernadette, who smiled serenely back at her. "It's nobody, Mrs Poole. Just a traveller. He stopped in and bought a book to read on his journey, that's all."

"If that's all, why are you blushing?" Bernadette asked with a teasing grin.

"Just you wait until I catch you looking twice in a man's direction," Louise warned her sister. "Fine, yes, he was… rather attractive," she admitted to Mrs Poole, who looked absolutely gleeful. "But please don't make anything of it. He was on his way to London, and doubtless I'll never see him again."

She tried to ignore the pang of regret she felt at the thought.

CHAPTER 4

Damages

Saturday morning was the Baxter sisters' usual cleaning and washing day, but thanks to their brother-in-law Felix Yates, they now had the very welcome assistance of Rosie. She and Mrs Poole did the bulk of the chores, and although the young lass barely said a word to the Baxters, Louise often overheard Rosie and Mrs Poole exchanging breathless town gossip as they scrubbed and cleaned. The fires were more than gossip, though, they were quite real, and quite frightening to think some ne'er do well was causing havoc.

Louise was sure it was a returned soldier, because why would someone from Hatfield damage their own town?

She and Bernadette had the much more welcome task of sorting out the crates of books that had arrived from Father and Minerva Press. Before they could make a start, she walked out the front door and checked the fire insurance shingle was still attached to the front wall. In daylight, she could see one of the screws securing it in place had come loose, and Louise humphed under her breath before going inside, finding another screw, and fixing the shingle straight again.

Satisfied with her handiwork, she then walked back in and made sure neither Crafty nor Pie could escape. Then she grabbed their mouse-entrail-collection tools and looked for dissected rodents. To her surprise, there were none behind the counter. She tapped the top of the counter to 'touch wood' that there were no remains, and then spotted not one but two murky furry remnants in *front* of the counter.

This would not do! How dare they change positions! And right where potential customers would stand, too! Cursing the pair of them, she wondered whether she should place a note outside the shop offering an excellent mouser to a good home? Maybe Bernadette might offer Pie to a farming family the next time she visited one?

Mess cleared up, she checked the hessian at the bottom of the stairs. It was shredded beyond repair. Bernadette walked down from the kitchen at that point and they wished each other good morning.

"I'll replace the hessian, then we can sort the books," Louise said.

Bernadette nodded and made her way over to the counter. She grunted as she lifted the ledger from the shelf to record the newest arrivals.

The two had a good routine now, checking each book and writing down the title, the condition of it and whether it needed repair, then assessed it against the London Catalogue of Books to see how much they could charge.

Even more importantly, they carefully turned through the pages to see where the note from their father might be, if he had included one.

"Oh dear!" Bernadette said as she opened a book to look inside.

"Gosh!" Louise agreed as she took in the sight of the illustrated plates. It appeared to feature people from the Indies in scandalously strange positions. "Best put that behind the counter in the locked section."

Bernadette turned back to the title page and read out, "'Camma Suttra?' Is that how you say it?"

Heat stole over Louise's face. "I'm just as puzzled as you. Any more like that in the crate? Pile them up over here so we can put them under lock and key."

"But then how do we sell them if they're locked away?"

Well, yes, her sister had a point. "Perhaps Papa has a client already and he just needed to get them out of France before anyone else could get them? Have you found any notes yet?"

"Not yet," Bernadette looked through another title, this one with illustrations and diagrams of flower segments, labelling each section. "Oh, this is glorious. May I keep it?"

"Botany? It's like Papa was thinking directly of you," Louise said with a smile. "Go ahead."

"Another one for the lock box," Bernadette said when she opened the next book. "Heavens, if people found out about these, we'd be run out of town!"

Louise peered over Bernadette's fair head to see what book she was looking at. She caught an eyeful of illustrated internal organs. It was enlightening. "Is that what we look like on the inside?"

"I think so," Bernadette said as she turned the page to see a much closer illustration of a male appendage. "I wonder if Doctor Rasley would like this one?"

"Into the lock box," Louise recommended. "What kind of estate did Papa raid to find these?"

"Not a vicar's library, I'll guess!" Bernadette said with a giggle.

Lead poured into Louise's belly at the mention of the vicar. "Old Brimstone already can't stand the Minerva books in the lending section. Can you imagine how much of a hue and cry he'd make if he knew we had these?"

"He'll be the one leading the mob running us out of town!"

They carefully sorted through the rest of Papa's crate and put several more books in the locked cabinet.

"What a shame there's no note from Papa," Bernadette said as they reached the bottom of the crate. "I checked every book, ever so carefully."

Louise sighed in frustration. A small note shouldn't be such a hard thing, but it seemed beyond their father's abilities. She was amassing quite the list of grievances to deliver upon him when he returned.

The shop door tinkled as someone came in. Louise stood up from behind the counter and said, "Terribly sorry we're clo..." before she realised it was Cousin Joshua, with Phoebe holding their youngest son Little Sticky, and Benjamin.

She cursed herself for forgetting to lock the shop door. But then, even if it was locked, he probably would have banged on it until she had to answer it lest he break the glass in the little window.

"Cousin Joshua, Phoebe," she deliberately left out their son, "To what do we owe this visit?"

Mercifully, Bernadette remained crouched down behind the counter, where they couldn't see her. A soft click she hoped only she could hear told her Bernadette had locked the cabinet. Not a moment too soon.

Phœbe placed Little Sticky on the ground and he charged directly over to where Crafty and Pie were nestled on a gap in the shelves. Crafty immediately scarpered, but Pie sniffed the toddler's hands and began licking whatever was on them. Sticky, whose real name was Barnaby, giggled with glee.

"This!" Joshua thundered as he held up a book. "You gave this depravity to my son!"

Louise gulped and had to think quickly. She was confident Brutus hadn't taken anything from the sorting piles from the night before.

Benjamin's grin of superiority grew. He clearly enjoyed the way his parents treated Louise and her sisters, and was learning far too eagerly how to follow in their footsteps.

"I did not think Benjamin was interested in reading?" Louise said, stalling for time to think.

Spittle formed at the corner of Joshua's lips. "I'm not talking of Benjamin. You gave this moral excrement to Brutus to bring into our home! What kind of depraved mind does that? You bring shame to the name of Baxter at every turn. Being in trade isn't enough for you, you have to drag us all into the gutter with this depravity!"

Phebe joined in, "We've a mind to inform the vicar. You should not even possess such things!"

Louise wracked her brain wondering what book it could be for them to form this objection. Not that it had to be much at all for Joshua and Phoebe to complain. Joshua took a step closer to the counter. Louise could almost make out the title on the spine if he stopped waving it about.

"This is bestiality!" he roared, right in her face.

CATHERINE BILSON & EBONY OATEN

"Ohhhhh," Understanding dawned. "The book on horses! Yes, it's about types of horses and such… what could possibly be concerning about that? Brutus is quite enamoured of horses and the illustrations are rather good. From what I saw they were accurate. I said he could borrow it so long as he took good care of it so we can sell it later."

To Louise's mind, there was nothing depraved about the book whatsoever.

"So you admit you gave it to him! That it came from these premises?"

She was getting very tired of this, and poor Bernadette was still crouched down behind the counter, possibly losing the feeling in her feet at this rate. "Fine, you've made your point. Leave the book and get out." This routine of Joshua's of coming into their lives, blowing fury their way and making them miserable had to stop. If things became too bad, they did have Felix's grandfather, Lord Ferndale in their corner, but she hoped it would not come to that.

In any case, Marie would be home before Christmas with enough money to keep them going for months, and with any luck their father himself would be home any day. They could endure this for a little longer. She scowled at Benjamin, knowing full well this was revenge for her chasing him out of the shop with a broom.

Benjamin appeared to take delight that she'd looked his way. He stepped forward and took the book from his father and opened it to an illustrated plate.

It was a stallion covering a mare.

Benjamin leered at her.

Louise sighed and shook her head. It was literally nothing they hadn't seen in person; they lived in a country town, for heaven's sakes!

Benjamin snapped the book shut. Joshua and Phoebe stood beside him with smirks of confidence.

Louise had to fix her eyes forward in order not to roll them.

Then Benjamin threw the book down on the ground with such force it broke the spine.

That was a step too far for Louise. They could tear strips off her for whatever reason they liked, and it mattered not. But damaging books was beyond endurance! Not taking her eyes off Benjamin, she reached under the counter for the crowbar she'd used to open the crates and pulled it out with one hand. She held it up so all three could clearly see what it was and take in its significance. "If you damage one more item of our property, I will damage your head, young man!"

Phoebe shrieked. Benjamin, to his credit, took a step back, alarm dawning in his expression. He knew she meant it. Good.

Joshua puffed his chest out and blustered for a moment until he could make proper words. "You cannot threaten us like this!"

Louise's heart raced in her chest, but the crowbar remained steady and sure in her hand. She had no intention of retreating. "I have the right to defend my property. We are closed on Saturday, as everyone in Hatfield well knows. You are the ones trespassing."

"It's not your property, it's your father's property," Joshua countered. "For all we know he's dea…"

"I grow weary of that silly claim. That crate, right there? Arrived from him just yesterday. Now get out, the lot of you. I'm sick of your hollow threats. I am absolutely prepared to follow through on mine!" She marched past them and banged the crowbar against the now empty crate. To

Louise's satisfaction, it smashed through the strong timbers as if they were little more than kindling.

Phoebe gave one more warning as she scooped up Little Sticky and Joshua herded them out, "The vicar will hear of this!"

Mercifully the door closed behind the four of them with a merry tinkle. Louise made sure to lock it firmly so they couldn't come back for the rest of the day.

"Are you all right, 'Dette?" she called back to the counter.

Bernadette stood up from her hiding spot, her cheeks a little pale. "I'm so glad you were here," she said.

"I'm not scared of them, and you don't need to be either," Louise said. "There's nothing they can really do to us." She still held the crowbar in her hand, and the weight of it finally registered.

Feet shuffled from behind a bookshelf and young Brutus and Ruth poked their heads out.

"I hadn't realised you were here!" she said, horrified, wondering how much they'd seen or heard.

"Rosie let us in earlier, so we could do some dusting," Ruth said. "We didn't mean to eavesdrop."

Brutus looked at his feet. "I'm sorry my parents are so mean to you."

The words, "I'm sorry your parents are so negligent towards *you*," were on the tip of her tongue, but she held it back. The poor lad knew that for himself.

"You were so brave with that crowbar," he said, looking up at her with shining eyes.

Louise wasn't sure she was an appropriate target for the kind of hero worship he seemed to be developing, but Lord knew the boy didn't have any good role models at home.

With a smile, she held the crowbar out to him. "Want me to show you how to use it?"

"Would I!" Brutus looked eager. He took it, but it was obviously too heavy for his spindly boyish arms, and Louise took it back with a grin.

"We'll start with some smaller tools. Build up to that one."

To his credit, he didn't look disappointed, just nodded, happy to accept that she would judge when the time was right.

"I'm awfully sorry about that book," Brutus added. "I didn't realise it would get you into trouble."

"No real harm done," Lousie said, finally putting the crowbar down on the counter and shaking her arm out with relief. "I'm sure they would have found something else to complain about in any case."

Ruth moved in to deliver a hug of relief to Louise. "You were incredibly brave. But I fear they will still tell my father. Please be careful."

Louise nodded. "Even your father can't do much to us, Ruth, I promise. There's nothing criminal about selling books." At least, *these* books. The ones in the locked cabinet might be another matter.

Bernadette asked carefully, "Did you hear us talking about the other books before?"

Ruth and Brutus looked to each other, and then back to Bernadette. Then they nodded. It was a relief they were honest, but awful that they'd overheard.

"Ah well," Louise said. "We didn't order them, they simply arrived. And we do not have customers for them either, so they'll remain locked away until Papa comes home. I do need you to promise me something, though."

Both Ruth and Brutus nodded solemnly, eyes wide.

"Promise me that not only will you never attempt to open that cabinet, you won't even speak of it. Not to each other, not to anyone. What's in there *could* get us in trouble, maybe. It's for my father to deal with when he gets home, do you understand?"

Both of them fell over each other promising her that their lips were sealed, and Louise nodded, satisfied. Neither of them were the type to brag to friends, and though Brutus might be curious enough to try and sneak a peek, she believed he wouldn't do so now he'd given her his word. Handing them much safer books which could be shelved, she sent them both on their way. Then she retrieved the damaged book and added it to her pile for repairs.

Sunday morning brought heavy rain, making the familiar and usually pleasant walk to church cold and miserable, huddled under umbrellas. Usually they'd take time greeting friends outside, but Louise, Bernadette and Mrs Poole quickly headed in. Their housekeeper diverged to greet her friends and sit with them, while Louise and Bernadette walked farther ahead to the Ferndale pew. How quickly they'd become used to sitting with Lord Ferndale and Miss Yates, their new family, welcome benefactors and in some ways, protectors. At times, Louise suspected that Lord Ferndale's patronage over the years had been the only thing between the bookshop and ruin.

Looking over the congregation, Louise noticed a taller man in the crowd, a full head taller than everyone around him. Her breath stilled as she recognised the magnificent former soldier who had been in the bookshop only a couple of days ago. He was still in Hatfield! He turned her way at that moment. Her heart soared as he returned her welcoming smile.

The Ferndales arrived and were full of smiles, although Lord Ferndale wore a thick scarf that he did not remove. Louise didn't remove hers either, despite the church being full of warm bodies. Louise's shoulders remained tense for the whole service, partly through cold, partly through fear of what kind of sermon they were in for.

Old Brimstone droned on, but thankfully it wasn't as bad as she thought. If Phoebe had whispered in his ear after their altercation yesterday, she felt sure the entire town would be getting a lecture on the dangers of unsuitable reading materials and the like. The hymns were familiar and she enjoyed adding her voice in song.

By the time worship was complete, Louise allowed herself a sigh of relief. She stood with Bernadette and the Ferndales, then turned slowly to see if she might catch sight of Mr Jackson. Thankfully the rain had eased, so she might catch up with him in the churchyard before he wandered away.

Stepping out onto the soggy grass, Lord Ferndale coughed into his gloved hand. A moment later, Bernadette reached into her pocket and produced a small bottle of tonic, which she pressed into Miss Yates's hands for safe keeping. The winter months were a worrisome time for the town elders, and people would certainly not blame them if they called the vicar to Ferndale Hall's private chapel for services instead of making their way into town in such miserable conditions.

Oh dear, there was Phoebe, striding up the vicar to bend

45

his ear. There could only be one thing Mrs Baxter had on her mind.

Louise turned her back on the unfolding situation so that she could appear to not be listening. Meanwhile her ears strained for morsels. If only Mrs Poole and her friends were nearer, they'd overhear everything, without doubt!

Some words did reach Louise's ears. As she suspected, they were terrible.

"You must speak with Lord Ferndale," Phoebe said with a loud hiss of urgency.

An ominous start.

Then there was more about, "Being the only one who can rein them in," which amused Louise greatly. Joshua was the head of the Baxter family, yet it was up to the vicar to plead with Lord Ferndale to pull Louise and Bernadette into line? If Joshua knew what his wife was saying about him behind his back, he'd be utterly humiliated.

For a moment, Louise smiled to herself, wondering how she might make sure Cousin Joshua *did* find out what Phoebe was saying without his knowledge.

As amusing as this exchange was, it definitely would not be good for Bernadette and Louise to endure the vicar's wrath. She looked over her shoulder when Phoebe finally stopped talking and realised with a gulp that Reverend Millings was coming directly their way, a grim expression on his face.

Bless Lord Ferndale, he stepped forward to the vicar and greeted him with a hearty shake of the hand. "Marvellous sermon, marvellous," he said with commendably well-acted enthusiasm. Without missing a breath, he kept talking and extolling the man's virtues. Bernadette gave Louise a look of confusion and concern, and Miss Yates politely giggled into her handkerchief, pretending she had a cough. The three of them would fall about laughing if Louise didn't look away right this minute!

Their run of luck had to run out, however, as the local solicitor, Mr Burton, and his wife walked over to speak to Lord Ferndale and Miss Yates about the Hatfield Hospital Committee.

This gave Reverend Millings the opening he needed. He cornered Louise and Bernadette before they could get away.

"It would be remiss of me if I did not express my grave concerns with the reading material you are trading. Especially to the younger minds of the town."

Grave concerns? What an exaggeration.

"Do not disrespect your betters," he demanded suddenly, raising his voice.

Bernadette must have rolled her eyes, because Louise was sure she had kept hers steady and her expression smooth.

On he went. "It is a serious undertaking to be alert for signs of moral decay, and there are a great many signs that decay is alive in Hatfield and must be stopped. Beginning with the books you make so freely available to all and sundry." He was really hitting his stride now and loving the sound of his own voice. "I've a mind to start a new committee for the maintenance of Christian welfare of Hatfield. I'm sure Mrs Baxter would be eager to join!"

Louise had absolutely no doubt of that. Phoebe would be the first in line to boss people about if she so much as suspected they might be doing anything she didn't approve of.

CHAPTER 5
Shaun Steps In

Seeing the pretty young lady from the bookshop at the front of the church, standing with a very well-dressed older couple in a private pew, had immediately made Shaun feel as though the sun had broken through the heavy grey clouds hanging over Hatfield. She had even smiled at him before the service started, when he caught her eye! Shaun had to school his expression to a properly sober and serious one, lest he be caught grinning like a fool in church.

He wasn't even quite sure why he was still in Hatfield. He could have caught another stage coach on to London on Saturday, but the bed at the Red Lion had been warm and comfortable enough he'd lingered late in it, and then an excellent breakfast had him feeling frankly lazy. Another night or two in a most comfortable spot would be a decadent pleasure, he decided, and the inn had the room available when he inquired.

And now here he was, loitering around outside the church while Miss Louise Baxter spoke with the older couple and another younger woman, who Shaun decided after a moment must be either a sister or a cousin. A good deal shorter than the statuesque Miss Louise, and Shaun thought a year or two younger, the other girl had a similar shape of face and the same hazel eyes.

Shaun was just trying to pluck up the courage to go over and speak to Miss Louise - he had charged French lines without fear, but going over to talk to a pretty lady struck terror in his heart and made his knees shake - when the vicar went striding past, cassock flapping, and stopped in front of her.

Shaun frowned. It looked very much like the vicar was berating the two young women. Snippets of his raised voice drifted to Shaun on the gusty wind, and then two more people joined the vicar, a middle-aged man and woman in clothes that spoke more to consciousness of fashion than practicality for the wintry weather.

When the man began to shout at Miss Louise and shake his finger under her nose, Shaun decided he'd seen quite enough. While Miss Louise didn't look intimidated - more annoyed - the other young woman with her was beginning to look quite miserable, and Shaun didn't like seeing young ladies berated anyway, certainly not in public. Striding forward, he deftly inserted himself between the shouting man and Miss Louise, offering his hand to the vicar to shake.

"Reverend Millings, is it? Thank you for your kind welcome to your church, sir. A stirring sermon."

"Ah, well... thank you, Mister...?" The vicar actually stuttered slightly, taking a step back, obviously thrown off guard by Shaun's sheer size.

"Jackson. Shaun Jackson." Shaun grabbed the vicar's hand and shook it vigorously, making sure to squeeze just a touch harder than really necessary. "And a pleasure to see you here too, Miss Baxter." He smiled broadly at Louise.

"You've met?" The middle-aged woman's voice was shrill.

"The gentleman made a purchase in the bookshop on Friday," Miss Baxter said, offering a polite little curtsey in response to Shaun's bow.

"Nothing illustrated I do hope!" the woman said, with a censorious frown.

"A thoroughly excellent fictional adventure it was," Shaun said. "Do you have more by that author? But where are my manners? I shall not ask you to discuss business on a Sunday."

"Allow me to introduce my sister, Mr Jackson." Louise indicated the pretty girl standing slightly in her shadow. "Bernadette. And our cousins, Mr Joshua Baxter and Mrs Phoebe Baxter."

"A pleasure to make your acquaintance," Shaun said generally, but in truth he only meant it to Bernadette. Joshua was still red-faced and scowling, as though he would like to shout at Louise some more, and Phoebe looked rather as though she was sucking on a lemon.

Over Joshua's shoulder, Shaun spotted the boy he'd spied in the bookshop on Friday, being pushed around by a rather larger boy, and wondered if he'd need to step in there, too. A grin came to his face as the boy looked after himself quite adequately, though, stamping hard on the bigger boy's foot before dancing back and running nimbly off, leaving the bigger boy to limp off with a face like thunder.

"Oh, well done, Brutus," Louise murmured under her breath beside him, and he realised she'd been watching the little fracas too.

"Father!" the bigger boy snapped, limping up to Joshua Baxter. "Can we go home now? It's raining!"

Mild drizzle, not exactly the same as the rain that was falling before the church service began.

"What happened to your foot?" Phoebe immediately fussed.

"I stubbed my toe," the boy lied, and Shaun had to swallow a laugh. Louise didn't even bother, laughing aloud, which made the boy - who must also be a cousin, he supposed - shoot her a nasty look.

"Let's get you home, come along then." Joshua nodded rather curtly before turning away with his wife and son. The vicar had already beaten a retreat to speak with other parishioners, and Miss Bernadette slipped away with a quiet murmur in her sister's ear, leaving Shaun and Louise alone.

Or as alone as one could be in a churchyard with about forty other people exchanging pleasantries, anyway.

"I thought you were leaving again," Louise said after a brief moment of excruciatingly awkward silence.

Shaun stuffed his hands in his pockets. "Well, that was the plan." He glanced about, suddenly quite unable to meet her eyes. "Except, I had a really good night's sleep at the Red Lion and woke up with the realisation that I'm not in a great hurry to be anywhere. I was going to London because it's where I left from, but there's nothing in particular for me to do there."

"I see." She tilted her head slightly, examining him thoughtfully, and he felt rather like a bug trapped by an entomologist's pins, being inspected from every angle. "You don't have any family? Or a..." she paused delicately.

"Job?" He smiled to show he took no offence. "Neither. Not since the Army released me. With Napoleon safely imprisoned on Elba, they've no need for such a large force of fighting men. I sold out and honestly, I'm looking for what to do with the rest of my life. I have a legacy from my father, as well as the money from the sale of my commission, so I expect I shall buy a house and settle down somewhere. Try my hand at a little farming, perhaps."

"Do you think you should like to be a farmer?"

"I don't know. I'd probably be a bad one," he admitted. "I don't know much about sheep, or cows. A little about horses."

"We sell books on animal husbandry." She smiled, as though at a secret joke.

"Perhaps I might buy a house in Hatfield." He tasted the idea, found it didn't displease him. Quite the contrary, with Miss Louise Baxter standing in front of him. "Would you… would you care to take a walk with me? Show me around the town a little?" It was only after the question had slipped out that he felt silly asking. "Although, it's still raining a little, maybe another day…"

"I think it's stopped, actually." Her smile had widened, and now seemed directed at him. He couldn't look away. "I should love to take a Sunday stroll with you, Mr Jackson."

Somehow, she had tucked her hand into the crook of his arm and they were walking out under the lych gate, Shaun having to duck his head just slightly to avoid knocking it on the supporting beam.

"This way." Louise pulled on his arm a little, and he turned obediently in response to her direction.

Misty drizzle dressed everything in sparkles, especially Miss Louise's enchanting eyelashes. Each person they passed wished Miss Louise a good morning, and she introduced them to "Mr Jackson, returned from the army and keen to explore Hatfield," or variations thereof.

Despite the chill, Hatfield readily warmed itself to him. It was cleaner and quieter than London, but not so small he'd be isolated from the world. There was a steady, even pulse to the place, with carriages regularly coming up the High Street, even on a Sunday.

"I take it your family has been in town for many generations?" he asked after another polite and welcoming introduction.

"What gave it away?" Louise delivered him the most glorious smile, and his heart staggered.

"Everyone knows you and is most convivial. Which is in stark contrast to the way your cousins were behaving after church."

"Well yes," she acknowledged, as they made their way along a pretty street lined with pine trees, whose green boughs provided a spot of colour all year round. "The bookshop, which you know…"

"Baxter's Fine Books, if I recall correctly," he said with a grin.

"The very same. The building is included in the entail of my great-grandfather's estate, to his youngest son, and heirs male of said son. My father, unfortunately, was blessed only with daughters, those dratted things," she said, looking up at him with what sounded very much like sarcasm colouring her tone. "Without a male heir, it goes back to the male descendants of the eldest male son, along with the rest of the estate's properties."

"I see."

"Whom you've met, just this morning."

The penny dropped. "That would be Joshua Baxter and

his … *charming* brood," he said, with a chuckle on the word charming.

"Terribly observant of you," she said.

"Your father is still alive, is he not?" he asked.

"We very much hope so," she said. "He's in France at the moment. The same reason you sold your commission is why he is on the continent right now."

"Napoleon," Shaun muttered under his breath. "At least he'll cause no more trouble now."

"Exactly," Louise agreed. "But Joshua has been getting, shall we say, pushy. He wants the property for himself. A few months ago, he had the temerity to begin measuring the windows for drapes!"

"How very presumptuous!" Shaun said, warming to the story. That old sense of protectiveness came over him, and he couldn't help wanting to protect the Baxter sisters. Miss Louise especially. Even though he was sure she was more than a match for her annoying cousins.

"As long as the crates of books keep arriving, we know our father is alive. That's enough to keep Joshua at arm's length for the time being. There is also some detail in the entail about the building needing to have a viable business operating, and it is at that."

"And there's unlikely to be a male heir any time in the future?"

She ruminated for a moment and he wondered if he'd overstepped the mark.

"Our mother died several years ago, and our father gave no indication he was interested in remarrying. The entail includes only direct male heirs, so unfortunately even if I or one of my sisters had a son, they could not inherit. But in any case, we are in a much better position than we were when Papa left England. Lord Ferndale is our dear friend and benefactor. Our eldest sister, Estelle, recently married his grandson Felix Yates, who is heir to the Barony. Lord Ferndale now insists we sit with him and his sister, Miss Yates, in the Ferndale pew in church."

It was all making so much more sense. The cousins felt they were being slighted, it was entirely predictable they would want to retaliate in some way.

Battlefields took many different forms.

They turned into another street and saw the bright blue and white shingle for The Swan. The place Louise had not recommended.

"I thank you for warning me away from that establishment," he said. "The Red Lion is warm and comfortable, and no sign at all of bed bugs, thank goodness. I suffered enough fleas and other biting creatures in the army. If I wanted to keep sleeping with them, I wouldn't have sold my commission."

Leaving The Swan behind, they continued to chat and walk, and greet people, as they made their way to the High Street.

"I'm sure you know the way from here," she said as they reached Baxter's Fine Books.

Did she shiver? He looked at her clothes and realised they may have been warm enough for a crowded church, but they'd been in the elements all this time and he hadn't offered his coat!

"You must be chilled to the bone! Would you allow me to buy you luncheon at the Red Lion, as thanks for the personal tour of the town?"

He expected her to demur or shy away.

"That would be delightful," she replied in ready agreement.

He held his arm out and she put her hand on his elbow again. Right where it belonged.

"These are the livery yards," she pointed out as they walked past the archway to the back of the inn. "They hire horses here, if you need one."

"I'll take a closer look when it's a little warmer," he said, noting how pink her cheeks were from the cold.

Opening the door to the Red Lion, they were assailed with delightful cooking aromas, slightly less delightful warm bodies and a welcome warm fire in the hearth. "Two for lunch, landlord," he said.

The landlord nodded and wished Miss Baxter a good afternoon.

"I hope I haven't put you in an awkward position," he said to Louise.

"Not at all, we are on very good terms with Mr and Mrs Haye. They send a lot of travellers our way so people have something to read on their journeys. You have already met Mr Thomas, he's the muscle who gets the crates of books off the carriages."

Understanding dawned. Everybody knew Louise, and Louise knew everybody.

Who needed a chaperone when you had the whole town looking out for you?

CHAPTER 6

Louise Approves

For a day that had begun with gloom and apprehension, Louise appreciated her rapid change in fortune with Mr Jackson's intervention outside the church. She was used to defending herself, and was far from a timid lass in need of rescue. However, having someone of Mr Jackson's stature realise what was happening and intervene had been welcome.

His actions had shown her Mr Jackson knew how to size up a situation quickly. He'd also given Bernadette a chance to slip away from their cousin's and the vicar's verbal attacks. No doubt Joshua and Phoebe would be back in the bookshop during the next week to deliver another stern talking to … but that would be private, in their shop, not in front of the church with everyone in town bearing witness.

Reverend Millings certainly had plenty of fodder for next week's sermon, no doubt. Louise could only hope some of the returned soldiers in town would cause a fracas between now and then. Surely a brawl would fit his definition of moral failures more than their humble literary trade?

The soup and crusty bread warmed her all the way through.

"It's an interesting dish," Mr Jackson said, "Filling, yet not too heavy."

Lousie couldn't help smiling. "It's my late mother's family recipe! She shared it with Mrs Haye long ago."

"Then I am honoured!" he said, tearing off a chunk of bread to soak up the thick layer from the sides of his bowl. "What is it called?"

Wistful pride and nostalgia gripped Louise. "*Pommes de terre et de poireaux,* otherwise known as potato and leek. Mama said all French families have their own version of it."

"It is good," he said. "I might order another. Would you like more?"

"I would, thank you."

There was something so lovely about being in his company. Their walk through town had raised Louise's hopes he might consider moving to Hatfield. It was as good a place as any other, after all, perhaps better than most… but then she was probably biased.

"Tell me about being a soldier," she asked as their second serving of soup arrived. She wasn't really that hungry, truth be told, but she wanted to delay returning home. Would he return to London on the morning coach? He'd already mentioned he didn't like that city.

"Well, I wasn't really a regular soldier in the end."

That surprised her, so she raised her brows in question and remained quiet so he would go on.

"You see, I ended up in far more battles with accounts, than the enemy. My father was a banker, and I learned numbers at his knee. Some of my army superiors recognised I was good with adding things up in my head and made me a quartermaster. My accounts were so accurate, they began to suspect others were not, so they sent me to investigate them."

This rang true for Louise. He'd spotted her mistake in the ledger, from the opposite direction, in dim light. "That sounds like it's something of a problem in the army?"

"Indeed it is. People make mistakes, that's understandable, but some were helping themselves to His Majesty's treasury."

Louise wanted to gasp, but she held it in. He'd been a thief-catcher!

He must have read her expression because Mr Jackson nodded and said, "Exactly that. I was good at going unnoticed, but I do still need to watch myself and mind my company. It's why I'm seated facing the door, so I can quickly check who's coming and going."

"Goodness." Louise kept her voice low. "How does someone as large as you not get noticed?"

He demonstrated by slumping in his chair to the point where his knees came into contact with hers under the table. She found that rather thrilling. Then he spoke using a Cockney accent asking which way to Piccadilly and Regent Streets, before returning to his faintly Yorkshire brogue.

A soft giggle escaped. "That is indeed a neat trick. I wish I could do that."

He straightened himself and coldness replaced the warm sensation where his knee had been touching hers.

"You did it yourself not long ago, when you gave the French name for the soup. You sounded like a different person."

"Oh, goodness, I did, didn't I?" she realised. This man was entertaining and enlightening. "But all the same, you

59

are rather tall. I spotted you easily in church. How do you not get noticed? I've never been able to do that."

"I'm quiet and have a slouch, people assume I'm a bit simple. They completely ignore me and speak far too freely. If I'm slumped in the corner of a taproom, looking like I'm in my cups, I'm practically invisible."

"You're living the life of an adventure hero," Louise said, her heart racing. "Like in a book!"

"Most of the time I am completely sober, while my back aches like the devil," he said with a chuckle. "They don't put the details about sore backs in the books, do they?"

Louise laughed along with him.

"Shall I walk you home?" he offered.

Louise grinned and joked, "But it is so far! Are you sure?"

He laughed at her jest and nodded. "I am a gentleman, perhaps contrary to appearances, Miss Baxter. I know how to behave, and that includes walking ladies home."

He paid for their lunch and as they stepped outside he put his coat on her shoulders instead of his own.

The smell of him enveloped her senses. "That is very kind, but it is only a few steps," she said. "I'm already warmed through from the soup." Not that she had any intention of taking his coat off.

"I have nearly finished my novel," he remarked, as they sauntered to the bookshop door. "I shall call in tomorrow for another, if that's all right?"

"You would be most welcome," Louise said, trying not to sound too eager.

"Do you have any books about Hatfield itself? Or the region?"

"We do indeed. They are popular with travellers."

They were dawdling now, Louise not wanting to open the shop door and end this lovely day. The sky filled with dark clouds, mist swirled in the air, but they were in a bubble of sunshine of their own making.

Mr Jackson appeared to be stalling for time.

She asked, "Is there anything else you'd like me to set aside for you?"

"Well, I mean, we shouldn't really talk about work on a Sunday, but I was…"

Louise held her breath, waiting for him.

"… wondering whether you knew of any houses for sale. I'd ask Mr Haye, but he might jump to conclusions or want a commission on the sale or something, and he might talk too freely."

"Whereas I can make subtle inquiries?" Her heart raced at the idea of Mr Jackson moving to Hatfield. He was already turning her head, and now she was beginning to hold out hope he might stick around.

"Exactly that. I'd be most appreciative."

Louise shrugged out of his coat and gave it back to him. "I shall make those subtle enquiries and with any luck I might have news for you tomorrow."

"Thank you, Miss Baxter." He gave her a gentlemanly bow.

She bobbed a curtsey in return and wished him a lovely afternoon.

As she moved to open the door, he said, "Watch for the cat."

Louise could well have been walking on clouds. She opened the door and took Mr Jackson's advice to watch for the cat. Well, the two cats. They both leapt down from their perches and ran to her, but she closed the door just in time.

For a moment, she leaned against the door and simply breathed.

Replaying the day with Mr Jackson filled her with strange sensations and something she identified as hope.

Then she stepped on a pile of mouse entrails in the middle of the floor and yelped in shock and disgust.

"Oh good, you're home!" Bernadette said as she made it down the stairs. "Come on up and tell us all about that lovely tall man."

After she'd cleaned the cats' ghastly 'gift', Louise walked upstairs to find Mrs Poole had the kettle on.

"You must be famished," Mrs Poole said, "I'll get you some soup."

"Oh, no Mrs Poole, no need, I've already eaten."

Mrs Poole and Bernadette looked at her with raised eyebrows.

Heat stole over her face. They'd find out soon enough; it was good gossip that she'd been seen dining with a man.

"Mr Jackson kindly asked me if I would offer him a tour of Hatfield, and I obliged. Then he invited me to lunch at the Red Lion as thanks."

Bernadette grinned and asked, "Did he really want a tour of the town or was that a ruse to spend time with you alone?"

More heat stole over Louise's face.

Mrs Poole nudged Bernadette and chided, "Mustn't tease."

Louise had to press on and follow through on the promise she'd made to Mr Jackson, though her face fair burned at this point. "He did want a tour of the town, and he asked me to inquire discreetly if I knew of any properties that were for sale. I said I would ask you, Mrs Poole, as you'd probably know more than I."

The dear woman looked thoughtful for a moment, "I don't know of any right now, but I can ask. Why doesn't he enquire at the Red Lion? The Hayes know everything about the town."

Louise nodded as she thought back to the activities he'd undertaken for the army. "I asked him that too, and he mentioned something about not wanting anyone to ask for a commission on the sale."

"Does he not have funds?" Bernadette asked.

Mrs Poole tutted at that. "It's rude to ask about people's finances."

Louise gave it some thought. She didn't know what kind of funds he had, but he hadn't worried about the cost of their meals, and they'd eaten enough for four. "I don't believe that's the case. He strikes me as the kind of person who keeps to himself and doesn't want to be the centre of speculation."

"You know him really well, don't you?" Bernadette giggled.

Louise wished this conversation would end. "Perhaps I am speaking of myself too, I don't like to be the subject of speculation either!"

Bernadette made a sing-song chant, "Lou's in lo-ove, Lou's in lo-ove."

"Stop it!" Louise cried, covering her ears.

"You are! You are in love with Giant Jackson! Oh my goodness, I never thought I'd see the day! So, he's moving to town and that can only mean one thing, he's going to propose! Oh how exciting! I can't wait for Marie to come home… maybe I'll write to her about this development!"

"Stop!" Lousie pleaded again. *Giant Jackson?* She could see the name sticking to him like book binding glue. "Don't you have families to deliver herbs to or something?"

"Leave your sister alone," Mrs Poole warned Bernadette, who quieted, but still smirked at Louise.

Louise finished her last sip of tea, while Bernadette kept giggling behind her hand. She loved her little sister quite dearly, but if Bernadette kept this up, Louise would be threatening her with the crowbar next.

"I'm excited for you, Lou," Bernadette said when Mrs Poole left the room for a moment.

"Please don't be. Nothing has happened. I only met him a couple of days ago. For all we know, he might already have a sweetheart in London that he's promised to."

For that was the truth, and her belly flipped at the thought. She had met him only the day before yesterday. Whatever feelings she might have were strange and unusual, but there was a high chance she had read the situation incorrectly.

"You owe Mr Jackson your thanks for interrupting the vicar this morning," Bernadette said. "He came to your rescue."

"I did not need rescuing, I had the situation well in hand."

"You didn't send him away, though."

"I did not," Lousie confirmed. "I don't deny his timing was welcome. He also created a distraction so that *you* could slip away unnoticed. You would do well to thank him when you see him next."

Bernadette's eyes shone with mischief. "So he is staying around?"

"He could be purchasing a house for his mother for all

we know," Louise said. All the same, her heart would break a little if he did not appear tomorrow to purchase another book. Not that she should set her well being on the appearance of a customer in the shop, but he'd said he'd like to buy more books. He truly was the first man who'd turned her head. It would be such a shame if this was the end of their association.

CHAPTER 7

A Restless Night

The Red Lion was crowded with people that Sunday night, awaiting the morning coaches to London. Shaun sat in a corner enjoying a pork pie and some ale, content with his decision to remain at least one more day in this pleasant town. A pair of bright hazel eyes teased the edge of his common sense. He'd been out of women's company for so long, he hadn't a clue how to proceed. And did he want to? It would not be fair to lead a lass on, but he found Miss Louise such excellent company. He was used to moving from place to place with no attachments, but something niggled at his conscience, like his gut was telling him to stay in town for a while.

His instincts had served him well in life so far, he'd be foolish to ignore them now.

Keeping himself inconspicuous, he picked up the conversation further down the table as he slowly sipped his beer. Letting a little slip from the side of his mouth so that those nearby might think this tankard was his seventh instead of his second.

They were saying something about wondering where to sleep this night.

It was already an hour into the darkness, Shaun thought, the men best have some kind of plan.

"Shame the one who done it din' set us a fire to warm ourselves by first," one mumbled.

The others laughed and said, "Aye, that's our lot."

At the mention of a fire, Shaun tilted his head to angle his ear more closely, hoping they wouldn't notice.

Somebody at another table called out, "Were you the men sleeping in the old cottage t'other night?"

"Aye," they answered.

"Damn shame, and don't judge the town by one bad act. We're not known for fires in these parts," the man at the other table said.

Shaun was definitely listening hard now.

"Back from France, defending His Majesty, and this is our thanks," one of them said.

Peering over his tankard, Shaun looked at the poor men who were so down on their luck. Back from France could only mean they'd been fighting on the continent, and from their broad accents they were from the North. They were wearing tinkers and ragmen's clothes, but he could imagine they would have made an impressive sight in uniform.

He decided it would be safe to engage them in conversation. "Wassis 'bout a fire?"

"We were staying in a ruined empty cottage, sleeping out, saving our coin for the journey home," one began.

Another chimed in, "We gets lucky sometimes and we picks up work along the way, but we're used to sleeping rough so we don't mind barns or old buildings and the like."

The first man finished the story. "Then some blighter set fire to it and there's no coach north till the morrow."

"Have my room," Shaun said. These men must have served honourably and needed a proper roof over their heads tonight. One that would not catch fire - or if it did, there would be dozens of witnesses. "I don' need it," he hoped he slurred his words just enough to sound pleasantly drunk, but not out of his mind. He grabbed the key from his pocket and handed it over. "Room 9, help yourselves."

"Where will you go?" one of them asked.

"Nah, I'm going for a walk," he said, pushing himself away from the table and staggering toward the front door.

"Do you want the rest of your pie?" another asked hopefully.

He waved his hand, then veered toward the bar and caught Mr Haye's attention. He handed over a couple of shillings and said, "Give those men a hearty meal, if you please. They've seen service."

"Right you are then," Mr Haye said, giving him back half the money. "We have a returned soldier special deal just this very night," he added with a wink.

Outside, Shaun turned his coat collar up against the cold and breathed plumes of steam. The air was still and he saw the familiar constellations twinkling in the sky. No cloud cover explained the icy temperature. He shuffled his feet to keep warm and found himself looking up and down the high street. What he was hoping to see was anyone's guess.

Fires made him nervous. Fires in the army were danger-ous, and they were often used to destroy evidence. "So sorry, we don't have the ledgers any more, a lamp broke and burned the office…" was a lie he'd heard over and over.

Unless the soldiers had lit a fire to keep warm and hadn't

put it out? Surely they'd know better. Far more likely to be deliberately lit, especially if people were becoming frustrated with the number of wandering soldiers in a district.

He was a wandering soldier himself, come to think of it. Perhaps that's why he'd taken the men at their word so quickly.

Looking the other way, down towards Baxter's Fine Books, he caught movement. A dog? No, far larger. A tall, thin man.

His heart leapt into his throat at the thought of somebody loitering about the front of Miss Louise's shop.

"What are you about?" he called out.

The shadow stood stock still, to the point where Shaun wondered if he was imagining things.

Then the shadow dropped something, spun around and tore off like a startled hare.

Instincts kicked in; nobody ran if they weren't up to something. Shaun gave chase. It was a man, slim and gangly. He already had a head start and ran as fast as a bolt of lightning.

Despite mainly taking care of numbers in the army, Shaun had kept himself fit, on the off chance he'd need to flee if people knew he was on to them, or occasionally to chase down fools who tried to run. It never did any good. The army's reach was extremely long.

Shaun barrelled on, determined to catch his quarry, but the man was too fast and obviously knew the town well. He ducked in and out of alleyways, and eventually Shaun lost him in the unfamiliar streets.

Frustrated, he turned and retraced his steps, his breath making thick clouds as he puffed hard from the exertion. He would need to maintain his training in the days to come, because he would definitely catch the next miscreant who crossed his path.

When he reached the darkened front of Baxter's, he found the object the man had dropped.

It was a tinder box. And the only thing a tinder box was good for was starting a fire.

He opened it to find it fully stocked with all the necessary items to make a blaze. The flint and char cloth looked well used, as did many of the match sticks. It had clearly been used often. Was this the same one that had set the soldiers' refuge alight the other night? Highly possible, but there was no way to know for sure.

His blood turned to ice when he noticed the bookshop's fire insurance shingle had been unscrewed and lay face down on the ground.

He traced his hands over where the shingle should have been and felt the holes where the screws should be, but as much as he searched in the dark, he could not find the screws themselves. Without the shingle, it was very possible a fire brigade would not come.

Dear heavens, it wasn't his imagination, he really had interrupted an arson attack! There were no lights shining through the upstairs window. Miss Louise and her family must be asleep upstairs, unaware it could have been their last night on earth.

If only they'd had a dog instead of two cats. A barking dog could have awoken them.

Damn and blast, if only he'd caught that ne'er do well.

All the same, he had the man's tinder box, so unless the fire starter had more - which could very well be the case - he at least would not be setting any fires in the High Street this particular night.

And certainly not to Baxter's Fine Books, not if Shaun had to stand guard in the street until the sun came up.

Which was exactly what he planned to do.

His nerves in a jangle, he pulled his coat tightly around him and grabbed his gloves from the inside pocket. Standing still would not do, so he paced back and forth from the corner of the Red Lion and back. Looking above the Red Lion's doorway, he saw a fire brigade shingle firmly affixed, which gave him some comfort. Of course, there were far too many people coming and going at this place, they would have noticed someone loitering about, trying to remove the shingle.

He walked down the street, to the building on the other side of the bookshop. It was so dark he couldn't make out much, and he thought about striking a light from the tinder box. But if someone left or arrived at the Red Lion as he did so, they might think *he* was an arsonist.

He'd wait until the morning.

When he paced back to the Red Lion, he checked in with Mr Haye and was satisfied the soldiers had enjoyed a good meal and gone up to sleep in his room. He ordered another pork pie, to keep him alert and fed during the night. He wrapped it in a handkerchief for later.

Using the light from the taproom window, he examined the tinder box for any initials or signs of an owner, but found nothing. The silver box was beaten and scuffed in many places.

For the rest of the night, Shaun paced and quietly seethed that somebody in Hatfield was deliberately lighting fires, and they were either targeting Miss Louise directly, or the bookshop.

Hours later, there were no lights shining from any

windows as Hatfield went to sleep. Shaun bit into the pork pie. It was delicious. In the distance, he heard some cats fighting and a dog barked. Perhaps the dog was alerting his owners to that arsonist he'd startled earlier. He could live in hope.

I will get you, he silently promised to himself, and Louise.

He leaned against the shop wall and drifted off a little, confident his presence would warn off anyone who might dare approach. The army had taught him a valuable lesson, to sleep anywhere he could, even if he was standing up leaning against a wall.

A cockerel crowed in the distance, although it was still dark. He could have sworn he heard some cows mooing as they woke. He tried checking his fob watch but it was too dark to see the placement of the hands.

He heard the distinct noise of someone feeding the horses in the livery stables behind the Red Lion. From the direction of the church, someone rang seven bells. There would be no usable light on the horizon for at least another hour at this time of year.

In the neighbouring windows across the street, he saw candlelight peeking through. He crossed over the street to look back up to the second floor of Baxter's Fine Books and was relieved to see light in their window as well.

Somebody was awake.

The whole town would be up soon and he'd be able to share what he knew with Miss Louise.

Mr Haye stepped out of the Red Lion and shook the dust off a rug. "My word, did you stay out here the whole night?"

Shaun nodded. "Was keeping watch."

"Anything we should be aware of?" Mr Haye asked.

Shaun walked closer and showed him the evidence; the

shingle and the tinder box, and he quickly explained their significance.

"Heavens!" Mr Haye said, then he turned to check his own shingle and sighed deeply on seeing it was firmly in place.

"I've not seen him come back this way, but you can never be too sure. Lanky tall man, fast on his feet. He got a good head start, otherwise I could have caught him."

"Breakfast is on the house," Mr Haye said with appreciation. "The Baxters are good folk and make no mistake. Couldn't live with meself if anything were to happen to them, what with their father not back yet and all."

"You're a good man, Mr Haye," Shaun said, giving him a friendly pat on the shoulder, "I'm glad the Baxters have people watching out for them."

"Well, not to mention a fire lit there could easily spread!" Mr Haye gestured to the narrow archway which was all that separated the bookshop from the Red Lion.

They parted on good terms and Shaun strolled back to the bookshop, his eyes tired and his body longing for a proper sleep. It could wait, because there were more important things to discuss.

He gave a knock on the shop door when he heard footsteps of somebody inside.

"We'll be open in an hour if you can wait," he heard Louise say on the other side.

"Miss Louise, I'm sorry to knock so early, but I have news-"

The door swung open with a tinkle and a worried frown marred her delightful face.

"It's not news of Papa?" she blurted.

"No, it's not," he said with a sigh. "May I come in? This

is something you probably don't want passers-by to overhear."

"Of course." She opened the door wide and the bell above tinkled. He turned his foot sideways just in case a cat should run out. None did. They were probably still asleep, smart creatures.

He stepped in and she closed the door, making sure the 'closed' sign remained facing outwards.

A soft yellow lamp lit the counter and he walked over to it, producing the tinder box and the shingle. "Last night at the Red Lion, I heard people talk about someone lighting fires. I went outside to get some fresh air a little later, and I saw someone loitering out the front of your shop. He ran off when I called out, and he left these behind."

"That's our shingle!" Louise picked it up. "It fell off again?" She looked puzzled. "How…"

"It didn't fall off, someone deliberately removed the screws, and when it's lighter out, I'll have another look to see if I can find them."

"This is a tinder box," she said, picking up the object and prising it open. "Well stocked too," she added.

It was clear from her expression that she believed him and did not think him to be imagining any of this.

"Whoever dropped it ran off. I gave chase for a good while but he had too much of a head start. Tall, though not as tall as me, and thinner. Fast on his feet too. Lost him in an alley somewhere… he knew where he was going, so he knows the town."

"He might not have been alone! You could have run into a trap," Louise pointed out.

"I hadn't thought of that," Shaun admitted. "I figured he was alone."

"Mr Jackson, you must be careful," she said.

He'd come here to warn her of the same. "I can handle myself," he said to reassure her. All the same, it warmed him that she cared about his welfare.

"I don't wish to upset you but... do you have any enemies?" he asked, trying to phrase it gently but unable to put the thought out of his mind that she could easily have been killed last night.

"Yes we do," she said, straight away. "The vicar doesn't like us one bit. I dread to think what we'll hear in next week's sermon now that Cousin Phoebe's been in his ear!"

Shaun pressed his lips together in thought. He'd met the vicar, and Phoebe. Although the reverend blew hard, so to speak, he appeared physically harmless. He was older and walked more slowly, Shaun was sure he wasn't physically able to run as fast as the man from last night.

"It definitely wasn't a woman in the street last night," he said. "And the vicar couldn't be that spry. Can you think of anyone else?"

"Cousin Joshua?" Louise offered with a shrug. "He wants us out... but wait, he actually wants the building itself. He will eventually get it when Papa dies. Why would he damage his inheritance?"

Shaun shook his head and ruminated. He'd met Joshua as well, but the man was too short to match the culprit from the night before. Unless he'd hired someone? But as Louise had said, Joshua wanted the building. Why would he try and destroy it?

It didn't make sense, but he had to keep an open mind about what strange motives people had.

"Do you think the person you startled set fire to the barn that burned, and the cottage?" Louise asked.

"I really don't know. I've not much experience in arson, I'm not sure how common it is. Have there been many fires in Hatfield before?"

"Well yes, especially in winter when people fall asleep with a lit candle nearby, or they forget to put the screen in front of the fire at night. We're always scrupulous about the screen around the fire here, and we blow out our candles in the kitchen and then go to bed, to make sure nobody stays up reading, what with all the books… oh no, the books! Maybe Joshua is so angry with us he doesn't care about the building any more and just wants to hurt us?"

She appeared to need comfort, and he wasn't sure what to do. Should he hold her and offer reassurances?

CHAPTER 8

A Job for Mr Jackson

Louise looked up into Shaun's eyes as her world splintered. Surely Joshua wouldn't be so mad as to want to set fire to the building he was so keen to inherit? It made no sense. But then... the fires that had occurred so far didn't seem to make any sense at all. Would an arsonist care about a specific target? A madman who just wanted to burn things would probably think a bookshop a wonderful target; so many books would create quite a bonfire.

"It can't be Joshua," she said slowly. "Why would he burn down a barn, and a cottage? That makes no sense."

"Ah." Shaun frowned thoughtfully. "You're thinking the attacks are random?"

"Perhaps?" She shrugged a little helplessly, feeling as though she was floundering about in the dark. "I don't know."

"Tell me about the previous attacks," Shaun requested, and Louise wracked her brain to recall the gossip Mrs Poole had shared.

"*Two* barns," Shaun said thoughtfully after she'd told

CATHERINE BILSON & EBONY OATEN

him everything she knew. "And an abandoned cottage. And now, he's tried for the bookshop. He's escalating."

"Esca…" she frowned. It wasn't a word she was familiar with, at least not in English. "From the French, *escalier…* stairs?"

"It means to do things in a bigger way, so yes, probably does come from escalier… to climb stairs. I mean that he's getting worse, he's stepping things up. From a barn he may have thought was empty, to an abandoned cottage, then to a barn full of hay… and now to a business with people sleeping above."

"Oh, I see what you mean!" Louise steadied her breathing, "As if the first few were a rehearsal of sorts."

"He won't stop." Shaun said it with a dark certainty, and Louise felt a shiver run down her spine. "I've seen men like this in the army… not necessarily arsonists, criminals of all sorts. They start small and get bolder and nastier, and they don't stop, not until someone makes them stop. This is a serious matter, I'm afraid. Who is your local magistrate, would you introduce me?"

Louise winced. "I have bad news on that front. You already met him, outside the church yesterday. It's my cousin Joshua."

The bell tinkled as she said it, but Louise couldn't look away from Shaun's face to see who had come in, even though the Closed sign was still on the door. Shaun's expression went from curious to horrified, before a kind of resolution dawned and he stood up even taller, if that were possible, his head almost brushing the shop's ceiling beams.

"Then I'll be staying in Hatfield until I've caught this miscreant," Shaun said, and his voice was like the low, distant rumble of cannon fire. Grim and dangerous. "I'm an investigator. I'll find him. I'm certainly not leaving y… this town to be terrorised by an arsonist."

Had he almost said he wasn't leaving *her* to be terrorised? The squirmy, delicious feeling was back in Louise's stomach again, and she wanted to smile, despite the grim topic of discussion.

"Excellent," another voice said, a familiar one, and Louise finally managed to tear her gaze from Shaun's face to see that it was Lord Ferndale who'd come into the bookshop. The elderly baron was smiling up at Shaun with apparent delight. "It appears you're just the man I'm looking for, then."

"I beg your pardon?" Shaun turned and stared down at Lord Ferndale, and Louise realised she had better make introductions.

"Lord Ferndale, this is Mr Jackson. Formerly with the army as a quartermaster and investigator, he's passing through Hatfield and has heard about the fires."

"Not just heard about," Shaun rumbled. "Darn nearly caught the scamp trying to burn the bookshop down last night!" He held up the tinderbox to show Lord Ferndale, who looked grave.

"Dear me, how dreadful! Are you quite all right, Louise? And Bernadette, Mrs Poole and Rosie?"

"No harm done, though I need to affix our fire shingle in a more permanent manner." She lifted the shingle off the counter. "The culprit unscrewed it!"

"Outrageous!" Lord Ferndale huffed in annoyance, before turning his attention back to Shaun. "An investigator, hm?"

"Of a sort. I was more what you might call an auditor, mostly looking for financial discrepancies… but I can handle myself." Shaun gave a self-deprecating little smile, and Lord Ferndale laughed aloud.

"Oh, I have no doubt of that, young man, no doubt at all. Well, I do believe you might have been delivered to me by Providence, because I was just about to request an express rider at the inn to take this to the Bow Street Runners for me." Lord Ferndale held up a letter. "Requesting that they send me a man to find this blasted arsonist before he burns down any more of my property or anyone else's. But since it seems there is an investigator here in town already... are you interested in a job, young man?"

"I feel like I'd be cheating you, to take your money for something I already planned to do," Shaun said.

Louise honestly suspected she might have fallen in love with him at that moment. What an honourable thing to say!

"Nonsense," Lord Ferndale said briskly. "At the very least, you must permit me to cover your bed and board, and shall we say perhaps a bonus to be paid when you apprehend this miscreant? Twenty pounds?"

"That is more than generous, my lord!" Shaun looked at Louise, as though to ask if Lord Ferndale meant what he said.

She offered an encouraging smile. "Lord Ferndale owned one of the barns that burned down. I'm sure he will consider you a bargain if you can bring in the arsonist for that price."

"Both of the barns, and the cottage!" Lord Ferndale corrected her. "I was beginning to wonder if my property was being targeted specifically, but perhaps not, if they made an attempt at the bookshop last night. Either way, I want this man stopped, and I cannot trust our magistrate to get the job done." He gave Louise a meaningful look.

She winced. "I was just explaining to Mr Jackson that the magistrate is Cousin Joshua."

"Ah." Lord Ferndale looked back at Shaun, catching the cynical look on his face. "You are an excellent judge of character, I see."

"I like to think so." Shaun offered his hand to Lord Ferndale to shake. "And talking of that… there are some men at the Red Lion. Returned soldiers, down on their luck a little. I'm wondering if you might see your way clear to letting me hire a few of them to help me out? Hatfield's a fair-sized town to cover on my own, and if I'm asking questions during the day, I'll want some men available to patrol at night."

"An excellent notion! Why don't we walk next door, and you can introduce me to them?"

Shaun and Lord Ferndale left the bookshop together, after polite farewells to Louise, and she sat with a silly grin on her face for quite a few minutes.

Shaun was staying, possibly for some time. Lord Ferndale had clearly taken an immediate liking to him, too.

Her gaze fell on the fire shingle on the counter, and she hummed thoughtfully, picking it up. "Maybe some glue," she said. "And new screws." She'd send Brutus over to the ironmonger when he came in, and she had some older glue which had dried quite hard upstairs. A hot-water bath should soften it enough to make a nice thick sticky paste, and it would dry again quickly. Let the arsonist try to get it off the wall then!

The bell jingled again, and Louise glanced up, expecting to see Ruth or Brutus - it must be almost time to open the shop. But it was neither of the youngsters; it was Shaun coming back in.

"Mr Jackson!" She shot upright. "Was there something else?"

"There is, actually." He leaned on the counter and smiled down at her. "While Lord Ferndale has generously offered to cover rooms at the Red Lion for me and the three men we've just hired, I don't actually want to stay there. Too many folk passing through, and," he looked a little conspiratorial, "I did make a fair few enemies, while I was in the army. I'd rather not be in quite such an obvious spot. Could I press upon you to make enquiries of whether anyone has any rooms to rent?"

"I shall make it my utmost priority," Louise beamed at him. "I already asked Mrs Poole yestereve about a house to purchase, and she knows everyone who's worth knowing in Hatfield. I'd wager I'll have an answer for you in two shakes of a lamb's tail."

She was bragging now, because those fluttery feelings were making her silly in the head. Mr Jackson was staying in Hatfield and he was performing important work. He was already possessed of so many excellent qualities, but if he brought down an arsonist he'd be a true hero, not just in her eyes but to the whole town.

"Much appreciated," he said with a slow and warm smile that made her tummy flip again. How utterly glorious!

She waved him off again, content they would see each other very soon. Then she luxuriated in her present situation. Yes it was dangerous, but she was starting to think herself properly in love with someone.

Were these the same feelings Estelle had experienced with Mr Yates? When she wasn't being an idiot about things, of course. To think, her eldest sister had fought with these same emotions and hadn't wanted them. What a silly goose

Estelle had been. Louise was going to be ever so much smarter about her predicament. In fact, she was determined to do the opposite of everything Estelle had done, skip the messy confusing parts and get straight to the happy bits.

Bernadette came down and delivered a stern look. "You're wool gathering. I don't suppose a tall man is the one with the wool?"

There was little point pretending anyone else had caught her fancy. Bernadette would tease her forever if she denied it, so Louise smiled and said, "Mr Jackson is staying in Hatfield, and I for one am delighted. Lord Ferndale has tasked him with finding the arsonist."

Bernadette pulled up short and looked confused.

Louise made her way to the door and turned the sign to Open, as she was fully awake now and may as well open for customers. "I'll fill you in, and I do hope Mrs Poole knows of someone with a spare room."

For the next few minutes, Louise showed Bernadette the shingle and explained all that Mr Jackson had told her, plus the very recent intervention of Lord Ferndale.

Bernadette looked confused. "I thought it was the returned soldiers who were up to no good. As did you for a time, too. Do you think Mr Jackson would turn in one of his own?"

It was on the tip of Louise's tongue to explain that Mr Jackson had spent the last few years turning in 'his own', but she kept that to herself. It made him sound a little less heroic. "He says to keep an open mind, so that's what I'll do too."

"You really like him, don't you?"

Louise grinned and those lovely fluttery feelings spread through her tummy again. "I really do."

"You take all the fun out of mercilessly teasing you, you know that," Bernadette confessed.

"*Quelle dommage!*" Louise said, fairly dripping with sarcasm. It was their late mother's favourite expression when the girls didn't get exactly what they wanted. "What a shame!"

The door opened and the bell above tinkled, as Brutus and Ruth came in to do a little work and enjoy the quiet reading time.

Louise lit up. "Ah, Brutus, just the lad I need. Our Fire Insurance shingle needs new screws. Would you take this to the ironmonger and purchase four long screws so we can fix it back to the wall?"

The lad nodded and asked, "Do we have an account with them?"

Louise thought for a moment. "I'm not sure we do, we seldom need screws or nails." She fetched some money from the locked box and gave it to him, to cover what she supposed would be the fee.

"Do you have the old screws to measure the new ones?" Brutus asked.

That was rather sensible of him. "Let's have a look out on the footpath and see if we can't find one."

They spent the next few minutes examining every crevice and crack, but there was no sign of the missing screws.

"I'm sure it's no problem, Miss Louise, the ironmonger probably has a set size for the fire insurance shingles."

She'd tell him about the arsonist later, when there was time.

He headed off down the street to the ironmonger, at the same time as Mrs Poole approached with a plate of breakfast for her. "Come in and eat, I'll put this on the counter."

Her tummy rumbled in anticipation of buttered toast and hot tea.

"When you see your Mr Jackson, tell him Mrs Bell across the street has a room she'd be happy to let. Oh, here he is now!" Mrs Poole fairly beamed as Shaun entered the shop for the third time that morning, and Louise smiled too.

My Mr Jackson. How nice that sounds!

She took a moment to introduce Mrs Poole, who inexplicably rushed straight off again, but her disappearance was soon explained when she dashed back down the stairs two minutes later with a second plate of toast and jam for Shaun, who thanked her heartily.

"Mrs Poole has given me the good news that Mrs Bell across the street has a room to let. Mrs Bell is a local midwife, so does keep odd hours, and I'm sure she won't mind you coming and going whenever you wish so long as you're quiet," Louise said, thinking even as she said it that this was a very good solution. As a midwife, Mrs Bell knew everyone in Hatfield - well, every woman, at least - and was even more familiar with comings and goings around town than Mrs Poole. She could be a very useful source of intelligence for Shaun, as well as a kind landlady.

"Well, that sounds tremendous," Shaun said, after polishing off the bread and jam. "Conveniently close too." He gave Louise that slow smile again.

"Convenient for, ah?" She was too dazzled by that smile to think straight.

"For meeting with my men at the Red Lion, of course."

"Oh, of course."

"And for keeping an eye on the bookshop. In case the arsonist makes a second attempt."

She felt a bit deflated. How very businesslike of him.

"Well, let me take you across the street and introduce you to Mrs Bell," she suggested. "If she's home, that is. If not I shall write a note and ask her to come and find you at the Red Lion."

Bernadette and Mrs Poole had been standing there the whole time listening to the conversation, and Ruth was probably hiding behind a bookshelf listening too, so Louise left them in charge and walked outside with Shaun, just as it started to snow.

"Oh, dear." She looked up into the grey sky full of swirling flakes. "I hope it's not doing this in the north. My sister Marie should be arriving in Cumbria today or tomorrow."

"A miserable time of year to be travelling in the north," Shaun noted, offering his arm to cross the street. They had to wait for several carriages to pass before making their way safely across.

"I'm afraid so, but when an earl orders more than a hundred pounds' worth of books and demands they be personally delivered… one of us had to get on a coach."

Shaun whistled between his teeth. "Whew. That's a lot of money to spend on books, he must be very rich."

"Very entitled, you mean." Louise cast him a sideways grin. "It's probably a good thing Marie went and not me. I might have told him what I thought of him."

Shaun laughed, rich and low, as Louise knocked on Mrs Bell's door.

Mrs Bell was at home, fortunately, and more than happy to rent Shaun a spare room when she heard Lord Ferndale had hired him to search out the arsonist. Louise left them negotiating about which meals might be included in his bed and board and made her way back to the bookshop with a spring in her step.

Shaun was staying.

Brutus arrived back just as she managed a safe crossing of the street, and she accepted the four screws and change which he handed to her.

"Shall we screw it back in now, Miss Louise?" he asked. "You did say you were going to show me how to use the other tools…"

"And I certainly shall, but first I want to prepare some glue. We're gluing that shingle to the wall as well as screwing it in. Let anyone try to remove it then!"

Louise looked back at the other side of the street, and up to the window at the front of the upper storey of Mrs Bell's house. The massive figure of Shaun was quite visible inside as he talked with his new landlady.

And let anyone try anything with my Mr Jackson on the case, she thought with a private little smile. Surely, with an expert investigator to hunt down the arsonist, he would be caught well before Christmas!

CHAPTER 9

A Budding Romance

The happy expression did not leave Louise's face for the next few days. It might have been getting colder outside, but a warm inner glow radiated from her for all to see. Shaun called in regularly each morning, his presence welcome and calming as gossip about fires swirled around the town. Louise had no doubt at all Mr Jackson would succeed in his investigations. The approval of Lord Ferndale further confirmed her high opinion of the man. If that was even possible.

He would come into the shop, always checking first to prevent the cats running out to the street and scaring the horses.

"That reminds me, we really must find a home for Pie," she mused as he wished her good morning.

"He truly deserves his name, he does appear to have run all the mice out of town," Shaun said, avoiding stepping in entrails as he approached the counter.

"Oh dear, is there something on that side?" Louise asked.

"There is, although this one has feathers," he said.

Oh dear, the cats must have run out of their regular mouse supply if they were bringing in birds now. Pie really needed to be on a farm somewhere. After she cleaned it up, she set to the ledger again and then stopped herself.

"I do feel nervous doing the sums, they're really not my thing," she said. "Would you mind ever so much?"

"I'd be glad to," he said, turning the ledger about and checking the numbers. "Also, the fire shingle looks sturdy on the wall out the front."

Brutus, who was helping Ruth dust the shelves, piped up. "Thank you, Mr Jackson."

"Oh, hello there lad," Shaun said, looking around and greeting Brutus. "You did a fine job, the glue is an excellent addition."

Brutus beamed with pride. "Miss Louise's idea. But I helped."

"You are always a great help. I have some more folios we can bind this afternoon," Louise said warmly.

"Shakespeare?" Brutus asked with a cheeky grin.

Louise shrugged. "Alas."

The two of them laughed in a shared joke.

Shaun finished with the ledger and asked, "You're not fond of Shakespeare?"

Louise grinned to herself. "I really do love Shakespeare, and I should not complain, because the bound folios provide steady income. But it does feel like that's all people want, and it's either red or green leather…" She couldn't even muster up a dramatic sigh though, because Mr Jackson had finished the ledger and was here in the shop and all was right with her world.

Brutus asked, "Can we do some binding now?"

She would much rather stay and chat with Shaun, but

Brutus was right to encourage them to get through their tasks.

"I'll need to be off in any case," Shaun said, "But before I go … would it be all right if I joined the lending library? Now that I'm staying in town awhile?"

Music to Louise's ears! "Of course you can, I think Ruth is dusting those shelves now." Then she grabbed the library ledger from behind the counter and opened it to the latest page. "I'll write the book details in, when you find something you like."

They stood there making calf eyes at each other, until Brutus coughed theatrically and said, "Miss Louise, we probably should get on with the binding."

"Oh, of course!" Lousie and Shaun said over the top of each other, remembering they had an audience.

It was lucky she had Brutus to help her today, as her concentration was in tatters and they had several orders for binding and repairs to fulfill.

Her concentration was no better the next day, and the day after that it was even worse. Mrs Poole had no doubt informed the entire town of her emotional attachment by now, and she found herself rather enjoying that thought.

It meant the rest of the single ladies of Hatfield would know he was spoken for.

More or less.

A letter then arrived from Marie, which had her suddenly paying attention to the world outside her loved-up bubble.

Her elder sister had arrived at the Earl of Renwick's estate, which was welcome news. She hadn't called him Demanding, but Louise could hear their pet name for him in her head. Even better, the books were all in excellent condition and had not been damaged in transit.

However, Marie had badly sprained her ankle falling on slick ice and was now stuck in Cumbria until she could cope with the rigours of travel again. Louise's heart ached for Marie, who must be feeling dreadfully alone and would not be home in time for Christmas now. And the money for those valuable books would not arrive until she came home either. Silently Louise prayed her sister would recover quickly and not be too miserable. Selfishly, she couldn't wait to tell Marie everything about Mr Jackson.

A man wearing a dark suit and clerk's attire walked into the bookshop the next day, with the classic appearance of a traveller who'd just stepped off the mail coach. He was rumpled and walking slightly stiffly, as if his joints had been cramped.

"I'm looking for Miss Louise Baxter," he said upon entering.

Her stomach fell. It could only be bad news. With a shaky voice, she replied, "I am she," and then sent Ruth to call down Mrs Poole and Bernadette for reinforcements. If this was bad news about her father, she needed family around her.

Mrs Poole definitely counted as family these days.

"Then I am in the right place," he stepped forward with what looked like folded papers. Official-looking papers that might contain terrible news about their father.

Bernadette and Mrs Poole arrived quickly with worried expressions. Brutus stepped out from behind the shelves as well, his face showing not curiosity but concern.

"It is good news," the man said, suddenly paying attention to their fretful expressions. "Lord Renwick has sent me,

91

with instructions to pay his accounts in full." He pronounced it 'Rennick' and it took Louise a moment to match the name to the Earl of Demanding.

"Oh!" Louise said, suddenly able to breathe again. "Thank the Lord for that!"

The man winced. "The Earl always pays his bills, why would you ever have doubts?"

"No, no, you misunderstand!" Louise gushed, hugging Bernadette and Mrs Poole with relief.

Ruth and Brutus exchanged glances and returned to their quiet tasks.

"We thought it was bad news about our father. He's in France at the moment and we feared something had happened."

"Oh, I see," the man said, his expression clearing. "I had no idea a clerk's uniform was so funereal."

"It is dark in here," Bernadette said, "And you looked like you'd travelled a great deal."

"That I have," he agreed. "Because Lord Renwick was keen to clear his account with you. His message required speed so that he was not in arrears."

"It is a boon to have the accounts taken care of," Bernadette said, accepting the papers. "We have been waiting to hear from our father for several months, you see, and… anyway, I thank you."

Louise had been so caught up in her romance with Mr Jackson, she'd quite let that worrisome aspect of their lives go to pasture. "I shall write up a receipt for Lord Renw-*Rennick* for you," she said.

It was true they were no longer as desperate for funds as they once had been, but the handsome pile of money would pay several bills that would fall due between now and the New Year, and leave them with plenty to spare.

She called Brutus over and handed him the money to pay the bakery account, and sent him off with permission to return with currant buns. The printers she would visit herself. It would be so satisfying to settle that account in full and early, with a little on top to thank them for sending work their way. The butcher was next on her list, but she would visit him later, along with the tanner who supplied her leather, as she didn't want to be carrying around so much money in one purse. Shaun would be too busy investigating the arsonist to accompany her about town paying accounts. And although he might have hired some returned soldiers to help him, there were still too many of them in town who lacked gainful employment and income.

The rest of the money she placed in a small tin and hid under the floorboards in her bedroom, dragging the heavy bed frame to put one foot on the loose board. Nobody could move it easily - it had taken all of her strength - and certainly not quietly!

That afternoon while the shop was calm, Louise sat at the counter and wrote back to Marie, choosing her words carefully to appear bracing and confident. She told Marie not to worry about a thing, just rest up and recover from her injury with as much forbearance as she could muster. With the money Renwick's man had delivered, they were more than flush for some time now.

Nibbling on her lip, Louise wondered if she should mention the fires in Hatfield, which hadn't started until after Marie departed. Best not, she decided. It wasn't as though Marie could do anything but worry about it, being so far away. Certainly Louise had no intention of mentioning that the arsonist might have tried to burn down their family bookshop.

Which also meant she really had no cause to mention Mr Jackson, either. Although, how could she even put into words how Shaun's continued presence in town was affecting her? She wasn't sure even Lord Byron could have managed poetry heartfelt enough to express such feelings.

Marie might think Louise had taken leave of her senses if she tried, too. She signed the letter, sanded it to dry the ink and then sealed it.

"Ruth, would you watch the counter for a few minutes? I'm just stepping over to the Red Lion to get this letter in the mail," she said.

"Yes, Miss Louise," Ruth said obediently. The girl still looked nervous every time Louise asked her to take charge, but she had to learn sometime. Bless Brutus, he always came and sat behind the counter too so that Ruth didn't have to manage alone.

In the busy inn yard, Louise found Mr Jackson talking with one of the returned soldiers he'd hired to help him, a thin dark man who had the unfortunate name of Riot Jones. Short for Sobriety, Shaun had informed her; Mr Jones was from a Welsh Methodist family. He didn't speak particularly fluent English, but Shaun was full of surprises and had admitted that he spoke Welsh quite well.

Riot Jones tipped his hat politely to Louise as he saw her coming, and slipped away with a murmured "Bore da, miss."

"Good day," she replied politely, trying to remember if they had a book of Welsh phrases in the shop. It really was such a pretty-sounding language.

"And what brings you out? Though Riot just told me he's seen you all over town this morning, at the butcher, the baker and the candlestick maker." Shaun grinned down at her.

"Well, Brutus went to the baker, but I did visit the butcher and the printer." She smiled back. "We had a visitor. A clerk from the Earl of Renwick, paying the account for the books my sister Marie delivered."

"The one in Cumbria, who hurt herself?" Shaun had been the one to hand her Marie's letter yesterday, had seen her face drop and heard her concerns.

"The very same. We were a little concerned we wouldn't get the money until she returned, but the earl organised everything, so I have been keen to settle our bills." She waved the letter. "And now I have to send this back to Marie, to reassure her that we are quite all right and she is not to worry."

"Very good."

Shaun's forehead was creased, Louise noticed, and he seemed a little distracted, even as he walked with her over to the post-counter.

"Is everything all right, Mr Jackson?" she asked.

Shaun hesitated, before he leaned closer and murmured, in a voice meant for her ears only, "There's been another fire."

Louise immediately wanted to ask questions, but there were too many ears surrounding them. She handed her letter to the post-clerk and put her hand into the crook of Shaun's elbow, leading him firmly back to the bookshop. He developed a half-smile on his face, walking with her.

"What fire?" Louise hissed, once the bookshop door was safely shut behind them and she'd peered around to check that they were alone but for Ruth and Brutus. "Mrs Poole hadn't heard anything…"

"Only just heard about it myself. It's bad. A remote cottage."

From the expression on his face, and the way he was still speaking very quietly, Louise knew that this time, the property hadn't been abandoned.

"Was anyone hurt?" she asked, her voice shaking a little. "Whose cottage?"

"A retired schoolteacher and his wife, Mr and Mrs Flyte." Shaun shook his head slowly, his eyes holding hers. "I'm sorry to be the bearer of bad news."

Louise's eyes filled with tears. She remembered the couple; Mr Flyte had taught quite a few of the boys in town their letters over the years, and had been a regular customer at the bookshop. His wife was a sweet lady who was on several of the committees in town with Mrs Poole. "They didn't make it out?" she whispered.

The slightest shake of his head was the confirmation Louise dreaded. A sob caught in her throat and she automatically leaned against Shaun for comfort. His warm arms wrapped gently about her shoulders and she breathed in his strength. "It's not fair. It's simply not," she said.

"I know," he said, his voice croaking as he agreed with her. "I will catch the blackguard who did this. Excuse my language."

Ruth and Brutus appeared, staring, and she gently broke the news to them. "If you need to go home, I'll understand," she said kindly. They were both just children; tragedies like this were a shock.

"My mother might need comfort," Ruth said, her eyes

filling with tears. The poor girl probably needed some comforting herself.

"Yes, your mother will need you, and I suppose your father will need to prepare a service for the Flytes too. Brutus, would you be an angel and walk Ruth home?"

"Yes, of course, Miss Louise."

He was not looking as upset as Ruth, because the names were probably not as familiar to him. "I suppose you were too young to have Mr Flyte as a teacher?"

"I never had him, but I think Benjamin might have known him. Miss Louise, after I take Ruth home, may I come back here after?"

"If that's what you'd like to do. Maybe we'll mix up some fresh glue when you get back, to keep us busy?"

The lad was obviously delighted, but tried ever so hard not to smile at his personal good fortune at such a time.

Shaun stepped away from Louise and she felt the loss of his warm, reassuring presence.

"I can walk Ruth home, if you like? It's on the way to the Flytes' cottage. I will need to examine the scene. I'll take Mr Jones with me."

It meant an end to their embrace for now, which filled Louise with shame that she'd experienced something wonderful as a result of something so awful.

Making a big pot of stinky glue would be exactly the penance she should perform.

Ruth made a little bobbed curtsey, "Thank you, Mr Jackson."

"Do you have sturdier boots, Miss Millings?" Shaun asked her, looking at her feet. "They don't look warm enough for this time of year."

She looked up in shock at his noticing such a minor thing, and said, "I have thick socks on."

"Right then," he said, nodding to Brutus and Louise in farewell.

He left the shop with Ruth and would be gone until he ran out of daylight, most likely. Louise sighed a little wistfully. "Brutus, I'll need to tell Bernadette and Mrs Poole, and we'll have a cup of tea first. I'll be back down in half an hour, but call up straight away if anyone comes into the shop, all right? And then we'll get to making that glue."

"I'm happy to sit at the counter and wait," he said, holding up a book from the lending library that he'd been reading. "This is a bully adventure, and I was just getting to the good bits."

"Right you are," she said, and headed up the stairs to the kitchen with the solemn duty to bear terrible news.

The French word for stairs popped into her head as she climbed them. *L'escalier*. Mr Jackson had been correct in his prediction; the culprit, whoever he was, had very much escalated things.

She was glad Mr Jackson was investigating, but all the same, a shiver of cold fear ran through her that the turnip-head lighting the fires had escalated to murder.

CHAPTER 10

The Midwinter Assembly

A week had passed since the tragic fire at the Flytes' cottage, and the couple had been peacefully laid to rest. Shaun had braced for a nasty sermon at church, and feared the vicar might make some kind of veiled attack at the Baxter women. Instead, the Reverend seemed subdued on Sunday. He spoke of the fires, which had Shaun sitting up and paying attention. Alas, this veered off towards a lesson on the fires of hell that awaited those who fall into temptation, which Shaun felt free to ignore.

Hatfield had been quite a mournful place since the fatal fire, but a few days later, the townsfolk seemed to be finding a little seasonal cheer as Christmas approached.

As he enjoyed a meal in the Red Lion, he noticed everyone seemed to be talking about a dance that was to take place the following evening.

"You going, Mr Jackson?" Hugh Fox, one of the men he had hired, asked. Shaun was sitting in the dining room sharing a meal with his three men, that delicious soup which was a recipe from Louise's mother.

"Maybe you can dance with Miss Baxter," Hugh's brother John said slyly, and Riot Jones laughed, obviously comprehending well enough the direction of the conversation even though they were speaking English.

Shaun's mood dampened. "I don't know if a lady like her would even attend." He immediately started thinking about what it would be like to dance with Louise. It had been a long time since he danced, and although his mother had taught him well, Mrs Jackson had been the last woman he'd been able to dance with who he didn't feel like a giant beside.

"Faint heart ne'er won fair lady," Hugh said with a grin. "Why don't you ask her?"

"Why don't the three of you stop sticking your noses in my personal life and go find this damn firebug?" His heart wasn't in the reprimand, even as he repeated it in Welsh for Riot's benefit, and all three men grinned at him. Riot and John pretended to start dancing a reel as they left, and Shaun laughed quietly to himself. They were good men, and now extremely loyal to him and Lord Ferndale. Hugh and John had even begun to talk of staying, if they could get long-term work on the farms once spring came, though Riot still wanted to go home to Wrecsam. Shaun had promised to pay his passage once they caught the arsonist.

Finishing his soup, Shaun found his feet carrying him back to the bookshop. "No, you don't, Crafty," he said, bending to scoop up the black cat as she tried to dart between his feet. She purred at him when he scratched the heart-shaped white spot on her chest, quite used to him by now.

Louise was smiling at him from behind the counter in a way which made Shaun feel rather like purring himself, and he set Crafty down, tilting his head to look at Louise thoughtfully. "Is that a new scarf, Miss Baxter? Haven't seen you wearing it before. Suits you." It was a pretty colour on her, a lovely emerald-green.

"Oh. Well, thank you!" She touched it. "It's not new, but I did just find it in the bottom of my drawer today and decided to wear it. My sister Marie knitted it last winter."

"Brings out the green in your eyes." He leaned on the counter, gazing into said pretty eyes, and said hopefully, "I was wondering, everyone in the Red Lion is talking about the Midwinter Assembly dance tomorrow night. I was wondering if you'd attend? Or if it's just for the common folk, like…"

"Oh, no!" Louise beamed at him. "It's two shillings per person to attend, so not really for the common folk at all, though some do save up to go. The fee goes to the hospital committee fund, you see, and of course Mrs Poole is on the committee, so we Baxters definitely attend."

"Ah!" He'd heard all about Mrs Poole and the committees. His landlady, Mrs Bell, was an excellent source of local knowledge. She had nothing but nice things to say about Mrs Poole and the Baxter girls, though she was rather disapproving of Mr Matthew Baxter having pushed off to France on a book hunting expedition and leaving the girls on their own, capable though they seemed to be.

"Are you going to attend?" Louise asked, a little diffidently.

"Only if you'll promise to dance with me."

She blushed a very pretty shade of pink. "Well, I rarely dance."

"Why ever not? A beautiful girl like you should have suitors lined up down the street to dance with you!" Shaun watched in fascination as Louise's blush deepened even further, until she was quite red.

"Well, I… that's extremely kind of you to say so, Mr Jackson." She pressed her hands to her cheeks, in an apparently vain effort to cool them. "Nobody has ever said anything like that to me before."

"I can't imagine why, you're quite the prettiest girl in this town."

"I… I… I'm taller than all the men here." She sort of mumbled it, unable to meet his eyes.

"You're certainly not taller than me, and I'll be honoured to stand up with you as many times as you'll allow me to."

She laughed, he rather thought in disbelief, before flashing him a bright smile. "I think twice is probably as many as Mrs Poole will let me get away with, else she'll send me straight home to bed."

"Twice it shall be, then; I wouldn't want you to get in trouble with Mrs Poole. The first dance? And another one later."

Louise agreed happily, and Shaun made his way back out to the street with a spring in his step.

Her body fizzing with anticipation, Louise took a good while longer to dress for this assembly than she had at the summer event. The lovely dress that had been made for her for Estelle's wedding would be perfect for the evening. As much as she wanted to clip her hair up in the usual economical way she was used to, she sat, fidgeting the whole time, as Bernadette and Rosie fussed about, curling and pinning her tresses.

The result was rather lovely, as she looked at herself in the mirror. "Thank you, both. I would never have managed that myself."

"Thank you, for letting us try the style," Rosie said with a little bob of her head. "There are others we found in a magazine, we'd love to try them... if you'd let us."

"That sounds like too much fun," Louise said, glad the maid was saying more than two words at a time around her. Perhaps letting the young lass at her hair had done the trick?

"Pinch your cheeks," Bernadette said. "Like this. It brings on a rosy glow."

Mrs Poole laughed and said, "She doesn't need it, she's glowing already."

Heat stole across Louise's face, but she grinned at them all. "I must say, I do feel rather pretty. Thank you for indulging me."

At the Red Lion, a sea of familiar faces greeted them, including Lord Ferndale and Miss Yates.

"I'm so glad you're both here, and you look so well," Louise said as she greeted them.

"I never miss an assembly, they are far too important," Miss Yates said. "Your hair looks divine, as do you."

Louise was overcome with the compliment. "Thank you so much, Miss Yates, that means the world to me."

Lord Ferndale added, "Wouldn't miss this for the world."

Bernadette asked after his health, and had another bottle of tonic for him. "How is your cough?"

"I forgot I had one," he said, not yet accepting the bottle. "I haven't even finished the last one. You keep that safe for someone who needs it more than I."

"As long as you're sure," Bernadette said. "You need to be careful on the cold nights."

"Stop fussing, that's Florence's job," he replied with a fond glance at his sister.

The musicians tuned up their instruments and played a quick few notes to let people know the dancing would be starting soon.

Near the musicians stood their cousins, Joshua and Phoebe. To Louise's surprise, Benjamin was standing with them.

Surely he was far too young to attend an assembly, though his height gave him an older appearance.

"Urgh, look who's here," Bernadette said, as they both tried very hard not to look. Several of the younger ladies of Hatfield were fluttering about, giggling behind their fans and looking Benjamin's way. Obviously they had no idea of his bullying tendencies.

One of the local farmers approached Louise, a man she knew was named Mr Stratforth. He was another tall man but not quite as tall as Mr Jackson. He smiled and said, "You're quite the prettiest girl here tonight, Miss Baxter. May I please have this dance?"

Louise beamed at the compliment and said, "You are very kind, and I thank you, but my first dance is spoken for. Perhaps the next?"

"Thank'ee," Mr Stratforth said with a nod. "Much obliged."

As if he'd planned such an entrance, the crowd parted and Shaun Jackson strolled toward her, his hand outstretched to take hers.

Oh goodness, he scrubbed up well! He was wearing a different coat to the one he normally wore, dark blue, with a waistcoat underneath in a slightly lighter blue colour. Had he bought them new for the occasion?

"I believe I have this dance, Miss Baxter?"

Louise smiled and pressed her hands into his as the dancers made their way to their positions for the country reel.

For such a large man, he was grace personified and light on his feet. His confidence radiated out to encompass Louise, who for the first time in her life felt pretty and light; possibly approaching elegant.

All her life she'd felt like a clumsy giant, dull in comparison with her prettier, smaller sisters. Tonight, with Shaun Jackson dancing with her, she could very well be the belle of the ball. She whirled and clapped and smiled so hard she thought her face might crack in two.

As the set ended, Shaun bowed to her and extended his arm, nodding towards the refreshment table. Quite warm from the dancing, Louise thought that a glass of punch would be rather nice and took his arm with a murmured thanks.

Her steps faltered as Phoebe swept into their path and stood facing her with arms folded, glaring down her thin nose at Louise. Or trying to, at least. Since Phoebe was so much shorter, she just looked rather silly with her head tipped too far back, as though she might be about to topple over at any moment.

Shaun simply tipped his head with a pleasant "Good evening, Mrs Baxter. How nice to see you again."

"Mr Jackson." Phoebe raked her gaze up and down his tall form with a dismissive sneer. She stepped aside, though as Louise walked past her, Phoebe said quite clearly, "We really must increase the entry fee for the assembly, if any old riff-raff think they can attend."

Riff-raff! Louise was fuming. How dare she!

"Please ignore her," she said quietly to Shaun. "Phoebe is a crashing snob at the best of times."

"People have said far worse about me." He gave an entirely unbothered shrug. "I don't let such things concern me unless they're accompanied by threats of violence."

"Has that happened to you a great deal?" she asked curiously.

"Enough," was all he said, handing her a glass of punch.

Bernadette came up then, smiling, and Shaun asked her if she had danced yet.

"Not yet." Bernadette shook her head.

"Well, since your sister says I may only dance two sets with her, may I request one of yours?" he asked.

Bernadette hesitated, looking up at him, and Shaun laughed quietly. "I may be large, Miss Bernadette, but I promise I'm not clumsy. I won't step on your feet."

She looked a little sheepish, and held out her hand. "In that case, I should love to dance with you, Mr Jackson."

Louise smiled as Bernadette cast her a sparkling, cheeky glance over her shoulder as she made her way to join the second set with Shaun. Bernadette had been almost a little afraid of Shaun at first, perhaps because of his sheer size, but over the last little while of him coming into the bookshop regularly and being unfailingly polite and charming, she had warmed to him.

Of course, she'd been teasing Louise about her interest from the very first moment. Louise sipped her punch and stood watching them dance, feeling rather pleased with herself.

"He's a very good dancer, your Mr Jackson. Light on his feet for a giant," Mrs Poole said, coming to stand beside Louise.

"Indeed he is," Louise agreed happily.

"I hesitate to say anything to take that smile from your face, but Mrs Wellworth just raised a rather good point to me."

"And what was that?" Louise's eyes narrowed. Mrs Wellworth was one of Cousin Phoebe's cronies. What poison was Phoebe spreading now?

"What do we know about Mr Jackson, truthfully?"

Louise was just opening her mouth to say that she knew quite a lot about him, really, when Mrs Poole added gently, "That he hasn't told us himself."

Louise froze, her mouth still open, and turned her head to meet Mrs Poole's gaze. The older woman looked really quite concerned.

"We don't even know if it's his real name," Mrs Poole pointed out. "Nor that he even comes from Yorkshire. That accent of his comes and goes like the breeze."

She didn't know what to say. Didn't know what to think. "He has a gentleman's education," she finally said, a little numbly.

"I will certainly give you that," Mrs Poole agreed. "And a facility with languages. His French is almost as good as yours, and he certainly speaks Welsh well enough with Mr Jones."

Louise looked across the room, to where Shaun was smiling genially down at Bernadette as they danced. She despised that she was even entertaining the possibility, but it was true that nobody in Hatfield knew anything about Shaun Jackson for sure.

"Lord Ferndale employed him," she mused aloud. "Perhaps he gave Lord Ferndale references?"

"Now that's a very good point, Louise. I'm sure Lord

Ferndale would have checked them, too." Mrs Poole nodded. "I might have a word with Miss Yates…" She drifted away, leaving Louise alone with her thoughts.

"Good evening again, Miss Baxter," a voice said, and she summoned a polite smile for Mr Stratforth, the farmer who had asked her to dance earlier. "I don't suppose you're available for the next set?"

"I am, as it happens." She couldn't think of a good reason to decline to dance, and if she did, she wouldn't be able to give Shaun the second dance she'd promised him. Despite the doubts Mrs Poole might have planted in her mind, Louise still did want that second dance with Shaun.

Louise was half way through her dance with Mr Stratforth, busily turning over in her mind subtle questions she might ask Shaun to find out more about him, when she realised Mr Stratforth was not so subtly hinting that he was ready to take a wife. And that he had his eye on her as a potential candidate.

"Of course, my wife wouldn't have to do cooking and cleaning," he was telling her. "I've a cook and two housemaids."

"That's, ah, fortunate," Louise said, not sure how she should respond.

"An educated wife would be a boon, though. Help me write letters and such, to other breeders. Keep track of the cattle's pedigrees. I've three prize-winning bulls and I get a lot of requests for their services."

"How fortunate." Drat, she'd already used that word, but also, this was something of an inappropriate topic for an assembly. He *was* a farmer, even if apparently a very successful one.

"I have a hundred and ten acres," he said proudly. "The

best grazing land in Hertfordshire, with good water even in drought; our dairy cattle have never dried up even in the worst years."

"That's…" she would not say *fortunate* again, "Providential."

Urgh! It meant the same thing! How was she going to escape what was possibly the dullest conversation she'd ever been subjected to?

"We're only about three miles out of town. I'd buy my wife a pony and trap, if she had family in Hatfield she wanted to visit, perhaps…"

"How generous." A thought struck Louise, and she had to suppress the urge to giggle. *A month ago, I'd never had so much as a sniff of a suitor. And now, it appears I might have two!*

As she danced, she caught sight of Shaun across the room, talking with Lord Ferndale. Shaun's eyes were on her, however, and his expression was… Louise wasn't quite sure how to define it, but he definitely did not look pleased.

Is he jealous? The thought was so startling - nobody had ever been jealous over her before! - that it took her a few moments to process how she felt about it.

Perhaps it was rather nice to have someone - to have *Shaun* - feel jealous over her. Louise smiled happily, and the hapless Mr Stratforth, who had been gazing hopefully at her while reciting a list of his favourite heifers' names - almost fell over his own feet.

What a lovely evening. And another dance with Shaun to look forward to! Louise firmly put any doubts about him out of her mind - blast Phoebe for spreading horrid gossip anyway - and decided to enjoy herself.

CHAPTER 11

Christmas at Ferndale Hall

The investigation was taking far too long, as far as Shaun was concerned. He thoroughly enjoyed the assembly and dancing with Louise, and was relieved his men had reported no new fires that particular night, but the next evening another barn had gone up in flames, this time with injured horses and a stablehand who Doctor Rasley had needed to treat. It had been the panicked horses who'd woken the stablehand, otherwise there would have been another death in town.

Shaun delivered his latest report to Lord Ferndale and Mr Baxter, the magistrate, and felt while the Baron was intent on pursuing the issue, the magistrate appeared uninterested in developments. But then, he knew more of the enmity between the two branches of the Baxter family, and understood the man was probably disinterested in anything Shaun had to say due to Shaun's obvious interest in Louise.

"A hurricane lamp, you say?" Lord Ferndale asked.

"Yes, we found the broken glass on the ashes. The same kind of debris we found at the Flyte cottage. I think we should ask around if anyone has been buying extra lamps lately."

"My stablehand has needed to purchase one recently," Lord Ferndale said. "On account of one of ours was missing. I hadn't put the two together …"

Joshua Baxter said, "I doubt the arsonist is showing his face and purchasing them for himself. Or herself for that matter."

"Herself?" Shaun and Lord Ferndale said together.

"It could very well be a woman!" Mr Baxter said. "We should not rule anything out. Why, Miss Bernadette gets about at night with a hurricane lamp herself!"

Shaun was all for keeping an open mind, but this was too much. "Miss Bernadette is helping ailing women and those in childbed. Do you expect her to go crashing about in the dark? Injuring herself?"

"You've lost your objectivity," Mr Baxter accused.

"But she's tiny!" Shaun said, incredulous that the matter could even be in question. It was a nonsensical suggestion.

Joshua pressed home his point, "And can you vouch for her on the nights of the fires?"

"I can for at least one, the night I found a tall, thin man loitering outside the bookshop with a tinder box. I was not chasing a small woman, that's for sure."

Joshua rolled his eyes and said, "Keep an open mind, that's what they say."

Lord Ferndale cleared his throat and said, "Now, my good man, I'm confident we'll have a breakthrough soon. In the mean time, Mr Jackson, what are you doing for Christmas?"

"Probably patrolling the town," he answered auto- matically.

"I'd very much like you to come to Ferndale Hall and spend it with us."

That brought him up short. "Goodness, I couldn't possibly impose."

"It would be no imposition at all! As you've no family here, I suggest you join mine, which will include the Baxter sisters as I consider them my granddaughters these days."

Louise would be there?

Joshua dramatically took out his gold fob watch and said, "Is that the time? I have another meeting to attend."

They nodded and wished him well. Ferndale sounded genuine, Shaun said it through gritted teeth.

Interesting that Lord Ferndale thought of the Baxter sisters as family, but not their cousin. Though Shaun admitted privately that he wouldn't be too hasty to claim Joshua as family himself, even if the connection were far more tangible.

When it was just the two of them, Shaun said, "In that case, my lord, I'd be honoured to attend."

"Most excellent!" Lord Ferndale said with a twinkle in his eye. It did appear as if the old man was matchmaking, and Shaun had no objections whatsoever to spending more time in close proximity with Louise.

"Now," Lord Ferndale probed. "Tell me more about your prospects."

Dear heavens, the man was direct!

Shaun answered his serious questions clearly and without hesitation. "I have been more fortunate than most, and have about twenty thousand pounds to my name, and plan to eventually purchase an estate of my own or a large house in town. I'd be able to support a wife and family in comfort."

"In which case, why are you renting a room with Mrs Bell?"

"That was for haste and convenience, not necessity. I needed to investigate the arsonist, especially after he threatened to burn down the bookshop. Mrs Bell answered my immediate needs, and her location is fortuitous as I can see the bookshop outside my bedroom window. This had the added benefit of disguising my true wealth from all in the town. I trust you to keep this knowledge between ourselves for the immediate future, as this may colour people's perceptions of me, and fuel gossip."

Lord Ferndale touched the side of his nose and said, "Understood."

At midday on Christmas Eve, Louise, Bernadette and Mrs Poole closed the bookshop and were ready with their travel bags. Lord Ferndale's coachman greeted them with the best wishes of the season and they travelled in comfort to Ferndale Hall. Louise thought of their sister, Marie, in an even colder climate and hoped fervently that she was coping with the Earl of Demanding as best she could. At least Marie had seemed otherwise well and in good spirits in her letter, and Louise hoped there would be another letter from her soon. How she ached to tell her sister about Mr Jackson.

They passed a bucolic meadow with cows clumped together under a copse of spruce trees and she giggled to herself about Mr Stratforth's rather stolid offer that he was ready for a wife. Louise could not imagine herself as a farmer's wife, not at all. Although perhaps if Mr Jackson were indeed to take up farming...

It sleeted all the way to Ferndale Hall and the roads were bumpy and wet, but it was a short journey and the hot stones in the footwell still had a little heat in them by the time they arrived.

Mr Thorne the butler greeted the three of them with a welcoming smile and directed them to the receiving room. "Mrs Sykes just took in tea," he said.

"How lovely," Louise said in anticipation. The moment she realised who else was in the room, a shocked "Oh!" fell out of her mouth.

For there, sitting beside Miss Yates and Lord Ferndale, was no other than Shaun Jackson.

"You've arrived!" Miss Yates said, as the gentlemen both rose from their seats to greet them.

Lord Ferndale said, "Welcome all. I trust you weren't too chilled in the carriage?"

Suddenly lost for words at seeing Shaun here, Louise kept her mouth shut. Mrs Poole stepped into the lull in conversation and said, "You're too generous. It was warm and comfortable. Thank you."

Mr Thorne came in and pulled out chairs for the new arrivals as Mrs Sykes poured more tea.

"You know Mr Jackson, of course," Lord Ferndale said, "I couldn't leave him by himself at Christmas, what with Mrs Bell gone to her sister in St Albans, and you're already acquainted so I thought we'd make a happy company."

Louise recognised a glint in Lord Ferndale's eye and wondered whether or not their self-appointed grandfather had given Mrs Bell some extra encouragement to visit her sister, in order to engineer this situation. She was well aware of how cleverly he'd arranged Estelle and Felix's romance. Not that she was complaining at all.

"Of course, Mr Jackson, it's delightful to see you," Louise said. "If I'd known you'd be here, I'd have brought more books."

"My library will have to suffice," Lord Ferndale said.

"Your library is a wonder, my lord, but I'm not too sure if you have many of the adventure novels Mr Jackson prefers," Louise remarked.

"Adventure novels, eh?" Lord Ferndale tapped his chin thoughtfully. "I've a few, I'm sure. Would you care to come with me to look, Mr Jackson?"

"I'd be delighted, my lord. After we've enjoyed this excellent tea Mrs Sykes has provided?"

Lord Ferndale laughed and said "Indeed, sir. I'm sure a gentleman of your stature requires regular fuel. Would you pass the fruit cake, Miss Louise?"

<hr />

Despite the only actual member of her family present being Bernadette, Louise thoroughly enjoyed Christmas. She spared a few thoughts for poor Marie, trapped in chilly Cumbria with the horrible Earl of Demanding for company, and several prayers for her father who-knew-where in France, but mostly she was too busy enjoying herself to think much about those absent. Especially Estelle, who would be having a wonderful time with Felix in Ireland.

Ferndale Hall was a delightful place to spend the holiday, full of good cheer and even better food. After a wonderful Christmas dinner of roasted goose with all the trimmings and more side dishes than even Mr Jackson had room enough in his stomach to sample, the party retired to the parlour and played a great many games, laughing all the while.

"Well," Lord Ferndale said as the laughter subsided at the end of a raucous game of charades, "I should like to thank you all for making this one of the most entertaining Christmases Ferndale Hall has seen in many a year."

"Hear, hear!" Miss Yates said happily, raising her glass of sherry.

"And I certainly hope you will all be here next Christmas with us too, when my grandson and his lovely wife will have returned, and hopefully dear Marie can join us, and your father too, my dears." Lord Ferndale gave Louise and Bernadette a benevolent smile.

"To absent friends." Shaun lifted his wine glass in a toast, and they all joined him, lifting their glasses and echoing the sentiment. "And though I do not know whether I will be here next Christmas, Lord Ferndale, I would like to repeat again my thanks for the invitation this year. I have enjoyed myself tremendously, though I really must point out one most egregious oversight in your arrangements."

Lord Ferndale paused with his glass halfway to his lips, arrested. "An oversight?"

"Indeed," Shaun said, a distinct twinkle in his eye as he glanced at Louise. "I have looked all about, and I cannot locate a single sprig of mistletoe within Ferndale Hall."

There was an instant of shocked silence. Louise gasped, and then absolutely everyone else burst out laughing.

Is he... did he just imply that he... would like to kiss me under the mistletoe?

She could not quite believe it. Her face must be as scarlet as the holly berries.

"Well, I do apologise for the oversight, Mr Jackson," Lord

Ferndale said, chuckling richly. "I shall ensure that my staff make up for it next Christmas, if you would care to join us again - I shall extend the invitation now!"

"I very much hope I will be able to take you up on your generosity, Lord Ferndale," Shaun said warmly, his eyes still on Louise.

Miss Yates made a funny little sound, and Louise glanced over, just in time to see the sherry glass topple from Miss Yates' hand and shatter on the floor, before the lady herself slumped against Bernadette's shoulder.

Everyone froze except Bernadette, who sprang into action with astonishing speed. Bernadette pulled Miss Yates' chair back, with the lady still on it, to create more room, before delivering a decisive rub onto Miss Yates' sternum.

The lady coughed and spluttered, her eyes springing open, then began apologising.

Louise sighed with relief.

"You passed out," Bernadette said. "Were you holding your breath?"

Miss Yates' hand fluttered about her chest and shook her head.

"There, there," Mrs Poole said. "Everything is all right."

"I was trying not to cough," Miss Yates said, then laughed at herself. "A little sherry went down the wrong way and... oh I've broken my favourite glass. That will teach me."

"You have a cough?" Bernadette's face filled with concern.

Miss Yates permitted herself a little throat clearing into her handkerchief. "Not at all, goodness I've made a hash of things. I was trying not to spoil the moment by coughing, so I held my breath and now I've ruined things."

Louise's heart tore a little at her dear friend's confession. "You haven't ruined anything, but we want to make sure you're well."

A few more slow breaths and Miss Yates asked, "My chest is sore, did I fall and hurt myself?"

"That was I," Bernadette confessed. "I learned it from the midwives, they give babes a little rub in the middle of the chest to rouse them if they're not immediately crying."

Miss Yates laughed and said, "I can see why that would make a babe cry!"

Relief flooded Louise as they relocated to the seats by the window while the maids cleaned the broken glass and spilled sherry.

Louise, Bernadette and Mrs Poole did not let Miss Yates out of their sight that evening and the next day. Miss Yates made soft noises of complaint about the attention, and by Boxing Day the novelty of being the centre of concern had completely worn off.

"You must go home on schedule. I am absolutely fine, you simply must stop fussing."

"Are you absolutely sure?" Louise asked, one more time. "We can send Bernadette home for more tonics. Whatever you need."

Miss Yates curled her hands into fists and pushed them into her hips, staring up at Louise as if she were a giant annoyance. "I am fit as a fiddle! Merry Christmas!"

Louise laughed, and then bent to fondly give the little old lady a kiss on the cheek. She'd become so fond of Miss Yates, quite as fond of as any of the family she was related to by blood, and fonder than several, considering Joshua and Benjamin. "Merry Christmas to you too, Miss Yates."

CHAPTER 12

Back To Business

T he journey back to Hatfield in the Ferndale carriage was far too short, in Louise's opinion. Shaun took the carriage back to town with them, and she savoured every moment with him and Bernadette and Mrs Poole, chatting and feeling completely comfortable in each other's company.

"I was very impressed with your skills, Miss Bernadette," Shaun said. "Miss Yates was lucky you were in attendance. You were so quick to bring her around."

"Truly, I wasn't sure it would work," Bernadette said. "We were lucky it wasn't anything serious."

"She gave me such a scare," Mrs Poole said. "She's been ever so kind to me over the years."

"In any case," Shaun said, "I shall use that chest rub technique in future, should I ever need to."

"And to think, she'd been trying not to make a scene," Louise said.

"How so?" Shaun asked.

"She said a little sherry went down the wrong way when

you commented about the absence of mistletoe. So she held her breath to stop herself from coughing and… she still ended up making a scene."

"That was funny," Mrs Poole said. "The look on his lordship's face when you said there was something amiss. He truly thought he'd make a mistake!"

Louise's memories were a little different to Mrs Poole's. As she recalled, Shaun had been looking at her with fondness at the time, making her tummy swirl in that lovely way. Just as it did when he was looking at her now.

The carriage slowed and they arrived at the bookshop. Shaun helped them out and encouraged Bernadette and Mrs Poole to get into the warm.

Riot Jones was there on the footpath, and he approached Shaun as the carriage rumbled away again. One of the Mr Foxes was also nearby, and he jogged up to Shaun as well. Louise wanted to get inside out of the cold, but she was madly curious as to what they could be talking about, especially as Riot had just mentioned the bookshop specifically.

Shaun nodded and thanked his men for their diligence, and asked them to continue monitoring the situation for the rest of the day.

"What's that all about?" Lousie asked, as the two men retreated to the archway.

Shaun smiled. "Good news. I asked my men to keep an eye on the bookshop because I'd be unable to, what with being at the Ferndales. At the time I hadn't known you'd be there too. I'm doubly glad I did, now, as the shop was empty for the best part of three days, though they said Rosie came in diligently each morning to feed the cats."

"I know I should thank you, but… this does not sit right

with me. The bookshop is my responsibility. Although… I should have thought of hiring some men to watch over it while we were away. We have the funds for that sort of thing now…" She trailed off, feeling at odds with herself. "Why am I not pleased? I should be. I think you should have asked me first, or let me know what you were planning."

Shaun's face looked stricken. "I have overstepped. Please forgive me."

"It was very thoughtful," she jumped in hastily, not wanting him to feel bad. "Oh goodness, I promised myself I wouldn't make Estelle's mistakes and fight with my sweetheart, and yet here I am!"

"Your sweetheart?" Shaun repeated.

"I don't want to argue. But this feels wrong."

Shaun smiled broadly. "I rather like the idea of being your sweetheart."

"But I'm cross with you!" Louise said. "And I don't like that you've made me cross, or that I am feeling cross. I wish these feelings would go away."

He pointed to the shop door. "Why don't we head inside? The fire shingle is still there, that's got to be a good sign."

An excellent idea. At least then she'd be warm and cross instead of cold and cross.

Inside, Mrs Poole was setting the fire and Bernadette lighting some lamps.

"We haven't checked the floors for entrails yet," Bernadette said. "We thought we'd take all the nice jobs and leave that for you."

Cheeky!

Louise watched her step as she and Shaun moved over to

the lending section of the shop and continued their fraught conversation.

"This is my fault entirely," Shaun said. "I'm so used to operating independently, and then having something to report at the end of it. I overstepped and I should have asked you first if my idea was a suitable plan of action."

"You are so kind," Louise said. "And... I think I'm mostly cross at myself for not having the sense to make sure the building was safe, considering what's happened."

Shaun stepped closer and tucked a stray tendril of hair behind her ear. The touch sent warm flurries through her. Very welcome warm flurries.

Anticipating a kiss, she said, "I'm sorry, we don't have any mistletoe either."

"We can pretend it's there," he said, leaning in closer.

Louise's heart nearly stopped in anticipation.

The front door crashed open and the bell flew off its screws and skittered over the floor.

Louise and Shaun leapt apart.

"Where the *hell* have you been?" Joshua shouted, storming into the shop with Benjamin on his heels.

"I beg your pardon!" Louise drew herself up to her full height. "I'll thank you not to use that kind of language here!" She scowled at Joshua. "And why do you care? It's not as though you and Phoebe were going to invite us to Christmas dinner, is it?"

Behind her, Shaun made a sound that could have been a snort but Louise was fairly sure was actually a laugh.

Joshua's mouth was flapping as though he hadn't a clue what to say, and Louise decided to press her advantage.

"Frankly, it's none of your business where Bernadette and I spent Christmas, and I must say that Brutus was well aware of where we've been, so if you ever talked to your middle son, you would already know!"

"Your reputation affects not just yourself," Joshua spluttered, finally finding his purpose for berating them this day. His face was red, and his chest was swelling up. "Your compcrtment at the Midwinter Assembly brought shame to the entire Baxter lineage. I'll not be surprised if the entire town of Hatfield, no, all of Hertfordshire, shuns this business! It's a blessed relief your father is not here to witness your fall."

"I grow tired of your theatrics, Cousin," Louise said, drawing in a deep breath. "And your barely-veiled threats. I supposed if I had refused to dance, you would no doubt accuse me of sulking. If I had not attended, you would accuse me of being remiss in my civic duties. The day you arrive bearing good news will be such a shock I shall no doubt faint!"

Pulse pounding in her ears, she felt so much better for giving him a taste of his own ridiculous medicine.

"As it so happens," Joshua blustered and began to stammer, "Th-the reason I came was t-to deliver you a boon. After the assembly, Farmer Stratforth asked my permission to court you."

The world tilted for a moment. Louise wondered whether she might indeed fall over in shock.

Joshua delivered a nasty little smile, as if he thought he had the upper hand. "I haven't yet made up my mind."

Benjamin, obviously not seeing Shaun in the shadows of the bookshelves behind Louise, took a couple of threatening steps towards her... and stepped in a pile of mouse entrails.

"Faugh, what's that?" Benjamin cried in disgust, retreating hastily.

Shaun did begin laughing then, moving forward to stand beside Louise. Joshua had apparently not noticed him either, because he took a step back, surprise coming across his still-red face.

"You haven't heard the last of this!" Joshua warned, wagging a finger at Louise, but he was already backing up.

"The last of what? I don't need your permission to go anywhere I please, whenever I please!" Louise snapped, thoroughly sick of her cousin's interference.

Joshua paused in the doorway, his eyes flicking to Shaun briefly, before he smiled victoriously. "You need me for one thing at least, miss, in your father's absence. You'll need my permission if you want to marry."

And with that parting shot, he slammed the door behind him again.

Louise found that her hands were shaking. She clenched and released her fists a few times, trying to release her anger.

"Are you all right?" Shaun asked quietly after a few moments.

"I have never resorted to violence in my life, but oh, I want to slap his face so hard I can almost *feel* it," she said through gritted teeth.

"I fully understand the sentiment." His hands landed on her shoulders, slowly rubbing, and she felt a little of her rage and tension fall away. "Why does he hate you so much? I know he wants the building, but from what you said about the entail, it seems he'll eventually get it anyway, when your father passes. Is he so short of funds that he needs to run you out of town sooner?"

"Quite the opposite, he's one of the wealthiest men in Hatfield," Louise said with a bitter laugh. She should turn to face Shaun, she supposed, but his large warm hands gently rubbing her shoulders felt so nice, she didn't want him to stop. "But he and Father have never seen eye to eye, and the entail does also state that our branch of the family must be running a viable business out of this building in order to keep it. The definition of 'viable', however, is a bit… loose. Cousin Joshua thinks it should not just support us, but enable Father to give us hefty dowries so we can move up in the world, or some such nonsense. Father - and all of us, I should note - disagree."

"And because Joshua Baxter's the local magistrate, the law's on his side," Shaun surmised.

"He *is* the law in Hatfield. He's only not pressed the issue because he'd have to pay to take it before Chancery Court in London, and he's too miserly to do that. And now, we haven't heard anything really from Father in months, but the books keep coming…" tears were running down her cheeks, Louise suddenly discovered, and she took a great gulp of air to try and stop them.

"Sh." Shaun's arms went around her, and he turned her round and pulled her close against him and just held her.

Louise buried her face in his neck and for a few, glorious moments let somebody else be the strong one, for once. "We'll be all right," she said finally, muffled. "Things were a bit shaky financially for a while because Father took out this huge loan to go to France, but Estelle's husband Mr Yates is so lovely, he paid several months' worth of the loan, and all these very valuable books keep arriving and are selling so well. And now the money's come from the Earl of Dema-Renwick, I mean, we're quite flush."

"And even if, Lord forbid, something has happened to your father, Mr Yates and Lord Ferndale will make sure the rest of you are secure," Shaun said.

"Yes." She sniffed a little and pulled back to look up at him, and he reached up to gently wipe away the tears on her cheeks with his thumb. "We'll be all right," she said, more firmly, and more to herself than to him.

"I have not the slightest doubt that even if you had nobody at all to help you out, you'd pull through, Louise Baxter," he said quietly. "You're really quite remarkable, you know."

She smiled shyly up at him, wondering if maybe he would kiss her now, but they were interrupted yet again, this time by Bernadette's cries of dismay on coming down the stairs and finding the doorbell on the floor.

"Let me fix that up for you," Shaun said, letting go of Louise and going to pick up the bell. She hugged herself, feeling the loss of his warmth, and then sighed and went to pick up the pan and rags to clean up the mess of entrails Benjamin had tracked across half the floor on his way out of the shop.

"Why do they always take it upon themselves to make every situation worse?" Bernadette lamented as she surveyed the chaotic scene. "If it's not one thing, it's another!"

Scraping entrails off the floor, Louise sighed in agreement. "I'm so tired of dealing with them. Father can't come back soon enough."

"And you, Pie!" Bernadette scooped up the half-grown cat as he dashed past her feet. "You're a menace!"

"Good mouser, though," Shaun noted, with a quiet laugh. "If he's still here when I get a house of my own, I'll happily take him."

That made Louise feel warm inside again; further proof that Shaun was thinking of staying in Hatfield long-term. He finished fixing the bell and departed with a cheerful farewell, saying that he needed to talk some more to his men. Louise didn't think it was only in her imagination that his final glance at her was filled with wistful regret for the kiss they still hadn't managed to steal.

CHAPTER 13
FIRE!

There was a certain rhythm to life in Hatfield that Shaun was beginning to thoroughly enjoy. Due to the constant passage of coaches - even at this time of year, when sensible folk avoided travelling unless absolutely necessary - there were always new faces at the Red Lion and strangers walking about the town. Underneath that busyness the townsfolk were a steady, hardworking lot.

Which wasn't to say they were all perfect, of course. There were at least four town drunkards who were regularly tossed out of the Red Lion or the Swan for instigating fights with unsuspecting strangers, but word had long since got about that Lord Ferndale had hired Shaun and his men to catch the arsonist, and from all accounts, petty crime in Hatfield had dropped considerably since the four of them had begun their regular pattern of nightly patrols.

The arsonist, unfortunately, remained at large. Shaun was more sure than ever that it was a local, someone who knew the alleyways and back gardens of the town and was clever enough to evade the patrols. There were several roads leading out of town and innumerable isolated farms and cottages on narrow lanes. It was here that the arsonist was choosing to strike for the most part. Almost every night another barn or stable caught alight, and often nobody realised it until the orange glow lit up the night sky and the building was beyond saving.

It was only a matter of time before someone else died, Shaun thought grimly, climbing into bed in the early hours of the morning. Every fire thus far had been started between the hours of nine and midnight, so he was reasonably confident that at three o'clock he could get some sleep without missing anything.

He had just drifted into that twilight state between waking and sleeping, his muscles slowly relaxing as his body warmed up under the covers after spending most of the night out in the wintry cold. A loud crash brought him to full wakefulness in an instant.

"What the hell was that?" He shot out of bed, grabbing for his trousers and shoving his feet into his boots. It sounded as though it had come from the direction of the bookshop. He didn't waste any time looking out of the window, just raced downstairs with his boots crashing on the wooden steps and wrenched the door open.

There were only two small windows on the ground floor of the bookshop, but even in the dark from across the street he could see that one of them was broken and there was a suspicious orange glow inside.

"FIRE!" he roared, racing across the street and hammering on the door. "FIRE! LOUISE!"

Running to the broken window, he peered in, wondering if he could get through the narrow gap, but it was barely big enough to admit his head, never mind his shoulders.

"LOUISE!" He bellowed her name again, and this time heard an answering call, accompanied by the sound of running feet.

The door rattled, and Shaun rushed back to it just as Bernadette pulled it open. She looked up at him white-faced, but Shaun had no time to do anything but run past her and head for the source of that orange glow.

He got there to find Louise on her hands and knees whacking at the fire with what he recognised as her thick winter coat. She already had it half out, and a bit of stamping from Shaun and a few more whacks with the coat extinguished the last of the embers.

Shaun spared a moment to be grateful that the narrowness of the window had meant the lamp the arsonist had thrown inside had landed in one of the few areas of the shop where there weren't actually any books, in a small nook with two armchairs and an old woollen rug on the floor. The rug had smouldered but was slow to truly catch alight, it was mainly the burning oil from the lamp itself that had caused the orange glow.

Louise knelt on the rug, singed coat clutched in her hands. She wore a thick robe over her nightgown, but her bare feet and hair tumbling loose about her shoulders said clearly that she'd been sound asleep in bed when the arson attack occurred.

"Mind your feet," Shaun warned as she stood up; there were shards of broken glass from the smashed oil lamp which seemed to be the arsonist's signature method of attack.

There were shouts outside and the ostler from the inn came in; Mr Thomas was a sensible man who Shaun had learned was quite sweet on Mrs Poole. Thomas stopped to check on the older woman, who stood huddled with Bernadette near the door, both of them looking a little faint, before coming over to Shaun.

"Bad business, this," Thomas muttered, and Shaun nodded.

"We need to cover over that broken window. Have you a board that would fit?"

"Aye, reckon I can find something."

Others were coming into the shop now, the landlord Mr Haye, followed by a white-faced Riot Jones.

"We thought it was too late for an attack!" Riot said in rapid Welsh.

"This bastard's got our patrol pattern figured out," Shaun responded grimly in the same language, and Riot looked sick.

Louise had walked to the counter and returned now with a dustpan and brush, kneeling back down to start sweeping up the broken glass.

Mr Thomas came back with a couple of boards, a handful of odd nails and a hammer, and he and Shaun set to boarding up the broken window.

"We could make some interior shutters for these," Shaun said thoughtfully. "So that you could open them during the day and close them at night. I'll do it tomorrow if you like, Louise."

Riot made an amused little sound. "*Louise* now, is it?"

Shaun suddenly realised that he was completely forgetting to call her Miss Baxter. She'd been Louise in the privacy of his thoughts almost from the moment he met her, and then when he saw the fire inside the bookshop he'd screamed her name repeatedly, and now...

She was looking at him very strangely, standing there

131

with the hammer and a couple of spare nails clutched in his fist.

And it was then that Shaun realised, in his haste to get to her, he hadn't remembered to grab a shirt.

Riot was openly laughing at him, Mr Thomas looked highly amused, and even Mrs Poole, now that she was past the worst of her shock, was looking at him with a twinkle in her eye and a smirk on her lips.

"I…" Shaun did not know where to put himself. "I… beg your pardon, Lou… Miss Baxter… I'll just…" He handed the hammer to Mr Thomas and retreated hastily, feeling her eyes on him all the while.

I must have shocked her almost out of her wits, Shaun berated himself as he fled back to Mrs Bell's, through a crowd of onlookers who'd gathered outside to see what all the commotion was about. And it was a good thing he'd been obviously outside the bookshop when the fire started, or considering his state of undress, he'd probably be dragged in front of the vicar later today and ordered to make an honest woman of Louise Baxter.

Not that he would in any way object to that, but being force-marched to the altar under a cloud of scandal was definitely not the way he wanted this courtship to go.

Deeply embarrassed, Shaun made his way back to Mrs Bell's to dress himself into respectability. As much as he felt stupid and foolish, he acknowledged the laughter - though directed at him - was also a form of relief that everyone was safe and there was no harm to the bookshop.

But he was especially relieved Louise was unharmed. At least physically. He hoped this incident would not plague her sleep and make this admirable woman afraid of people.

She was the most courageous woman he'd ever met.

Back in his room, he caught sight of himself in the small mirror and gave himself a shock. His hair was at all angles from sleeping, and he'd missed a button on his pants. What a mess! But speed was the enemy of sartorial elegance.

Properly dressed, he dragged a brush through his hair and sat up high in his bed so he could keep the bookshop in view for the rest of the night.

Determination thrummed in his blood, as he vowed to catch the arsonist. He would not rest until he stopped whoever he was.

It was obvious the arsonist was deliberately targeting the bookshop and Louise.

He thought some more and started to wonder... had his mind and heart been so captivated by Louise that he'd over-looked the true target? Was Miss Bernadette the real victim here and he'd overlooked her?

No, surely not. Bernadette helped people and they paid her in kind with baked goods and produce, so far as he could tell. Targeting Bernadette made even less sense. Had she slighted or rejected someone? That was a possibility. Perhaps a spurned lover had refused to accept her decision and was taking his anger out on the town?

He was mixing up real life with the dramatic events in novels. None of his theories about Bernadette held water.

The only people who publicly disagreed with the Baxters were Reverend Millings, via his sermons, and their cousin Joshua. Millings surely didn't have the strength for the efforts, and Joshua was far too short and wide.

Maybe it was a returned soldier with no prospects? Desperate people would do anything for money - and Louise had told him Joshua was one of the richest men in the town. Was Joshua paying someone to make their lives hell?

A chill spread through him that tonight the arsonist had taken advantage of their patrol movements and schedule. He trusted Riot and the Fox brothers, but was there a chance they'd let something slip to a fellow soldier?

Sooner or later, the arsonist would slip up, and Shaun would be there to catch him and bring him to justice. It could only be a matter of time.

CHAPTER 14
Another Crate

L ouise yawned and rubbed her tired eyes as she walked downstairs the next morning to let Rosie in.

"You look exhausted," the maid said. "I heard what happened. Let me help with the cleaning down here."

Louise was not at all surprised that Rosie knew about last night. Most of Hatfield must already know, and then in a couple more days at church everyone would be well informed.

Louise rubbed her eyes again and made a croaky, "Good morning." It had taken her forever to get to sleep after the attack last night. Even after everyone who'd helped had gone home and she, Mrs Poole and Bernadette had a sip of brandy each to calm their nerves, she'd had trouble falling asleep.

Each time she closed her eyes, they sprang open. Not from reliving the fire, but from seeing Shaun Jackson's delectable torso.

Suddenly she remembered to look down in case there were morbid leavings from Crafty and Pie. There were, so she mumbled something about fetching the ashpan and cloth.

"I'll do that for you, Miss Louise," Rosie said.

"You're too kind," Louise said, her eyes filling with tears. Rosie was such a boon to them, and ever since she and Bernadette had done Louise's hair for the assembly, the maid had become so much friendlier to her.

Bernadette came down and lit the lamps, Mrs Poole soon following with some kindling and a tinder box to start the fire in the small stove. She was placing a fire where it belonged, safely away from anything else flammable and protected with a sturdy guard around it.

All the same, the sight of the flames made Louise twitchy at first.

It had been so easy to dismiss Shaun as being overly protective when he'd chased the arsonist away. But now that arsonist had come back and struck a blow. A badly aimed one, but still a blow. Would he get bolder still?

The shop door opened, making the bell tinkle. In walked the man whose naked chest had robbed her of any chance of getting back to sleep last night, with a crate of books on his shoulder.

"Good morning, Miss Baxter," he said with all due formality for their audience.

As Louise steadied her heartbeat and replied a good morning greeting back to him, she then waited for him to greet the others. To her surprise, none came. The bookshop was silent. Louise turned around and realised everyone had quietly slipped away as soon as Shaun walked in.

Heat roared up her face, knowing they'd purposely left her alone with Shaun.

Shaun said, "This crate just arrived, so I thought I'd bring it in."

"Please, down near the counter, I'll grab the crowbar," Louise said, doing her best to sound business-like.

With delight, she recognised the writing on the box's labels as her father's. As she cranked the top boards off and the nails sprang free, she begged the Lord above that her father had included a note or letter this time.

"I hope you were able to get some rest last night, after the attack."

She popped the last few nails and put the crowbar aside. "Not a wink."

"I was the same," he said. "I'm starting to wonder if it might be a soldier, and maybe he got Hugh or John to let something slip? They've hired a couple more men as well, and they would have had to tell them what times we do patrols. Wouldn't take much for the arsonist to deduce when we're not patrolling."

"Well, we wondered about that from the beginning." The top of the crate was filled with rag scraps, her father's preferred method for safely packing books. They in turn were very useful for collecting Crafty and Pie's sloppy gifts. Louise plucked the rags out and picked up the first book. "But honestly, most of them do move on and go home. I think there would be very few who are still in town from the date of the first attack."

"What if it was a soldier for whom Hatfield *is* home?" Shaun argued. "There must be dozens of them."

Louise conceded that was true. "But then, why would he have such a desire to destroy his own town?" she asked.

Shaun sighed, leaning against the counter and folding his arms across his chest. That delicious, broad chest, which she'd got to see in all its naked glory last night. He wasn't chiseled like one of the Greek statues she'd seen in illustrations, more thick with muscle, dark hair curling from a broad mat on his chest and arrowing down to a thin line which led all the way to his waist... and presumably lower.

Heat seared her face at the memory. *I shouldn't be thinking about that.* She tried to focus on what he was saying, something about men whose reason had been broken by the horrors of war.

"And you think the only sign of such a broken mind would be a penchant for arson?" she asked sceptically.

"I... don't know," Shaun admitted. "Miss Baxter... Louise..."

The way he said her name made a thrill go through her, and Louise had to stop sorting books for a moment because her hands started trembling.

"Yes?" she said, her voice coming out thin and soft.

"I think you should leave."

"I beg your pardon!" She had been thinking, hoping really, that he might ask if he could kiss her, but what was this?

"The bookshop. That's twice you've been targeted. Three times if you count the fire shingle coming loose. I think you, Bernadette and Mrs Poole should move out, until the arsonist is caught. Lord Ferndale would be glad to host you, I'm sure..."

"Absolutely not!" Louise was horrified at the mere suggestion. She put her hands on her hips and scowled at Shaun. "Ferndale Hall is too far away. We wouldn't be able to open the bookshop. And if the bookshop isn't open, Cousin Joshua will be able to claim we're not running the business out of the building!"

"Somewhere else, then, somewhere closer," Shaun suggested. "The Red Lion - Mr and Mrs Haye think a lot of you, I know they'd find rooms…"

"You're being ridiculous," Louise said firmly. "This is my home. I'm not going anywhere."

"You're being stubborn!" He looked almost pleading. "Your safety, your *life*, is the most important thing here."

"I'm not leaving and that's final."

Shaun shook his head slowly, his mouth setting in a thin line. "This discussion isn't over."

"Yes, it is."

They were interrupted - again! - by Mr Thomas coming in with an armload of wood, and Louise thought glumly that the marvellous opportunity she'd been given to be alone with Shaun, maybe to be kissed, was once again going to be wasted.

For the next hour, the men busily constructed interior shutters for the small ground floor windows. They could be opened during the day to let some light in, but at night they could be bolted shut to prevent future attacks.

Removing the temporary timbers had the cold wind howling through, but it couldn't be helped.

Louise settled herself behind the counter and decided to write to Marie. She would need to mention the fire, but chewed the inside of her cheek thinking how she might word it. Marie was too far away to be able to help, and might injure herself further if she tried to rush home before her ankle was strong enough. "Nothing to worry about, just an arson attack from a man who's still at large and who is targeting us, according to Shaun," would definitely send Marie into panic.

It would mean having to explain Shaun Jackson, who was causing Louise not to know up from down half the time!

In the end she had to write something, so settled on some bland wording and said everything was well in hand and the rest of Hatfield was watching over them.

Brutus and Ruth arrived to dust the shelves, which would need a little more work than usual because the fire last evening might have left soot or oil residue on the shelves. When the glazier arrived, the place seemed even more crowded than usual. The glazier measured the window and removed the shards of broken glass still stuck in the frame. Louise paid him in advance and he promised to have the new panes installed within the week.

Bernadette appeared with her basket of herbs and tonics, rugged up warmly against the weather. "I shall be back later this afternoon," she said to Louise.

Shaun nodded a greeting to her and said, "Hold up. Take Riot or one of the Fox brothers with you for safety."

Bernadette frowned and said, "I appreciate the gesture, but ah, a man travelling with me would cause more problems."

Louise looked at Shaun, who was looking even more adamant than when he'd suggested they move out of the bookshop. Going over to him, she took his arm and drew him aside. "What's this about?" she asked quietly.

Shaun glanced at Bernadette, who was standing by the door, apparently not leaving just yet. Looking back at Louise, he answered in an equally hushed tone. "I've been thinking. The bookshop being targeted twice has made me wonder if it's someone with a grudge against one of you. Bernadette wanders about alone... and she's only a bit of a thing."

A cold feeling settled in the pit of Louise's stomach.

"Can you think of anyone who might have a grudge against her? A rejected suitor, perhaps?" Shaun asked.

Not a rejected suitor, not that Louise could think of, but there were certainly men in town who might think they had a grievance against Bernadette. Allan Jefferies, who'd wanted to marry Sally Lewis enough to plant a babe in her belly against her will… and Bernadette had made sure that a marriage wouldn't be necessary after all. And Allan was just the most recent name that came to mind.

She wasn't going to tell Shaun any of this, not without discussing it with Bernadette first. Every woman in town knew what Bernadette's herbs could do, and not even Phoebe Baxter would breathe a word of it to any man. A woman who dared break that code would likely find no help would come from a midwife when they most needed it.

"I can come, Bernadette," Louise said. "Give me a moment to grab my coat." She'd used her good winter coat to smother the fire and was using a thinner one that would have to do, despite the cold outside. It was just behind the counter and she grabbed her letter to Marie at the same time. Then she called out to Ruth and Brutus to mind the shop.

Shaun frowned at Louise and Bernadette. The youngest Baxter sister shifted her basket into her other arm, further away from his gaze. Louise delivered a bright smile his way and handed him her letter to Marie. "Would you mind getting this into the next post for me?"

"Of course," he said automatically, and although he still looked confused, he didn't ask any more questions.

Good. Bernadette's business was women's business. Men didn't need to know about any of it.

The next day the Ferndale carriage arrived outside the bookshop around mid-morning. Brutus and Ruth were quite confident now to mind the shop so that Bernadette, Louise and Mrs Poole could visit Ferndale Hall, and Rosie came down to sit with the youngsters too in case they needed someone a little older and with more confidence to help out.

Riot Jones was keeping watch outside the shop, standing in the street and nodding to passers-by. Louise was surprised Shaun wasn't with him, and she looked in the direction of Mrs Bell's house to see if he was watching the street from his window.

The reason for Shaun's absence became apparent when they arrived at Ferndale Hall. There was her protector, deep in conversation with Lord Ferndale.

Shaun smiled broadly when he saw her. "We meet again." He took her hand and bowed over it most correctly.

"I was wondering why I hadn't seen you this morning," Louise said, realising even as she said it that she was not just wondering about it, she had been disappointed. She'd grown used to seeing him come in first thing, often before she'd even finished scraping up Crafty and Pie's messes.

"I had to consult with Lord Ferndale. The lads I've hired are doing their best, but it's a big town and a bigger district to cover. We need a bigger watch crew, and the fire engine is antiquated… there are much better models available now."

"And Lord Ferndale will pay for it?" Louise glanced at the old baron, who was smiling genially as he listened to Mrs Poole chatter about something.

"Aye. He said it's cheaper than rebuilding more barns,

and you can't pay enough to replace people, anyway." Shaun's face was sombre.

"That's very true." Louise suddenly realised Miss Yates wasn't in the parlour to greet them. "Where's Miss Yates, Lord Ferndale?" she asked.

"Florence wasn't feeling quite the thing this morning. Sent word down with her maid she'd have breakfast in bed." Lord Ferndale looked a little concerned. "I missed her smiling face at breakfast, she rarely stays above stairs like this."

Bernadette was on her feet at once, and Louise followed her and Mrs Poole straight upstairs without waiting another moment. They were all very fond of the sweet old lady, and if there was anything they could do to help her feel better, there wasn't a moment to waste.

"Hullo, my dears!" Miss Yates looked up with a happy smile as they almost burst into her bedchamber. Far from lying in bed looking pale and wan, she was sitting by the window, fully dressed, a cup of tea at her elbow.

"Lord Ferndale said you weren't feeling well?" Bernadette said, a little out of breath from the rush up the stairs.

"Oh, Arthur, always making a fuss." Miss Yates shook her head with a cheerful little chuckle. "I stubbed my toe on the chamber pot and thought to rest it from walking downstairs for a little while!"

"Florence!" Mrs Poole gasped, clutching at her heart. "You gave us all a fright."

Miss Yates giggled a little and waved to the chaise opposite her. "My dears, really, do sit down. I shall send Anne for tea and cake."

"And you shall let me look at that toe," Bernadette said firmly. "Just in case you have done more than bruised it."

"Very well, very well." Miss Yates suffered Bernadette to look at her foot and wiggle her toe about while the others took their seats. "Now, Louise." Miss Yates gave her a little smirk. "How did you find our other guest this morning? I saw Mr Jackson arrive a little while ago. Such a fine figure of a man."

Louise could not help the slow red tide surging up her neck and onto her cheeks. "Mr Jackson seems very well," she answered sedately.

"I think the livery stables rented him a cart horse, a great beast he rode in on this morning!" Miss Yates smiled meaningfully. "I shouldn't wonder if he'll buy himself a horse soon enough, with the amount of travelling he does about the countryside. I think Arthur might have a nice hunter he plans to sell which would be up to Mr Jackson's weight; I might mention it."

Mrs Poole said what Louise was thinking. "I'm not sure if that would be within Mr Jackson's budget."

Miss Yates laughed aloud. "Not within his budget? Good Lord, Alison, have I not told you yet? Arthur asked him about his circumstances. The man has a nice fortune to his name!"

Louise's mouth fell open with shock.

Miss Yates eyed her with a widening smirk. "More than enough to buy a fine property... and support a wife."

Louise's blush, which had been fading, roared back up her cheeks as everyone looked at her and giggled.

"Why, I shall very much enjoy telling Phoebe Baxter all about that when I see her next week at the Hatfield Gardens

Committee," Mrs Poole said, clearly delighted, as Miss Yates' maid brought in the tea.

"She finally got onto a committee then?" Bernadette asked

"Yes, after we lost dear Mrs Flyte, may she rest in peace, we had a vacancy," Miss Yates confirmed, before she turned back to Mrs Poole and said, "Indeed, make sure you tell her how much." Miss Yates sipped her tea and smiled, looking very much like Crafty after getting into the cream. "Twenty. *Thousand*. Pounds."

CHAPTER 15

Where There's Smoke

F rustration gnawed at Shaun at how long the arsonist remained at liberty. When the next Sunday rolled around, he accompanied the Fox brothers to the Catholic service at St Peter's, to see if he could spot any people who might fit the same frame as the arsonist he'd chased away from the bookshop that night.

As much as he could describe the culprit to his men, he felt sure he'd know him if he saw him. As far as he could tell, Shaun had been the only one who'd seen the blackguard so far, not that it had been a very good look in the dark.

One man in church appeared to fit the bill, but as the man turned around Shaun quickly realised he was far too old, as he had a cane beside him. Definitely not the athletic young man he'd chased away.

After the service, he chatted with the Fox brothers as they walked back towards the Red Lion.

Hugh asked, "Does he have a horse? Is that how he's getting about? He almost has to, eh. The distances he's covering... a long way for a man afoot."

"Good point," John said. "We should see if there are any missing from the stables."

The news put Shaun on edge. The arsonist was playing with them, changing up his habits to keep them unsure of when he'd next strike.

Cunning as a rat.

He farewelled the brothers and went back to his room at Mrs Bell's so he could sleep for a few hours. He jammed a nail into a candle, about half an inch from the top, so that when it melted the wax as it burned down, the nail would fall away and hit the tin candle holder, waking him up.

This became his routine, staying awake all night watching over the bookshop, checking in on Louise in the morning, then grabbing a few hours' sleep during the day when there were far too many people out and about for the arsonist to do anything without being seen.

There seemed to be a fire every other night. A barn or an old cottage on the far edges of town, but completely different sides of Hatfield. It was sending the volunteer fire-fighters batty, as they were getting no sleep either. They were running all over finding the fires and then trying to put them out before it spread anywhere else. They also had jobs to perform during the day, but lack of sleep meant many were making mistakes or injuring themselves.

This in turn kept Doctor Rasley far busier than he was used to, and he was getting grumpy as well. The town simply wasn't functioning the way a town should with so much uncertainty and fear.

On his way to check on Louise the next morning, he saw Riot out the front of the bookshop, on guard as usual. Was it selfish of him to want to guard the Baxters while other buildings were going up in flames?

"Morning, Riot," he said. "I appreciate your diligence, but you don't have to guard the bookshop during the day. I'm sure they're safe in broad daylight, with all the passing traffic."

"Morning, Mr Jackson," Riot replied, with a slight blush. "Miss Louise… the Baxters are important to you, so that makes them important to me."

Shaun felt heated embarrassment spread up his face. Was he so easily readable these days? He truly was losing his touch, spending so long not solving a case. "I appreciate your concern, and I'm sure the Baxters do too."

A tall man walked past while Shaun was talking to Riot, and entered the bookshop. Shaun turned his head to watch him go, concluding regretfully after a moment that although the man was the right height, he was much too broad-shouldered and walked flat-footed, unlike the slender, agile arsonist. *Not the man I'm looking for.*

There was something familiar about the man, however, and Shaun spared a moment to think about where he'd seen him before.

The assembly! That was it. The man was the farmer who'd danced with Louise - who'd made her laugh.

And now he was going into the bookshop.

Where Louise was.

Shaun walked away as Riot was mid-sentence, leaving the Welshman staring after him in astonishment.

Mr Stratforth - Shaun remembered his name now - was leaning against the counter smiling down at Louise as Shaun hurried into the bookshop after him. Louise's gaze flicked to Shaun and she nodded slightly, in a gesture he'd come to learn meant, "I'm with a customer, I'll get to you in a minute."

Shaun stood awkwardly for a moment, unsure what to do with himself. Unsure of even why he'd rushed into the shop after the farmer. He didn't for a moment think Louise was in any danger. Not from this oaf, who was awkwardly asking if Louise had any books on dairy farming in stock. It was on the tip of Shaun's tongue to sarcastically ask if the man didn't already know how to look after his cattle, but Louise wouldn't thank him for being rude to a paying customer.

Louise fetched a book and showed it to Mr Stratforth, their heads bent much too close together for Shaun's liking. He couldn't watch. In the end he turned around and walked out of the shop again without waiting, before he said or did something stupid.

"Jealousy's an ugly thing," Riot said, and Shaun turned his back on the too-astute Welshman and stomped off down the street.

He found himself outside a shop he rarely frequented, the haberdashery, where the ladies of Hatfield bought their fabrics and ribbons and who knew what folderol. The shop had a larger window than most and he paused, caught by something displayed inside it. After a moment he pushed the door open and entered.

"Can I help you, Mr Jackson?"

He wracked his brain for the lady's name; he'd met her at church a time or two. Mrs Brownlee? That was it.

"Good morning, Mrs Brownlee. I, ah, that cloak in the front window. Is that for sale?"

"It is indeed." The lady smiled at him. "We don't sell much pre-made clothing, but I make a piece occasionally for display."

"It looks quite long…"

"Easier to make a piece too long and take it up than find it's too short for the lady who wants to buy it!" Mrs Brownlee chuckled richly.

"I was wondering if it would be long enough for Miss Louise Baxter." He looked more closely at the cloak as Mrs Brownlee took it off the dummy it was hanging on and offered it to him. It was a thick, quality wool, a practical dark blue colour, and had several mother-of-pearl buttons down the front and slits a lady might push her hands through to use them.

"I should think it might be, at that." Mrs Brownlee looked amused.

"Hers was ruined in the fire at the bookshop the other night," Shaun said hurriedly. "I… thought to replace it for her."

"That's very generous of you, Mr Jackson. What a kind gesture. I'm sure I could let you have it for a good price, considering…"

He was sure she could. They haggled briefly, and he pulled some coins from his pocket and counted out the agreed price before Mrs Brownlee wrapped the cloak in some brown paper for him and tied it with string.

With the package under his arm, he made his way back up the street, hoping the stupid farmer would have taken his book and gone by now.

He nodded to Riot again as they passed each other. By this point Rosie had arrived and was also greeting Riot, with a cheerful "Bore da," which had the Welshman smiling broadly.

When he entered the bookshop, he'd hoped Mr Stratforth would be long gone. No such luck at all. The farmer and Louise were having an animated discussion, and when

Shaun walked in, Louise immediately said, "You should tell Mr Jackson everything you can remember."

Parcel under his arm, Shaun stood there as the farmer relayed his tale.

"The lad was almost tall as me, he was," the farmer began. "Caught him trying to throw something on the roof. Ran over and called him out, then he turned and collected me on the head. Had some kind of cudgel. Knocked me out cold! By the time I came around he was long gone and the roof was alight. Others must have seen the flames because they rallied round quick and we got it out. There's damage aplenty, but not so bad as it could have been."

Shaun's blood ran cold. Jealousy forgotten, he put the parcel on the shop counter and interrogated the farmer with more questions.

"Did you get a good look at him?"

Mr Stratforth shook his head solemnly. "That I did not. He was wearing a cloak with a hood and it covered much of his face. But it were a man, I could tell by the shape of his jaw, and his height, near as tall as me! Slim fellow, but strong. When he hit me I blacked out and didn't see which direction he ran off in."

Shaun huffed out a breath. The arsonist was becoming even more dangerous, carrying weapons to disable and potentially kill people if he gave it enough force.

"How is your head?"

"It does ache, I'll give you that. Lad was strong."

"You should get Doctor Rasley to check you over, you might need laudanum to get you through it."

Bernadette walked in then with a small stoppered bottle in her hand. "Here you go, Mr Stratforth. I'd appreciate it if you could return the bottle when you're done."

"Much obliged, Miss Bernadette. And you too, Miss Louise, for the suggestion of your sister's tonic. I hear Rasley's working all hours treating people with burns and other injuries because of that blackguard, s'cuse my indelicate language. Young Miss Bernadette must be run off her feet helping folk too."

"I like helping people," Bernadette said with a pleased look.

"Well, I'm sure this will help," the farmer said, bidding all of them farewell.

Rosie came in and greeted them, then took the stairs to begin helping Mrs Poole with the cleaning.

Shaun searched through his thoughts, wondering if there was some kind of connection between the fires, Bernadette and the doctor. It didn't seem possible, but he couldn't rule anything out.

Were people going to Bernadette instead of the good doctor? He'd certainly been in high demand since the fires had started. It couldn't be the doctor himself doing the crimes, he was too short and stocky, not to mention old. Nowhere near tall enough to hit Farmer Stratforth on the side of the head or agile enough to run away afterwards. Perhaps the doctor had hired someone to do the dirty work, in order to lift himself into higher esteem amongst the townsfolk?

He was sending himself mad with these theories. Investigating accounts and badly-added books had been so much easier and faster to figure out!

The package on the counter remained where he'd put it. Goodness, where was his concentration?

"Ah, I got you this," he said, giving the parcel to Louise.

"Oh!" Louise's surprised expression delighted him. She

carefully untied the string and unfolded the brown paper. "Oh my goodness!" she said, lifting the cloak up. A moment later she moved over to the wall lamp to get a better look. "This is lovely!"

"You ruined your good coat, and the one you've been wearing is far too thin. If I'd been better at my job, you still would have had your old one to keep you warm."

"You are very kind," she said, beaming as she held the cloak up.

He could tell she was making sure the shoulders were wide enough before she tried it on.

"If it's not a good fit, Mrs Brownlee is happy to make adjustments," he offered.

Louise hugged the bundled cloak to her chest for a moment.

"Shall I help you get it on?"

She blushed deliciously and nodded.

He held it ready for her and she slid in one arm, then the other and he adjusted it onto her shoulders. This close, he caught a scent of lavender and lemons, and his brain very nearly shut down.

"This is a very good fit," she said. "And it will keep me so warm." She made a slow twirl so he could take in the sight of her.

He stuck his palms to the side of his body to stop himself reaching out to her.

CHAPTER 16

Another Fire

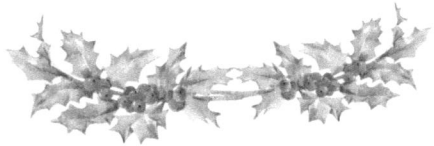

S unday rolled around again. Shaun waited outside the bookshop to escort Louise, Bernadette and Mrs Poole to church.

Louise was wearing her new cloak, and it looked regal on her. She looked up at him with a happy smile as he offered his arm. "I forgot to ask, but you didn't come to church or to Ferndale Hall last week. Were you on patrol?"

"In a manner of speaking," he said. "The Fox brothers are Catholic, so I went to their church to see if anyone matched the arsonist's description."

"I take it no luck?"

"No luck at all. It's so vexing."

"Mr Stratforth's description sounds very similar to yours, so I am hoping there's only one arsonist rather than two," Louise said.

Shaun pulled up short. "Why didn't I think of that?"

"But there aren't two, it's the same tall man, isn't it?"

Once again Shaun wanted to kick himself at being such a dunce. He'd become so focussed on Louise he'd forgotten how to do his job. Maybe there *were* two arsonists, which is how they managed to move across the town so quickly. Perhaps one of them had always had a cudgel, rather than this being a new development?

He would use his time at church to pray for answers, because his previously reliable methods were not working any more.

They found the Ferndales in good health outside the church, and they greeted them warmly. While the ladies spoke to Miss Yates, he relayed the latest developments to Lord Ferndale.

"As much as I don't like Mr Baxter," Shaun confessed, "he is the magistrate, so I've provided updates. He's not taking this as seriously as he should. More people might perish, and Doctor Rasley appears exhausted."

The doctor was walking their way, with Joshua, Phoebe and Benjamin Baxter bringing up the rear, the boy wandering along with his shoulders hunched against the cold and hands shoved deep in his pockets.

"Terrible things, these fires," Dr Rasley said.

"Indeed," Lord Ferndale nodded. "But I've no doubt Mr Jackson is close to a breakthrough and we shall be spared this almost nightly terror."

Lord Ferndale sounded confident, a direct contrast to Shaun's ongoing failures.

Joshua berated Benjamin and said, "Do stop slouching, boy!" Then he interrupted the conversation and directed his words to Lord Ferndale, "Can we not talk about something more uplifting on the Lord's day of rest?"

"Yes, quite right," Dr Rasley said, but then added in a tone which showed he was far from actually being in agreement with Joshua, "Far be it for us to show concern for our fellow townsfolk."

Benjamin muttered something that sounded like, "You're doing well out of it."

Dr Rasley's face flushed red and he raised his voice. "Hold your tongue! How dare you speak to your elders like that!"

Shaun had to cough to stifle a laugh, as Benjamin turned around with a huff. As they walked into the building, Joshua reprimanded Benjamin again, "Stand up straight, for goodness' sakes, and look at me when I'm talking to you!"

So, Joshua was capable of reprimanding his eldest son after all. Benjamin's face was red with rage, but he held his tongue. Trouble brewing there, Shaun thought. Benjamin was taller than his father already, despite the hunched shoulders. A few more years and some muscle on him and Joshua would have his hands full if the boy decided to fight back.

Louise touched Shaun's arm and guided him towards the Ferndale pew to sit with them, a pleasure he would by no means forego. Sitting beside her and sharing a prayer book was lovely, a little moment of peace in which he could forget everything that weighed heavily on his mind. Her face was serene in the dappled, coloured light pouring in through the stained-glass window behind the altar, and he lost himself in staring at her during the reverend's droning sermon, taken by surprise when she suddenly stood up and he realised the sermon was finally over.

Hastily, Shaun stood up too, and Louise cast him a laughing look. She knew he hadn't been paying attention, but did she know he'd been staring at her the whole time? He flushed red, hoping nobody else had noticed, but the amused look Bernadette sent him put paid to that notion.

They were invited to Ferndale Hall for Sunday dinner, and the Ferndale carriage to bring them back again. Shaun realised, about halfway through the excellent meal, that he was beginning to think of the Yates and Baxters as his family. Indeed, better than family; his father had been always busy with his banking business and his mother a quiet, distracted woman far too taken up with her own concerns to bother overmuch about Shaun. Here, Lord Ferndale was forever taking an interest in what he was up to and Miss Yates and Mrs Foole were both busily mothering him, telling him that he must have another slice of roast pork or to try the honey-baked carrots.

I want this. I want all of this.

Most of all, though, he wanted Louise, bright-eyed and smiling as she proudly told Miss Yates about her new cloak.

The arsonist, however, was making Shaun begin to feel like a failure. Would his suit of Louise be approved by Lord Ferndale if he couldn't catch the man? He needed to get it done, and soon, so that he could get on with the business of courting Louise properly with his full attention, as she deserved.

The ride back to Hatfield was a convivial one despite the snow beginning during the journey, so Shaun made no protracted goodbyes to the ladies. He saw them safely inside the bookshop and waved the carriage off before making his way to the Red Lion to find his men, who were just finishing a hot meal before setting out on patrols.

"Get some sleep, boss," Hugh Fox said cheerfully. "It's miserable out, and the arsonist don't like the cold or wet."

That was true; to date only one fire had occurred on a night when it was snowing or raining. Likely enough the arsonist would stay home warm and dry in his own bed tonight, probably smugly thinking of the patrollers soaking wet and chilled to the bone.

"I'll patrol with you until midnight," Shaun compromised.

Hugh and John had drawn the duty of riding about the district that night; the livery stable knew them well by now and provided a pair of quality horses on Lord Ferndale's account. The Fox brothers set off into the falling snow with lanterns, and Shaun and Riot spent a few moments to divide up between them which streets they'd patrol.

With the snow falling, Hatfield was quiet tonight, unless one was immediately outside either of the two inns, and even there the chatter from the taproom seemed muted, Shaun thought as he paced by the Swan, fists clenched deep in the pockets of his greatcoat so they didn't freeze.

Nobody was about. The only time he saw another person was Riot, at the far end of a street when their paths crossed. The Welshman gave him a wave and moved on.

He turned the corner and marched on, his boots striking the cobblestones in a familiar rhythm ingrained into his soul after marching across the Continent for the best part of a decade.

The church clock tolled midnight at last, and Shaun decided to turn in after finishing his current round. He was just passing the darkened bookshop and turning to cross the street to Mrs Bell's when a distant sound made him stop and turn.

Was that shouting?

"Fire!" he heard, somewhere to the west, and his blood ran cold.

The house was well alight when Shaun arrived at a dead run, out of breath. Riot was there already, banging on doors and yelling at the neighbours in English and Welsh, to get out lest their houses catch fire too.

"Is anyone in there?" Shaun shouted.

"I don't know!" Riot called back. His English was improving, but he forgot it at times of stress. "Couldn't get in!"

Shaun could see why. The house was an older cottage with a thick thatched roof which was already burning merrily. There were flames visible through every window, and the heat was high enough that he had to back off quickly when he tried to approach.

The front door was closed, so Shaun ran around to the back of the cottage. The little door at the back was firmly shut too. He didn't see a broken window, and wondered if this was actually a case of arson, or perhaps a faulty stove or some other sort of accident this time.

The creaky old fire engine arrived along with several men from the fire brigade, hastily unrolling their hose and dropping it down the well before starting to pump.

"Concentrate on the neighbours' houses," Shaun called to them. "Too late here."

Hugh Fox arrived at a gallop, jumping down off his horse and coming to stand by Shaun and watch as the flames raged higher.

"Mary, Mother of God," Hugh muttered. "You know whose house that is?"

Shaun shook his head, dread churning in his stomach. "Whose?"

"Doctor Rasley."

"Oh." Shaun didn't swear much, but he felt the occasion probably called for it. "Shite."

"Let's hope he was out on a call…"

They stood in silence, both knowing it was unlikely. The old doctor rarely bestirred himself after dark, leaving the sort of emergencies that occurred during the night hours to the midwives.

It was morning before the fire was finally out, and by then there was little left to burn. Shaun waved off offers from Riot and the Fox brothers and picked his way carefully into the still-smoking ruin, hoping a floorboard didn't give way under his foot and drop him into an unseen cellar.

A few minutes later he made his way out again and shook his head, expression grim. "Nothing anyone could have done. Let it cool before you go in to collect what's left."

He didn't stay to hear their quiet agreement, just walked away, weariness slumping his shoulders, and only one thought in his mind.

He wanted to see Louise. Wanted to see her smile, be in her calm, steady presence. His feet took him straight to the bookshop and inside, where she looked up at him with a sad look on her face.

"You've heard, then," he said flatly.

"That Doctor Rasley's house burned and nobody has seen him? Yes."

"I found him inside. Still asleep in his bed, from the looks of things, when the smoke overcame him."

"Oh, Shaun." She stood up and came around the counter and put her arms around him, and he held onto her as though she were an anchor in the storm, pressing his face into her hair and letting out a low groan of frustration and pain.

"I'll need to see Lord Ferndale," he said after a few moments, regaining a little of his composure.

"Of course you will." Pulling back, she looked at him, then reached up to frame his face with her hands, apparently uncaring that he was soot-smudged and stinking of smoke. "You'll find the arsonist, Shaun. I know you will. And this isn't your fault. His crimes? Are not your fault."

She always seemed to know the right thing to say to make him pull himself together, Shaun thought as he left the bookshop and headed for the livery yard to get a horse.

It wasn't until he was halfway to Ferndale Hall that the realisation struck him.

She called me Shaun.

───※───

Lord Ferndale was horrified to hear the news about Doctor Rasley, but then the old baron grew thoughtful, tapping his finger on his lower lip.

"Tragic as it is, this does present an opportunity I've been waiting for quite some time for," Lord Ferndale said. "Doctor Rasley had some… let's just call them *outdated* ideas. I know he and the midwives and the apothecary, and even Miss Bernadette, had some strong disagreements on how patients should be treated. I had some philosophical disagreements with him myself. We butted heads on the town council a few times."

Shaun nodded, being well aware of the latter. While Doctor Rasley hadn't exactly been one of Joshua Baxter's closest cronies, the pair had tended to agree more often than not, and Joshua seemed almost to enjoy opposing any idea Lord Ferndale might propose.

"So I think this would be an excellent opportunity to recruit a new doctor of my own choosing." Lord Ferndale gave him a direct look. "And I think you would be just the man to represent me. Would you go to London for me and visit the Medical and Chirurgical Society, Jackson? You could see about ordering that new fire engine while you're there, too."

Shaun hesitated, thinking. Neither of the errands Lord Ferndale was sending him on were simple; meeting and interviewing doctors would take days if he was to select a good candidate. He'd need to stay in London.

It shamed him that his first thoughts were of Louise, rather than of how much damage the arsonist might be able to do in that time.

"I know you're thinking about the arsonist," Lord Ferndale said, half-accurately. "But your men have just as much chance of catching him as you do at this point. Hire a few more, if you wish, to patrol while you're away."

"I don't know…" Shaun said. "Don't you have a man in London who could get this done, my lord?"

"You know this place, what Hatfield needs. My man in London doesn't," Lord Ferndale said. "I trust you to get it done right, Jackson."

There was little he could say to that. Shaun bowed, thanked Lord Ferndale for his trust, and made his way back outside and got on his horse again. He was bone-weary after the sleepless night, but the sooner he got to London the sooner he could get back again, so he rode back into Hatfield, returned the livery horse, and stopped in at the Red Lion to buy a ticket on the next southbound post-coach, which would leave in an hour. Just time to stuff a few things in a satchel and stop in to tell Louise where he was going. He could snooze on the coach, hopefully.

Louise was in her usual spot behind the counter, doing something with Brutus that involved some very smelly glue and leather and an old-looking book. She wiped her hands and came out when she saw Shaun come into the shop.

"I have to go to London," he said without preamble. "Lord Ferndale wants me to recruit a new doctor, and to purchase the new fire engine too."

"Oh." Her face dropped a little, but she smiled encouragingly. "It's good that Lord Ferndale is putting so much trust in you!"

"I feel as though I've let him down by not catching the arsonist yet," Shaun admitted.

"I know." She put her hand on his arm, patting soothingly. "But that's not the truth, you know that. Nobody could have done any more than you have. And you'll get him, I believe in you."

He looked down at her hand, frowning as he saw his filthy sleeve. He hadn't changed before going to Ferndale Hall, though Lord Ferndale had been polite enough not to mention his soot-stained state. He really needed to change his clothes and wash his face and hands at least before he got on the post-coach.

"I have to go. I'm getting on the coach at two o'clock, but I wanted to see you before I left, tell you I'll be gone for a few days at least."

"I understand." Her eyes were bright. "Thank you for telling me."

"I'm sure Riot will stop in later, would you let him know? He'll be sleeping right now, it was a long night. Lord

Ferndale said we can hire more men to patrol, Riot and the Fox brothers will know who to trust…"

She reached up as she had earlier, and framed his face in her hands. "You've had no sleep. Why don't you wait and go tomorrow?"

He shook his head. "The sooner I go, the sooner I can come back to you." He really hadn't meant to say the last two words, but they just sort of slipped out, and the soft smile that came across Louise's face made him quite glad they had.

"I'll be here," she said quietly. "And maybe, when you come back, you can start looking for a proper house of your own?"

"I think I'll do that." He could hardly breathe, with the way she was looking at him. Should he kiss her?

A slight scuff nearby made him tear his eyes away from Louise long enough to see Ruth walk out from between some bookshelves and freeze as she saw him, standing so close to Louise with her hands on his face. Brutus was staring at them from behind the counter too, eyes wide as saucers.

Our first kiss shouldn't be with an audience. Probably shouldn't be when I'm this filthy, either, Shaun thought as he stepped back and glimpsed the sooty smudges on Louise's fingers as her hands fell away. Nevertheless, he couldn't just leave it there, so he caught her hands in his and lifted them to his lips, kissing the knuckles of first one hand, then the other.

"I'll be back as soon as I can," he vowed.

He carried the memory of her smile with him through the next rushed half-hour of washing, changing, packing and scrambling onto the post-coach. Leaning against the side of the coach, he looked out of the window at the bookshop, wistfully hoping for one last glimpse of her face… and there she was, standing at the door to wave him off.

"Is that your wife?" an older woman seated opposite him asked inquisitively as Shaun waved back enthusiastically.

"No," Shaun said, grinning as he sank back into his seat. "Not yet." *Soon*, he promised himself. He'd handle Lord Ferndale's business in London, get back and catch this damned arsonist, buy a house so he had something real and tangible to offer Louise apart from his heart and then… yes.

Soon.

CHAPTER 17
Marie Comes Home

T wo weeks later, Louise scolded herself for being selfish about Shaun's absence. She missed him with an ache, which contrasted with her pride that Lord Ferndale had entrusted Shaun Jackson and only Shaun Jackson with the task of recruiting a new doctor for the town.

A great many people wore black armbands out of respect for Dr Rasley; Louise, Bernadette and Mrs Poole included. They may not have needed the doctor's services, but the rest of the town had and still did.

Privately, Louise admitted she had begun to wonder if Rasley might have harboured a grudge against Bernadette for her activities helping women. But those women would have suffered in silence instead of going to a man for their troubles, so she'd hardly stolen his business.

Still, she couldn't help ruminating that perhaps Dr Rasley had been somehow involved. Was this why he was never available to help injured people in the evenings? His housekeeper had always said he was asleep. What if he'd only told her that as an excuse, and was instead out at all hours lighting fires?

"I'm getting carried away." She shook her head as she entered some numbers into the ledger. Adding them up required concentration, which she utterly lacked as her head was filled with thoughts of Shaun and the mysterious arsonist.

After a fruitless few minutes, she shoved the book aside and left it for when Shaun came home.

Bernadette came in from the outside, her face pink from the cold. Brutus was only a step behind her and grabbed the door before it closed again, to stop it from jangling the bell so much. She hadn't wanted to take any of Shaun's army men with her for protection, so Brutus had volunteered instead. He wasn't as tall or as daunting as the former soldiers, and was happy to sit and read until he was needed to escort Bernadette back to the shop.

"Is it wrong of me to prioritise the Allom family because they pay in pork pies?" Bernadette said with a grin.

"It would be difficult not to have favourites," Louise agreed. "Save me a half, please."

The bell above the front door jangled again and Louise gasped in surprise at the sight of her sister.

"Marie!" All thought of pork pies vanished as she darted out from the counter to reach her sister for a welcome embrace. "Oh, Marie, I'm so glad you're home!"

Bernadette threw herself into the welcome with a cry of joy.

"I missed you so much," Marie said.

"How was the Earl of D…"

A large man, though not as tall nor wide as Shaun,

entered the shop on Marie's heels. He took off his hat to greet them.

"Louise, Bernadette, this is the Earl of *Renwick.*" Marie gave her a pointed look. "My lord, these are my sisters, Miss Louise and Miss Bernadette, and my cousin, Master Brutus Baxter, and this is Miss Ruth Millings."

Everyone made respectable curtseys and bows. The earl in turn delivered a warm smile that crinkled the corners of his eyes and said, "Delighted to make your acquaintances. Miss Louise, I understand I have you to thank especially for my books arriving in excellent condition."

"That is most kind, my lord," Louise said. "I was relieved when Marie relayed that good news."

Mrs Poole came down the stairs and said, "I thought I heard good news." She embraced Marie warmly. "It's so good to see you. How is your ankle?"

"It is very well, and fully healed," Marie said. "I have his lordship to thank for that."

"Miss Baxter was an excellent patient," Lord Renwick said, playing with the brim of his hat.

"Let me take that for you," Mrs Poole fussed, taking his hat and gloves and placing them on the counter.

It was a lovely reunion, and Louise couldn't help thinking the Earl of Demanding appeared so much kinder in person than in correspondence.

Two young boys had followed the earl in and were looking about, wide-eyed; Marie introduced them as the earl's sons, George and Richard. Louise thought they were around the same age as Brutus, and suggested Brutus show them about the shop, especially the shelf of adventure books which boys of that age seemed to particularly enjoy. Considering how much their father regularly spent on books, surely he could spend a few shillings on reading matter for his sons!

"Choose whatever books you like," the earl called after them, reinforcing Louise's guess, before he looked back at Marie, a softness coming to his face. "And where would I find the books you asked your sisters to set aside for me, Miss Baxter?"

Marie looked to Louise, who blushed, remembering the content of many of those books. "They're in the locked cabinet under the counter," she admitted. "Let me get them out for you, my lord."

Watching the way the earl and Marie bent their heads together over the books, a certain suspicion entered Louise's mind. The way Renwick had looked at Marie made Louise think of the way Shaun had looked at her, just before he had left for London. The way he'd looked at her on more than one occasion, when she'd suspected he might be thinking of kissing her.

But surely the Earl of Renwick and her sister… no. That was patently a ridiculous thought, and Louise set it aside.

"I can't believe that's the Earl of Demanding," Bernadette said quietly, coming up beside Louise where she lingered tidying the lending library shelf.

"I know! He's nice!" Louise peeked around the edge of the shelf to see the earl giving Marie that look again. She lowered her voice to a whisper. "And I think he might be sweet on Marie."

"What!" Bernadette's eyes went very round, and she too peeked around the edge of the shelf. "Well I never. He's looking at her just the way Mr Jackson looks at you, I think you're right!"

Eventually, the earl finished selecting his books and

called to his sons, saying a little regretfully that they needed to make their farewells and get a meal at The Red Lion, before they retired to their rooms. They would leave for Eton in the morning where he was taking the boys to school. George and Richard added several more books to the pile and the earl paid Marie with a cheerful smile.

Renwick reached for his gloves and hat, then suddenly stopped. "What's this?" The hat tilted and the weight was off balance. Pie the cat sat up from inside the hat with a loud "miaow" of discontent.

Renwick laughed heartily at the surprise. "Well, Miss Marie, you did say I needed a cat!"

Marie's hands pressed over her face in shock.

Louise said, "This is Pie, full name Pied Piper, and we do need to find a home for him. He is an excellent mouser." She refrained from describing Pie's penchant for leaving entrails of disembowelled rodents everywhere. At least Crafty had the good grace to favour one place for her remainders behind the counter.

Good-natured laughter followed as the earl gently shook Pie's paw.

"Oh, can we really have him, Pa?" one of the boys asked - the fairer one, Louise thought it was George.

"Well." The earl looked thoughtful. "I suppose I could come back this way, after I go to London. Would you keep him for me for a week or two, Miss Baxter?" he asked Marie.

"Of course! I am sure he'll have a wonderful life hunting down the mice in Alston Castle for you." Marie looked happy, and Louise rather suspected it was at the prospect of seeing the earl again when he returned. Whatever was going on between the two of them? She had a lot of questions to ask her sister!

"We'll call by in the morning before we leave for Eton," the earl said as they prepared to take their leave.

Just then, the bell jangled, and Shaun walked into the shop.

"You're back!" Louise cried in delight, and Shaun gave her a broad grin, before his eyes fell on Renwick and widened.

"My lord," he said.

"You!" Renwick looked equally surprised, though quite pleased, and held out his hand for Shaun to shake. "Very good to see you again, ah…" he paused, glancing around at the watching Baxter sisters.

"Jackson," Shaun said. "Shaun Jackson. And yes, that's my real name."

"Sergeant?" Renwick said.

"It was Colonel, actually, but now I'm retired."

This was quite the oddest conversation Louise had ever witnessed! It was obvious that the two men knew each other, but equally obvious that Renwick had not the slightest idea what Shaun's name was, or the army rank he'd held. Which, at Colonel, was significantly more elevated than Louise had ever suspected.

"What ever was that all about?" she asked when Renwick and his sons had left, and Marie went upstairs with Bernadette to unpack.

Shaun leaned on the counter, smiling down at her, the corners of his eyes crinkling in that way which always made her knees feel a little weak. "Renwick was quite highly placed in the War Office, overseeing supplies going all over the Continent. I reported directly to him on several occasions, but as I was an undercover agent being regularly relocated to different regiments, I was constantly changing my identity. He never knew my real name."

"How very cloak and dagger!" She was forever learning new things about Shaun, it seemed, and all of them fascinating. "*Colonel*."

"Retired," he said firmly. "I sold my commission. Just plain Mister Jackson. Or... Shaun, if you prefer."

Heat crept up her cheeks. She'd called him Shaun that morning after the fire at the doctor's house, quite unconsciously. It had slipped out when she saw him looking so exhausted, emotionally as well as physically wrung out.

The bell jangled as a customer came in, and Louise silently cursed the interruption. Was she destined never to get a moment alone with Shaun to tell him how she felt? He stepped back with a polite smile to let her see to the customer, who turned out to be a traveller passing through who was looking for rare books. Louise shot Shaun an apologetic smile, realising she would not be able to attend to the matter quickly.

"I need to go and speak to Lord Ferndale," Shaun said quietly. "I'll call in and see you tomorrow, you'll no doubt want to spend the evening with your sister, now she's home safe."

The following afternoon, Marie was upstairs resting - she seemed quite exhausted after her long journey home. Mrs Poole and Rosie were cleaning, Brutus had been assigned to walk Ruth home and Bernadette had gone with them to deliver some tonic for Mrs Millings' headaches. Shaun had come in and was now behind the counter quickly adding up the numbers in the ledger for the day.

Louise stood beside Shaun in the empty shop, her soul yearning.

"It's so quiet all of a sudden," Louise said in a wistful tone.

"Beautifully quiet," he said, placing the quill back into the ink pot. He turned to face her and reached for her hand. "Time is of the essence," he said, with a smile filled with promise.

Her hand in his felt so right. His thumb played over the top of her hand and he raised it to his lips. Louise's breath hitched and she silently prayed that nobody would disturb them, not even the cats. She stepped closer to him, her heart racing in anticipation.

He asked, "Should I lock the shop door?"

She shook her head and repeated his words back to him, "Time is of the essence," and tilted her face up to his.

His lips brushed hers in the softest whisper, proving once again this magnificent, strong man could be light and tender when the occasion required. Her hand reached his neck and she pulled him in closer. Heart leaping with joy, her body thrummed as they deepened their kiss. Nothing else mattered but his lips on hers. The scent of him teased her brain as her hands caressed his strong neck muscles. His arms came around her waist, holding them together.

Louise luxuriated in the beautiful moment. He pulled away for a second and she caught her breath, but Louise was not done.

She kissed him again, claiming him for her own. He utterly belonged to her now. As if there were any doubt.

And she belonged to him, heart and soul.

Making up for lost time, Louise wrapped her arms about his broad shoulders. Her lips parted with a sigh. Matching her enthusiasm, Shaun's tongue traced the edge of her lip.

Bliss!

Footsteps sounded on the stairs and they jumped apart.

"Oh!" Marie stood there, eyes round with shock.

Shaun cleared his throat, flushing red. A bubble of laughter caught in Louise's throat. "Far better it be Marie than Cousin Joshua!"

Shaun said nothing, but his shoulders shook in silent laughter.

Marie huffed and headed back upstairs.

Despite her bubble of happiness at having finally found time to kiss Shaun, and so gloriously too, Louise had seen tears in her sister's eyes. "She seems upset, I'd best see to her."

Shaun hadn't finished adding up the numbers, but he turned to Louise and delivered another kiss. He pulled away a little, their foreheads touching. "You're amazing."

Louise giggled and stole one more quick kiss from him before heading upstairs herself.

She could have been walking on air. Louise barely felt the steps beneath her feet as she climbed the stairs.

Marie was sitting at the table, her face resting against one hand.

Mrs Poole fussed over her. "You've hardly touched your currant bun."

To Louise's horror, Marie began to cry, great fat tears running down her cheeks. Louise rushed over and threw her arms around her sister.

"Oh Marie, I'm so sorry you walked in on me and Shaun kissing…"

"Wait, you were kissing Mr Jackson?" Mrs Poole said, startled, but Louise waved her off.

Marie shook her head, gulping back sobs. "It's not that, Lou, it's… oh, I love him, and… and…"

"And he's coming back in a few days to collect Pie, you'll see him again." Louise tried to sound bracing, but inwardly she wondered. She'd thought from the first moment she saw them looking at each other that something might be happening. Their eldest sister would be a baroness one day, so why couldn't Marie be a countess?

Renwick did indeed return several days later, buying some more books and taking Pie, but then he left again after he and Marie had some sort of fight! Marie seemed to spend all her time crying in her room, quite unable to take on her usual duties in the bookshop. Louise and Bernadette were desperately worried about her.

Shaun was so busy, Louise barely saw him; the new fire pumper was delivered and the fire brigade had to be trained in its operation. Adding to their woes, another new problem had presented itself; Benjamin Baxter was making a nuisance of himself around Ruth.

Louise had been concerned about Ruth for a while. The vicar's daughter was a quiet little thing who seemed withdrawn most of the time, rarely even cracking a smile. Her father was quite horrible, of course, the worst kind of fire-and-brimstone preacher, and her mother a downtrodden mouse of a woman who was forever taking to her bed with a headache, perhaps unsurprising with such a husband.

Ruth was, however, quite the most beautiful young

woman in Hatfield, even at only fourteen years old. She had a perfect pale oval for a face, large blue eyes and hair like spun gold. It was no surprise the young men of Hatfield stared when she walked past, but Benjamin was a canny boy who seemed to have infinite time on his hands and no scruples about taking things further than merely admiring looks. While he couldn't bother Ruth in the bookshop for fear of Louise and her crowbar, he would lurk around outside waiting for Ruth to come out on an errand and then pester her. It was a relief that he was going away to school soon, Louise thought.

"He can't go off to school soon enough," Louise said grimly to Marie, who had finally come out of her room after two days of crying, and was sitting behind the counter checking the account book.

"Who's going to school?" Marie asked drearily, not bothering to look up.

"Benjamin!"

That got Marie's interest. "Why?" She pushed her spectacles up her nose and peered at Louise. "And where?"

"Some school in Oxford. Joshua finally realised that Benjamin can't get a gentleman's education at university if he's barely literate. They found somewhere in Oxford for him. He's leaving soon, thank goodness!"

Crafty came padding around the edge of the counter and jumped up into Marie's lap. "Hello, girl," Marie murmured, cuddling the cat. "Are you missing your son?" She sniffled a little bit.

"If you're going to cry again, you might as well go back upstairs," Louise said.

Marie gave her a glare, though her eyes were watering.

"Just because your romance is going well! You might have a little sympathy."

"I'm sorry." She was; she hadn't meant to be unkind. Watching Crafty tolerating being cuddled - even the cat seemed to feel sorry for Marie - Louise hesitated, and then said, "Marie, I think you should write to him."

"To Renwick?" Marie gulped back a sob. "It's no use. He's an earl, and I'm… just me."

"You aren't 'just' anything. You're Marie Baxter; you're clever and unique and far prettier than you realise, and he was looking at you like you hung the moon and the stars. And so were his sons!" Louise bent down and brushed a strand of loose hair off her sister's wet cheek. "Your heart isn't here any more, is it?"

Marie shook her head wordlessly.

"You need to tell him," Louise said gently. "Take your chance, Marie. Tell him how you feel. What do you have to lose?"

"I suppose…" Marie said slowly. "Either he doesn't feel the same way and I'll never see him again, or…"

"Or he does love you and he'll come back for you. But if you don't write, how will he know that you want him to?" Louise asked logically, thinking that being in love appeared to have absolutely ruined Marie's normally excellent powers of deduction.

"You're right. You're quite right!" Marie jumped up, upsetting Crafty who streaked off with an indignant yowl, and ran off up the stairs, presumably to start writing her letter.

With a sigh, Louise picked up the overturned stool and sat back down behind the counter.

At least I'll have Shaun to help me with the accounts, Louise thought with a little smile, closing the book and setting it aside for later. She felt almost guilty for being so happy while Marie was miserable, but hopefully she'd been right about the way Renwick had looked at Marie. She rather thought that letter would find an eager reception, and then Marie would be off to Cumbria for good.

CHAPTER 18
Suspects and Suspicions

Ruth came back late one afternoon with a pale, worried face and one of the apprentice printers by her side.

"Whatever's the matter?" Louise's stomach roiled at how distressed the girl was.

The apprentice said, "Miss Louise, Mr Black asked me to make sure she got back safe and sound. Master Baxter was making a bother of himself."

Louise called out to Mrs Poole to make tea, and she locked the shop door and accompanied Ruth upstairs.

"That Benjamin is a menace," Louise said as they sat down at the table. "I should have gone instead. Benjamin knows I won't tolerate poor behaviour."

The delicate child buried her head into Louise's shoulder and said, "I tried to ignore him, but he would not leave me alone."

"He's a little pig," Mrs Poole said, handing over some shortbread.

"Well, my understanding is he's heading off to school

tomorrow," Louise said. "So he won't be around to bother you any more."

Louise and Mrs Poole both nodded their heads in agreement.

Louise made sure to walk Ruth home later, and they greeted many friendly townspeople along the way. Benjamin didn't show his face, which Louise thought was rather a shame. She was carrying her crowbar inside her cloak.

The next morning, Shaun informed her the reason he was later than usual was because there had been yet another fire overnight, and he'd had to inform Lord Ferndale. "I also tried to tell your cousin but he was busy seeing his son off to school on the coach and wouldn't give me the time of day."

Louise's heart leapt into her throat. "Is anyone hurt?"

"Nobody. In fact, the new fire pumper did its job magnificently and they got the fire out quickly."

"What a relief," she said, reaching for an embrace.

He held her tightly and said, "You haven't asked me where it was, yet."

Feeling guilty for only thinking of his embrace and not the property damage, she asked tentatively, "Not the Ferndales?"

"No, not them. This time he targeted the printer."

Louise's mouth dropped open in shock. "All that paper!" she gasped.

"Indeed. If it had been operating, the paper would have caught easily. As chance would have it, they'd finished with the press and there was no paper in it. The fresh stacks were still in storage."

"Thank heavens for small mercies," Louise said.

Shaun reached for her hand and she softened at his touch. "I'm sure you haven't slept."

"I can sleep some other time. Do you have a ledger that needs checking?"

Thrilled that he wanted to spend more time with her, Louise almost danced to the spot behind the counter. She came to a sudden stop when she stepped on mouse entrails. Cleaning that up had the effect of restoring mundane normality.

"It makes sense that an arsonist would target anywhere with paper," she said thoughtfully. "A bookshop and a printer. And of course barns made of old wood or filled with hay."

"Aye," Shaun agreed.

"But why target people? Especially an old teacher and his wife and the town doctor? Why would you hurt people who devoted their lives to serving the community?" The moment the words were out of Louise's mouth, roiling sickness burned the back of her throat. "I think I know who it might be."

Shaun's head whipped around, his eyes going wide. "What did you say?"

She had his complete attention, and she whispered it low so they would not be overheard. "I think it could be Benjamin."

"Your cousin?" Shaun's voice filled with concern. "The older boy who teases Brutus?"

Louise nodded. "You've seen him in action, then?"

"Well yes, but it's one thing to tease your little brother, another to burn down houses with people sleeping in them."

"I know, but… just yesterday, one of Mr Black's apprentices had to walk Ruth back to us because Benjamin was bothering her dreadfully. And then there's a fire in that same place, that very night."

Shaun's jaw clenched and he breathed hard. "Doctor Rasley sent him off with a flea in his ear, and then soon after…"

Louise slapped her hands over her mouth.

Shaun shook his head. "He seems too young. I would have thought school boys would have a curfew. I could kick myself for not paying attention. He does have the right build for the man I chased, but I thought because of his youth… In the dark I didn't get a look at his face."

Louise said, "I've known him for a lot longer, and I didn't suspect him either."

"Little consolation," Shaun made a heavy sigh. "The lad's gone now at any rate, his family waved him off just now outside the Red Lion."

"If it was him, that means we won't have any more fires."

"Can't fault your logic," he said. "All right, what about the old teacher, is there a connection to Benjamin?"

"Yes, Brutus said he thought Benjamin might have had a year or two of instruction from him before he retired. Probably told him he was wrong in front of the class or something."

Shaun buried his face in his hands. "Doesn't feel like enough motive, really. But perhaps the lad held strong grudges. You had his measure, that's for sure."

"And he targeted us three times," Louise said.

"That he did." Shaun shook his head and sighed heavily. "And for certain Joshua has no love for Lord Ferndale, which is why Benjamin might have targeted the Ferndale properties. I think you're on to something. For now, we'll keep this just between ourselves and wait and see what happens. I watched him leave town, so if it's him, we'll be free from fires for a good while yet."

For the next week, Louise's suspicions about Benjamin and the fires were validated. Each morning when Shaun visited the bookshop, he reported no activity the night before. It was a relief, and confirmation they were right to suspect Benjamin.

Proving they were right would be another matter, but it was at least an alarming coincidence.

The fires, or lack of them, were on everyone's minds as they gathered at church the next Sunday. An internal struggle consumed Louise. She was having such a hard time keeping this secret, but she knew she had to keep her suspicions to herself until they could catch Benjamin in the act. That could be a long time coming as he wouldn't be back from school until Easter at the earliest.

Mrs Poole departed to catch up with her friends, while Louise, Bernadette and Shaun chatted with Lord Ferndale and Miss Yates. A little way off, she recognised Riot Jones as he doffed his hat to Rosie.

The clouds parted and the sun briefly poked out, warming the gathering. It turned cold very quickly as Mrs Poole scurried back to them. "Louise, may I bend your ear?"

Their housekeeper appeared pale.

"It's about your Shaun, and I thought you'd want to know. Phoebe has been sharing a theory that the fires started when Mr Jackson came into town."

Ice filled Louise's veins. "No!" Her hands flew to her throat.

"Obviously, I don't believe her, but some might, and... well... we know what she's like."

It was on the tip of Louise's tongue to retaliate that

Phoebe was only accusing Shaun to keep attention away from her eldest son. Alas, she'd promised Shaun they'd keep this a secret. For now. And did Phoebe even know what Benjamin had been up to? Surely not.

"Oh dear," Mrs Poole said, "Joshua and Phoebe are on the warpath."

Turning back to Shaun, Louise's heart constricted at the sight of Phoebe marching his way.

She rushed back to be by his side.

"You should be ashamed to show your face here after all the damage you've caused!" Phoebe accused.

His face immobile, Shaun nevertheless bowed to Joshua and Phoebe. "Lovely to see you both. Is there something that's concerning you?"

"Now see here, Jackson," Joshua said, "You can turn yourself in, or I'll drag you in myself."

Louise interjected. "What are you talking about?"

"Your man here might have fooled some, but he does not fool me!" Joshua said. "He's only stopped this week because he knows we're on to him. Did you ever wonder why this man, who is such a clever investigator, can't work out who's lighting fires in a small town? It's been him all along!"

"That's not true," Louise declared. "He was in London getting better fire equipment, and there were fires while he was away."

Phoebe snorted contempt. "Probably got one of the lazy old soldiers to do that, to ward off suspicion. He's playing you for a fool, Louise. And you too, Lord Ferndale, you're the one funding his operation. Paying him to set up his own army when all along he's been the one to blame!"

"And what proof do you have of this, Mrs Baxter?" Lord Ferndale asked in his usual genial tone.

Phoebe hesitated at that, and Louise pounced. "Shame on you, Phoebe. If everyone took every unfounded suspicion as gospel truth, where would we all be?"

"I saw 'im," another voice butted in, and Louise turned in surprise to find the farmer Mr Stratforth behind her. He was frowning at Phoebe too.

"You saw Mr Jackson?" Phoebe said eagerly.

Louise thought she might pass out. Was Mr Stratforth siding with her cousins?

The farmer stepped up and said, "No, ma'am. I saw the arsonist, the night he tried to set fire to my house. Tall, he were, but a thin fellow, nothing like the size of Mr Jackson. He hit me on the head, the arsonist." Mr Stratforth gave a little half-smile. "If Mr Jackson had hit me, I dare say I wouldn't be standing here talking to you."

"There you go, Mrs Baxter," Lord Ferndale said firmly. "An actual witness, a man in good standing in this community, who I dare say has no particular reason to be fond of Mr Jackson." Unaccountably, he looked at Louise here. "And Mr Stratforth is very clear that the arsonist *isn't* Mr Jackson."

"Nor any of his men," Mr Stratforth put in helpfully. "None of them are as tall as the blackguard who hit me."

Louise wanted to cheer.

Phoebe huffed, looking thoroughly disappointed, but she and Joshua withdrew. They still whispered to each other, looking at Shaun, and Louise had the sinking feeling they would continue to spread the malicious lie no matter what.

Mr Stratforth doffed his hat and walked away, and Louise reached out to touch Lord Ferndale's sleeve. "Lord Ferndale…"

"How many times must I tell you to call me Grandfa-

CATHERINE BILSON & EBONY OATEN

ther?" he said with a kindly smile. "You are family now, my dear!"

He really was the dearest old man. She smiled fondly at him, but what she had to say was too important to get distracted. "Grandfather - did Mr Jackson tell you that we have a suspect in mind?"

"Louise..." Shaun began, shaking his head, but Louise hushed him.

"This is important. I think he should know."

Lord Ferndale looked from one to the other of them. "Spit it out, one of you!"

"We think it's my cousin Benjamin Baxter," Louise said, in a low whisper.

Lord Ferndale's bushy grey brows shot up. "But he's just a boy!"

"A boy with a grudge against everyone who's been a victim of the fires," Shaun said, looking resigned. "Whose parents are lax with him, whose window can be easily climbed in and out of at night, and whose father has a horse loose in a field behind the house that is a very easy creature to catch and bridle."

Louise looked at Shaun in surprise. "You've been investigating," she said.

He shrugged. "It's what I'm being paid for."

"I wonder why Mr Stratforth was targeted, then?" she mused, suddenly wondering. She couldn't think of a motive for Benjamin to target the farmer.

Lord Ferndale and Shaun looked at each other, and then they both laughed, confusing Louise mightily.

"Oh, I think we can guess exactly why he was targeted after he danced with you at the Midwinter Assembly," Lord Ferndale said pointedly. "I think the two of you might be onto something, especially since the fires have now stopped… since the boy went off to school, correct?"

"Indeed." Shaun nodded. "But we have no proof."

"And if you make a counter-accusation now, Mr Baxter will say that you're accusing an innocent boy, who's not even here to defend himself, to throw suspicion off yourself," Lord Ferndale said.

Louise felt sick. She hadn't even thought of that, but she could see from the look on Shaun's face that he had.

"All we can do is wait until he comes home, and see if the fires resume," Shaun said. "Though I will see if I can find someone in Oxford who will let me know if there are any unusual fires there."

"I suspect school will be a lot less easy to escape from to cause mischief than my cousins' house," Louise said miserably to Shaun as they walked back to the bookshop together. "And if there are no fires in Oxford…"

"It doesn't make any difference. Once Benjamin comes back here, we'll be following him day and night," Shaun vowed. "We'll catch him, Louise. I promise."

Louise looked as if she didn't really believe him, and Shaun had to admit he had been a dismal failure at his job so far. It was Louise who had begun to suspect her cousin, and though Shaun wasn't dismissing the possibility of a different culprit out of hand, the fact that the fires had stopped immediately Benjamin Baxter went away to school was telling.

"I've seen a house I like," he said, hoping to invite her to come and look at it with him.

"Really? Where?"

"It's a little bit out of town... a mile or so." It wasn't an ideal location, he'd prefer a house in town, but it was a nice property. He could see himself living there, with Louise as his wife, hopefully, though she'd been a little distant in the last few days. He knew she was concerned about her sister Marie, who seemed to have come back from Cumbria thoroughly miserable, and of course there was the ever-present concern about her father, who hadn't sent books in almost a month now. Perhaps Louise wouldn't accept him even if he proposed, wanting to wait for her father to return home, as well as her eldest sister, still in Ireland with her husband.

"Mm." Louise seemed to lose interest in what he was saying, looking away and smiling at someone ahead of them. Shaun's hands clenched on the brim of his hat as he saw Mr Stratforth standing at the lych-gate.

That damned farmer! He seemed to be in town an awful lot for a man who should be busy with his cattle, and in the bookshop far too much for Shaun's liking. Was Louise seriously interested in him? She was thanking him now for speaking up for Shaun.

"Not right, what Mrs Baxter was saying," Stratforth replied. "Had to speak up."

Well, that was jolly decent of him, even if Shaun was beginning to think of the man as a rival. Shaun gritted his teeth and shook Stratforth's offered hand.

"I'm not really all that concerned about what your cousins were saying," he said as Louise took his arm again and they walked on. "There are plenty of people who saw me literally miles away at the same time as fires started. The printer fire, for example... I was on the farthest distance patrol that night, and stopped at the inn that's almost to St Albans. A dozen people must have seen me there."

"Ycu don't know my cousins," Louise said, looking straight ahead. "Phoebe would just say you had someone else light it. At least Mr Stratforth could say it wasn't you *or* any of your men."

"And he'll be able to vouch for Benjamin being the right build too, when the time comes," Shaun noted thoughtfully.

"Yes, when the time comes." They'd reached the bookshop, and Louise let go of his arm. "Thank you for walking me home," she said, as her sisters came up behind them.

That was a discouraging dismissal if he'd ever heard one. He bowed, first to Louise and then to her sisters and Mrs Poole. "Good day, ladies."

A clatter of wheels behind him warned him it would be a bad moment to cross the street; he waited for the carriage to pass, but it pulled up right behind him. He was still facing the Baxter sisters, saw the dawning astonishment and delight on Marie's face.

"Renwick!" she cried, and then she ran past Shaun and threw herself into the arms of the earl, just stepping down from his coach.

CHAPTER 19
Separation

The wheel of fate turned, burning Louise's hopes of happiness with Shaun Jackson to ash. Napoleon's escape from Elba and triumphal march into Paris caught everybody by surprise with its terrifying speed. Papa was still in France somewhere, but where? With no correspondence or books now for nearly two months, she could only hope and pray he was somewhere near a port so he could sail away from danger. She checked an atlas for his last position, in Tours. It was far too close to Paris for her liking, and a great distance from the sea.

Bernadette was already heading around town with her basket of herbs and tonics, so Louise left Ruth to the books and set about making glue with Brutus. The activity would provide a welcome distraction.

"I have some gossip," Brutus said with a grin as he stirred the smelly glue.

"Goodness, have you been talking with Rosie?" Louise asked.

"No, this is from home, and it made me glad. But you can't tell anyone."

"I solemnly promise," Louise confirmed.

"We received a letter from Benjamin's school. Mama was reading it to Papa and it said Benjamin wasn't coming home for Easter. I wasn't supposed to be listening. But he's been troublesome at school so they're keeping him back while the rest of the boys have a break. Mama left the letter on the table so I read it later, and folded it back exactly the way I found it."

Ordinarily Louise would heartily laugh, but her spirits really weren't up to the task today. She searched for a diplomatic response. "He has not been the kindest of older brothers, has he?"

"I'm glad he won't be home for Easter, I wasn't looking forward to it," Brutus said.

Louise absolutely agreed with him, but for even more reasons. There hadn't been a single fire in Hatfield since he'd gone away to school.

Shaun came into the shop in the early afternoon, grim-faced. Louise's stomach churned at his expression.

"What is it?" she demanded, heart hammering against her ribs.

"I'm sure you've heard the news, it's all over town. Napoleon is back, I must re-enlist."

"You're needed here!" she challenged him, panicking suddenly.

He shook his head and half closed his eyes in frustration. "Please don't make this any harder than it needs to be."

"You're leaving me?" Her vision blurred and her eyes heated with unshed tears.

"I have no choice. I will be back, I promise."

He was leaving for France. The most dangerous place in the world! The words, "How dare you!" flew from her lips. Her hands balled into fists and she ran forward and started pummelling him in the chest. "How dare you even think of going!"

He caught hold of her, hugged her to him. "I would not be able to live with myself if I didn't go. The Fox brothers leapt on the first post-carriage to London, and Riot is saying goodbye to Rosie just out the front now."

"But it doesn't make any sense. You sold your commission. You were looking at a house to settle down in!" The unspoken part of that was a feeble "with me", which she said in her head. To her own ears she sounded desperate and pathetic.

"Things are safe in Hatfield now," he said. "No fires since Benjamin left. You were dead to rights about him."

Somehow, being right didn't make her feel any better. Plus, she knew Benjamin wasn't coming back between school terms.

"Did you already know? Benjamin's school is keeping him there because he's causing trouble?" It wouldn't be right to lie to him about the threat if there really wasn't one now.

"I saw a group of schoolboys alight from the coach yesterday. Benjamin wasn't among them. I began to wonder if he was being true to form."

"That figures," Lousie agreed. Shaun noticed everything. Of course he did. But drat the whole situation. Benjamin's non-return gave Shaun the extra permission he needed to leave England, knowing Hatfield was safe.

"Will you at least kiss me goodbye?" he asked.

Louise folded her arms across her chest. "No."

"No?" He balked. "Whyever not?"

"Because I'm furious with you, that's why. You sold your commission! You've done your duty to King and country already. You don't owe them anything more!"

Shaun took a step back and sighed with frustration. "I had thought we could part on better terms."

"You thought wrong. I'll thank you to leave, now, I have work to do."

She turned and headed up the stairs, holding back the tears until she heard the bell from the shop door telling her Shaun had departed.

Louise's words burned acid in Shaun's belly. He'd upset her terribly, but he truly had no option but to rejoin and head to France. There simply wasn't enough time to explain everything to her; he had to be on the stagecoach this afternoon. Napoleon had to be stopped; he only hoped she'd forgive him by the time he got home. Whenever that time might be.

Some things really were that important.

All the same, he had a few minutes to speak with the new doctor, Glynn Williams, about keeping an eye on Louise and Bernadette while he was absent. He found the doctor finishing his meal in the Red Lion.

"I'm afraid I can't stay," Shaun said, crushing his hat in his hands. "I've rejoined the army, and I must be off."

"Goodness, are we at war again?" Glynn asked. "Who's it with this time?"

The doctor's face was pure innocence. How had he not heard? But of course, he was not spending all his time with returned soldiers, who could only talk of one thing.

"Napoleon escaped Elba and is raising merry hell," Shaun said.

The doctor looked aghast, obviously understanding how serious this had become. Glynn paid for his meal and followed Shaun back to Mrs Bell's so he could finish packing.

"I must ask you a favour," Shaun said. "Would you please look after Louise and Bernadette while I'm gone?"

"That virago?"

Shaun's eyes rounded in shock. Not the reaction he was expecting - but then nothing had been as he'd expected this morning. "Louise?" Louise could be stubborn and occasionally bossy - but a virago? Never.

"No, not her. Miss Bernadette."

Shaun stopped packing, confused. "She's a sweet, quiet little mouse."

"She's a harridan," Glynn objected. "Meddling with people and playing with medicines she doesn't understand."

Shaun sighed and shoved the last few items into his bag. "I've spoken with Mrs Bell, and she's more than happy for you to have my room. She offered her front room as your consulting room."

"Until my house is ready?"

Shaun shook his head. "The men repairing the doctor's house are joining up as well. There won't be any more work done on repairs for a while, unless you're good at carpentry yourself?"

Glynn sighed and shook his head in annoyance. "Well, needs must. Good luck, Jackson. Come home safe."

Louise sat behind the counter in a pit of despair. All that confidence about how good her romance was had come back to bite her, hard. How often had she been smug and lofty in believing she'd avoided Marie and Estelle's mistakes to find happiness without complications? Far too often.

Now fate dealt her the most cruel blow.

Marie had been miserable, that was a fact, but the Earl of Renwick had come back for her and they'd eloped to Scotland together and were no doubt living in wedded bliss in his Cumbria castle by now. Estelle and Felix had created silly arguments, but they'd figured themselves out and were now happily married.

She and Shaun had been happy from the beginning, but now she didn't know if she'd ever see her beloved again.

She'd sent him off without so much as a kiss!

She hadn't told him she loved him, she'd been too angry with him. Foolishly angry and petulantly silly.

Or she chastised herself, all the while reading every scrap of terrible news that arrived from the continent. It was terrifying, what with Napoleon amassing a vast army in an alarmingly short span of time. Meanwhile the leaders of the Congress of Vienna seemed unable to put aside their differences in order to stop the horrible little Corsican.

Every time she read a new article, shakes of pure terror overwhelmed her whole body. But she was powerless to stop reading the newssheets, as if the mere knowledge of what was happening was somehow keeping Shaun alive.

And their father had not managed to get a letter out in months, much less any more crates of books.

"Why did he have to go?" Louise sobbed into her hands one morning at breakfast. "One man isn't going to make any difference and I - *we* - need him here!"

Bernadette patted Louise's shoulder. They also needed their father, and the longer it took for him to come home, the worse their fears became.

"Why don't you stay upstairs today?" Mrs Poole suggested kindly.

"Someone has to mind the counter," Louise sniffled.

"I can do it," Bernadette said stoutly. "I'm not as busy now that Dr Williams is in town. You stay upstairs and just rest. I know you're not sleeping well."

Louise lowered her hands and looked at Bernadette from reddened eyes, before nodding.

"And tonight, I'm going to give you a tea before bed and you're to jolly well drink it," Bernadette added firmly.

"All right," Louise conceded quietly.

"And you're going to eat this breakfast, too!" Mrs Poole added, pushing the plate of buttered crumpets under Louise's nose.

Louise picked up a crumpet and nibbled at the edge, and Mrs Poole and Bernadette exchanged another worried look.

"I was so stupid," Louise said miserably, picking crumbs off the edge of the crumpet. "I never told him how much I loved him."

It was quite apparent that neither Bernadette nor Mrs Poole had any idea what to say to comfort her. Bernadette retreated to mind the shop and Louise made herself eat the rest of the crumpet, to appease Mrs Poole, before retreating to her room.

She should do some book-binding work, to try and keep her hands and mind busy, but she couldn't make herself do anything but lie on the bed and worry.

Crafty came in and jumped up on the bed, purring softly and coming to rub the top of her head against Louise's chin.

"Hello, old girl," Louise whispered, trying not to sniffle. "Do you miss him too? I know you liked him, even though he always made sure not to let you out." She petted the cat, and Crafty flopped down on the bed beside her and rolled over to show her belly.

Her distinctly round belly.

"Oh, Wollstonecraft." Louise sat up. "How?"

Despite being a mighty huntress, Crafty only got fat when she was having kittens. They'd only just managed to find a home for Pie, the last kitten from her last litter! Though at least Pie had found the very best of homes, with Marie and Renwick.

Stroking Crafty's swollen belly, Louise thought again of Shaun... because Shaun had said once that he'd take Pie if the young cat was still available when he found a house.

"Maybe he can have one of these kittens instead," Louise whispered, before the tears began to fall in earnest again. "If he ever comes home!"

Bless Crafty, she didn't even meow a protest when her fur began to soak up Louise's tears.

Even at home, nothing seemed to be going right. Reverend Millings was being downright horrible in his sermons, undoubtedly egged on by Joshua and Phoebe; every Sunday brought a fresh tirade clearly directed squarely at Bernadette and Louise. Lord Ferndale even said quietly to Louise one day that he would quite understand if they wished to skip church.

"My mother would roll over in her grave," Louise said

stoutly. "We have nothing to be ashamed of, Grandfather. There is nothing Reverend Millings can do to us."

"Unfortunately, there is not much I can do to him, either!" Lord Ferndale looked grim, before conferring a kindly pat on her hand. "I hope the rest of Hatfield are far too sensible to listen to his nonsense."

"Our business has not decreased," Louise said, though she had privately noted that a few of Phoebe's cronies who used to come in to look at the fashion journals had stopped frequenting the shop. Not that they ever bought very much anyway! "Have you received any letters from Mr Yates?" she asked, changing the subject.

"Indeed… and you from Estelle?" Lord Ferndale looked at her cautiously, and she beamed at him.

"Indeed, we have. With good news that they are expecting!" The letter had come a couple of days previously, a small bright spot in Louise's glumness.

"But they cannot come home yet because poor Estelle has the sickness. A shame Bernadette is not with them, I am sure one of her tonics could bring your sister aright."

"I'm sure she'll be well enough to travel soon," Louise said optimistically. "Bernadette says the sickness ofttimes passes soon after the quickening."

"Let us hope so; I should very much like the next Yates to be born at Ferndale Hall!"

Thinking of that brought a smile to Louise's face, and she accepted Lord Ferndale's offered arm to walk beside him to his coach, and to their regular Sunday dinner at Ferndale Hall.

Another letter arriving a few days later bore far less pleasant news. A courier came into the bookshop and asked her name before handing her the letter; addressed to The Misses Baxter. It looked strangely official. The courier even required her to sign a paper stating that she had received the letter.

Curious as to what it might be, Louise picked up a letter-opener and slit open the envelope, sliding out the thick paper within and unfolding it. Her eyebrows shot up as she read. A cry caught in her throat.

"Are you all right, Cousin Louise?" a voice asked anxiously, and she looked up to see Brutus staring at her. "Is that... bad news?"

She could not look him in the face just now, not with that letter in her hand. Shaking her head spasmodically, she somehow managed to gasp out an instruction to watch the counter before taking to her heels and fleeing up the stairs.

"Louise!" Mrs Poole looked up from where she was cutting out scones at the kitchen table. "You're white as a sheet, what's the matter?"

"Bernadette," Louise gasped, unable to think. Was her sister home?

"She's out..."

Louise ran from the concerned look on the motherly housekeeper's face, desperate to be alone. In her room she sank down on the edge of the bed and read the letter over again, scarcely able to comprehend what it was saying.

A strange squeaking noise drew her attention, and she looked around, puzzled. "What was that?"

The squeak came again, from under her bed. Crouching down, Louise peered at the boxes and trunks stored there, before beginning to pull them out one by one.

"Oh, no!" she shrieked, on making another dreadful discovery.

Crafty had given birth to five squalling kittens... in the box of beautiful fabric Miss Yates had given them for Estelle's wedding. The fabric Louise had been saving to make her own wedding dress.

"Whatever is the matter?" Mrs Poole asked, coming to the door of her room, and then looking down at the box on the floor. "Oh... dear."

"Louise?" Bernadette called from the kitchen, sounding anxious.

Louise picked up the box, trying to hold back the tears. Carrying it into the kitchen, she set it on the table.

"Oh dear, oh dear. That's ruined that, then," Mrs Poole said, and Louise bit her tongue so she didn't snap.

Dr Williams was there with Bernadette, looking guilty, as well he might. He was the one who'd let Crafty out for her fateful night of passion with a local tomcat! Louise wasn't even sure why he was there, but he beat a hasty retreat, to her relief. She couldn't hold the tears in any longer, just collapsing to sit in a chair at the table and beginning to sob hopelessly.

Bernadette put an arm around her shoulders and tried to be comforting, but she didn't even know the whole of the bad news that Louise had to impart. Trying to pull herself together, Louise put a hand in her pocket and pulled out the letter she'd stuffed there when she'd been distracted with Crafty's kittens. Sliding it across the table to Bernadette, she met her sister's eyes.

"It's from Chancery Court, in London. Cousin Joshua did it, 'Dette. He went to Chancery Court and... and he told them that Father is missing in France, probably dead, and that the two of us are running the business."

"It's not illegal for women to run a business. Is it?" Bernadette looked uncertain.

"It is if we're not of age, and neither of us are. It was different when Estelle and Marie were here, but I'm not twenty-one until October."

"So…?" Bernadette looked puzzled.

"So Cousin Joshua has asked the Chancery Court to appoint him, as our nearest male relative, and as the heir for the entail, as the trustee for Father's estate. Because *obviously* we, as women, can't be trusted not to destroy the valuable property which will be coming to him when Father is declared dead." Louise tried for sarcasm to mask her rage and fear, the terror she could see beginning to dawn on Bernadette's face.

"Is he going to win?" Bernadette asked in a thin whisper, as though she couldn't make her voice come out quite right.

"Probably, yes!" Louise clenched her fist on the table, thinking it was lucky for Joshua he wasn't in front of her right at that moment. She'd have blackened his eye. "We have thirty days to produce either Father, alive and well, or legal documents from him appointing an acceptable trustee."

They were both silent for a few minutes, both trying to think.

"Could we forge…?" Bernadette began.

"Wouldn't work." Louise had already considered and discarded the idea. While they had plenty of samples of their father's handwriting to mimic, the document would have to be notarised by a solicitor or magistrate… and since Joshua was the local magistrate and the solicitor, Mr Burton, was one of his closest allies, they would be very suspicious of a document supposedly notarised by someone else. Being caught forging documents would only add to their troubles.

"We could close the bookshop..." Louise said, but Bernadette was already shaking her head.

"We can't! Remember? The entail says our branch of the family has to be running a viable business out of the building, or Joshua gets it at once! If we close the bookshop, we're handing it over without even trying!"

They both shuddered, knowing what would happen. Joshua would probably have a bonfire of books in the middle of the street, sell the building to the highest bidder, and they'd be thrown out of the home they'd grown up in. At least they'd have somewhere to go, thanks to Lord Ferndale, but the idea of Joshua getting his way was unthinkable.

"We need help," Louise said finally. It went against the grain to ask for it, but she didn't see that they had any choice; they were in an untenable position with the law against them.

"But how? Joshua holds all the cards!" Bernadette looked a bit terrified, and Louise had to admit she was trying not to panic herself.

"We can't produce those documents, or Father, unless he turns up. So instead we need to gather other evidence... that contrary to what Joshua is trying to claim, the business is doing just fine. And," she grimaced, "I'm afraid we need a man to act for us."

"Lord Ferndale?" Bernadette suggested.

"I have no doubt that he'll offer help if we ask for it, so yes. If only Mr Yates were home, or Lord Renwick were closer!"

"I'll write to them. To Estelle and Marie, anyway,"

Bernadette said. "We can't keep this from them, Lou, and they'll want to help. Even if Estelle can't travel, Mr Yates could come home, and as our brother-in-law, and a baron's grandson, he'll have just as much claim to be our guardian as Joshua."

"And Lord Renwick even more, being an earl," Louise mused. She might not like the fact, but peers definitely received preferential treatment. An earl speaking for them to the Chancery Court might make the court think twice about handing everything over to a local magistrate, who was a mere 'gentleman'.

"I'll write to them both today. And, tomorrow's Wednesday, when I go to see Lord Ferndale," Bernadette said firmly. "You leave this to me, Lou." She put a hand on Louise's arm gently, looking at her seriously. "You've got enough to deal with."

Bernadette left her, going to fetch her writing materials and then downstairs to sit at the counter to write letters. Louise sat alone at the kitchen table, watching the mewling kittens rolling around on ruined silk which had once been worth a small fortune.

The stained, ruined silk seemed a metaphor for the death of all her hopes.

No wedding dress.

No wedding.

No Shaun.

And maybe soon, the loss of everything else she held dear.

CHAPTER 20

Waterloo

Waiting for a battle, waiting for news, Shaun kept busy organising troops as best he could. The less experienced men were eager to "Take the fight to Boney" but the seasoned soldiers remained calm.

Or, appeared calm on the surface, anyway. Shaun too did his best to calm his nerves as they waited, and waited some more with Wellington's army in Belgium.

At least his quartermaster skills were proving useful, and were keeping him busy. Too many of the experienced fighting men had been sent off to the Americas with their rifles and equipment for the War of 1812, and what was left was a ragtag bunch of those who'd sold out and come back - like himself - green lads, and a few experienced regiments being rushed in from elsewhere and trying somehow to integrate all together with not much time and definitely not enough equipment. Just trying to find every man a uniform, a rifle and enough shot to be useful was quite a task, not to mention keeping them all fed.

He'd been welcomed back at his former rank with open

arms, and had been able to keep the Fox brothers and Riot Jones with him by virtue of simply insisting that he needed them. He'd managed to get them all ranked as sergeants, too, which meant they got better treatment than most, a tent to share between them and decent rations.

The first qualms of doubt had hit Shaun on the ship heading across the Channel. The white cliffs of Dover were receding in the distance, and Shaun was standing at the ship's stern. Several of the soldiers were noisily casting up their rations into the water. 'Feeding the fish' the captain had called it.

What difference was he really going to make? It wasn't as though he was going to personally collar Boney and drag him before Wellington by the scruff of his neck, as some of the silly young boys were bragging they'd do. Shaun knew better, it would be muck and blood and, from what he was hearing the more serious older men saying, he'd be lucky to get home alive this time.

He cast one more look at the distant cliffs, before they vanished below the horizon and all that was left to see was churning grey waves.

"Thinkin' of Miss Baxter?" Hugh Fox stepped up alongside him, leaned on the rail.

"Aye." There wasn't much point in denying it, after all. "Wondering if I should have left her. If we were right and Benjamin Baxter was the arsonist…" He'd shared his suspicions with his men weeks earlier.

"He didn't come home for Easter," Hugh pointed out.

"Looks like his school got wise to his temperament. But they'll not keep him over summer." Shaun sighed, looking out at the rolling waves. Holding the thought of Louise close. She knew about Benjamin, at least, and forewarned was forearmed.

He just couldn't keep from thinking that he'd made a mistake. That she might need him far more than His Majesty's Army did.

Two months later, Shaun's doubts only grew stronger as he looked about the gathered men before him. They were not battle ready. In fact, they were hardly trained at all, but Napoleon wasn't waiting. His Armée du Nord was marching towards them, over a hundred thousand men strong from all reports, and growing by the day.

The days were filled with exercise and marching, weapons cleaning and preparations, and charging into strawmen with bayonets.

Each night, he wrote to command, pleading for more ammunition and weapons, rations and uniforms. He had no idea if any would arrive in time, but he had to try. After sending his reports, he would write to Louise and beg her to forgive him, promise her he was doing everything to keep safe and hoping this madness would be over soon.

He was not expecting his notes to Louise to have any chance of arriving. He only hoped that if he wrote enough, one of them might get through. She would know he was still alive.

The fear of never seeing her again sat like a rock in his throat.

The world turned to hell before dawn the next day, when word spread through the camp that Napoleon had turned aside from the expected course and taken Charleroi.

"The Dutch are at Quatre Bras," Shaun's commanding officer said grimly, hunching over the map spread over a camp-table in his tent. "We're heading there to reinforce them."

"Where are the Prussians?" Shaun asked.

"Ligny, and they've got their own battle to fight. Gather your men, Jackson. You're with the 3rd Division, and Count Alten will tell you where to march." The general straightened and looked Shaun in the eye. "It's time to face the French. And may God preserve us all."

It was a long march on foot; they were out of position because of the French army's quick, unexpected manoeuvres, and most of the 3rd Division was foot troops. Shaun marched with his men, refusing to ride when they could not.

They began to hear the guns mid-afternoon, and soon the smoke from the cannons was visible, along with the continuous crack of rifle fire. Shaun saw faces pale, throats convulsively swallowing, and exchanged glances with Riot and the Fox brothers.

"Make your way along the line," Shaun said quietly. "Stiffen the spines of these young lads. For God, England and King George, men."

"Sir!" They saluted him and marched away, and Shaun watched them go, wondering if he'd see them again before the battle.

Or after.

"Louise," he breathed to himself, pressing a hand to his heart. He had nothing personal of hers to carry with him, had never asked her for a token. What he would not give for a lock of her hair! But all he had was a book, the one she'd sold him that very first day, tucked inside his coat over his heart.

He doubted it would stop a bullet or a bayonet, but perhaps it would bring him luck, all the same.

It was all over by dark; short and sharp, and by the end of it there were almost nine thousand dead on the field and huge numbers of wounded. The French had retreated, though, at least for now.

Shaun was exhausted, filthy and entirely out of ammunition, but he was alive and, miraculously to his way of thinking, completely unharmed, with not so much as a scratch on him. He was gathering up what remained of his regiment when Riot Jones came marching up, no smile on the Welshman's face.

"Riot, thank God," Shaun said, but his relief died when he saw Riot's expression.

"Come," was all Riot said, and Shaun followed.

Hugh and John Fox lay side by side, as close in death as the brothers had been in life. A cannon blast had taken both of them in the same moment, from what Shaun could tell.

The backs of Shaun's eyes burned, but he refused to let the tears fall. He stood in silence for a moment.

"Make sure they're picked up," he said hoarsely to Riot at last. "Make sure all our men are picked up." They'd not get much more dignity than a mass grave and a chaplain's hasty prayer for their souls, but better that than being left out here like carrion.

Riot saluted him in silence, the Welshman's brown eyes wet. Shaun gave a jerky little nod and turned away.

There was no time to grieve.

The next day was a blur of exhaustion; there was no time to rest. Shaun identified and recorded the name of every man dead or injured in his regiment, and by the time he'd passed that to the clerks to send on, Wellington had ordered the retreat from Quatre Bras, to regroup in greater strength on better ground. The Prussians had not done well at Ligny, despite having a numerical advantage, and had splintered. Wellington was determined to pull together the largest force he could manage at Mont-Saint-Jean escarpment, and when the Duke set his mind to something, it was as inevitable as the dawn.

The march back the way they'd come was even worse, through a torrential rainstorm. Tired and mourning, Shaun and Riot marched side by side, grim-faced.

Shaun had seen some terrible battles in the Peninsula, but he had never seen anything like the battle of Waterloo. More than 500 cannon and almost 200,000 men clashed in one of the bloodiest days the world had ever seen, and by the end of it the French were routed, but at a shocking cost.

Near-deafened by the constant boom of guns, utterly exhausted, Shaun wandered the battlefield afterwards, searching for his men. Too many dead, they numbered in the thousands, and many more wounded. He could not find Riot anywhere.

Dark was falling, and the cries of injured men around him were weakening. Many were in French, but he hardened his heart, looked away, though he didn't join those who made sure the Frenchmen would call no longer. It was nearing midnight when a lilting Welsh voice called his name.

"Riot!" Shaun scrambled over bodies, at last found Riot lying in a shallow ditch.

"Took your bloody time, didn't you?" Riot was filthy, covered over in mud and blood and who knew what else.

"What's been keeping you?" He knew it was serious. Going to his knees in the mud, he reached for Riot's hand, relieved at the strength in his grip.

"My leg." Riot grimaced. "Fell in this bloody ditch and broke it, didn't I. Can't stand."

Relief flooded through Shaun. Riot could and would survive a broken leg. "Is that all?" he almost begged.

"Bloody enough, isn't it!"

Shaun laughed, suddenly feeling a weight lift off him. "Come on. Let's get you out of here."

Riot wasn't a big man; Shaun had carried bigger off battlefields. The gutsy Welshman didn't make a single sound as Shaun lifted him up and carried him almost a mile to where the field hospital was set up, though his leg must have been sheer agony.

The doctors were run off their feet, but one of them looked at the bars of rank on Shaun's shoulders and at the sergeant's jacket on the man in his arms. "What's wrong with him?"

"Broken leg. Clean break, I think." He hoped, anyway.

"I'll set it if you'll splint and wrap it and take him away again," the doctor bargained, and Shaun nodded.

"I can do that."

The doctor was quick, but Riot still screamed and fainted as the leg was straightened.

"Best thing for him," the doctor said briskly. "Here's your splints and bandages," as a young apprentice hurried up with them.

"Thank you," Shaun said humbly, reaching out to take

the items. The doctor looked down at his hands, reached out to take his left one.

"Did you realise you've got two broken fingers, Colonel?"

Shaun blinked. "I… what?"

He had no idea when it had even happened, but looking down now he saw that his ring and pinky fingers were indeed bent outwards at unnatural angles.

"Do they not hurt?" The doctor probed lightly.

"Ah, they do now!"

"Well, no nerve damage, then." The doctor smiled tightly. "Need something to bite down on?"

Shaun clenched his teeth and shook his head. Two horrible crunching sounds later and his fingers looked almost normal. Shaun let out his breath, spots briefly spinning before his eyes.

"Jacobs, splint those, and help the colonel splint his man's leg," the doctor said, before nodding briskly and walking away.

The young apprentice stepped forward hesitantly - he couldn't have been more than fourteen or so, Shaun thought, not much older than Brutus Baxter. He hoped the boy had been far away from the battlefield today, though the lad's eyes were haunted by what he'd obviously seen in the hours since.

"Thank you," he said quietly as the boy slipped two thin shims of wood between his fingers and carefully bound up his hand, before turning to Riot. "Have you eaten today, lad?"

The boy shook his head.

"If you'll help me get Sergeant Jones here back to my tent

CATHERINE BILSON & EBONY OATEN

once his leg's splinted, I'll have a hot meal brought. Enough to share."

The small bribe was eagerly accepted, and the lad found a stretcher. Shaun's fingers hurt now, but he was still able to keep his end up and the two of them carried Riot to where Shaun's tent had been set up. Shaun kept his promise, and by the time the food arrived Riot had woken up.

"Smells bloody good, at least," Riot said, accepting the bowl of stew and spoon Shaun held out.

"We've barely eaten more than stale bread in three days," Shaun pointed out dryly. "I wouldn't ask what's in it."

"Wasn't planning to." Riot tucked in, as did the young apprentice, who handed his bowl back afterwards and disappeared into the night.

Shaun ate more slowly, almost too exhausted to lift the spoon to his lips. The stew wasn't bad, but he thought wistfully of the potato and leek soup from the Red Lion, Louise's mother's recipe, or of the wonderful Sunday dinners at Ferndale Hall, Louise sitting beside him with her eyes alight with joy. It was Sunday today, or had been, it was long after midnight by now, and all he could think of was her, his beautiful Louise, far away from this hell of death and horror.

Enough of this.

He was going home.

"Two broken fingers?" the general said the following morning. "Can you fire your rifle?"

"I doubt it," Shaun said honestly. His fingers hurt like the devil this morning, and he could tell they were swollen beneath the bandages. He could barely use his left hand.

"It's your left hand, you can still write… your skills would be useful with the quartermasters, Jackson. I'll reassign you."

Shaun swallowed a protest. He nodded, slowly. "Very well, sir."

Riot wasn't fit to travel anyway, Shaun consoled himself as he made his way slowly back to his tent, and there was no way he could leave the Welshman who'd followed him into hell and out again.

The Prussians were pursuing Napoleon, though Wellington would no doubt follow, wanting to be there when Boney was finally run to ground. But there was so much to be done here; Shaun had heard figures of ten thousand men injured, and somehow they would all have to be doctored, fed, and returned to England to recuperate. The logistics of that alone would be a staggering task.

Well, once he could manage it, he'd assign himself and Riot aboard a ship to go home. And when he got back to Hatfield, the very first thing he was going to do was lay his heart at Louise Baxter's feet and beg her to be his wife.

CHAPTER 21

Misery Loves Company

The days passed in a blur of loneliness for Louise. She spent every day working in the bookshop trying to wear herself out, and then still couldn't seem to get a good night's sleep for worrying. She couldn't stop jumping from one fear to the next. Her father, Cousin Joshua's horrible plan to seize the bookshop out from under them, and most of all, Shaun.

Bernadette seemed less concerned, insisting that they had allies in Lord Ferndale as well as Mr Yates and Lord Renwick, who would surely be hurrying to their aid. Lord Ferndale had already written to his man of business in London instructing him to create a second petition to Chancery Court to be made guardian of Louise and Bernadette, which would protect them at least, even if he couldn't protect the bookshop.

Louise had suggested transporting some - if not all - of the books to Ferndale Hall for safekeeping, but Lord Ferndale had pointed out that unfortunately Cousin Joshua might be able to accuse them of stealing his property if he got his way with the Court.

Thwarted at every turn. Louise tapped her quill on the counter, trying to think. Maybe if they *sold* the books to Lord Ferndale for a fraction of their worth? But the ledgers would prove otherwise and Joshua would say they had cheated him… unless they burned the ledgers… no. Everything in her cringed away from the thought.

The door crashed open, the bell flying off its hanger and hitting the floor, and Louise sighed, remembering the last time that had happened. Shaun had fixed it for her. Well, she'd have to fix it herself, just like everything else around here. She braced herself for yet another Cousin Joshua confrontation - he was the only person who'd push the door open so violently - and was utterly shocked to see Bernadette rush in, white-faced.

"What's happened?" Louise stood up, sudden terror bolting through her.

Bernadette didn't seem to be able to speak, her mouth working soundlessly, her whole body shaking violently. Grabbing her sister's arm, Louise kicked the door shut, grateful that it was a Saturday and the bookshop was closed. Nobody would come in to interrupt them.

"Sit down before you fall down, and tell me what's happened!" She pushed Bernadette onto the stool behind the counter and crouched in front of her, chafing Bernadette's cold, shaking hands between her own.

Louise wasn't sure how much more bad news she could take.

"Re-Reverend Millings," Bernadette said between chattering teeth.

"What's he done now?" Rage flooded Louise, replacing

her fear. Reverend Millings was a petty annoyance compared to everything else, but she was reaching the end of her tether. Perhaps it was time she gave the man a real piece of her mind; she'd held her tongue until now, but enough was enough!

"He's d-dead."

Louise stared at her sister in shock. "*What* did you say?"

"He - he just fell over dead. Right in front of me and Glynn, I mean, Dr Williams, he was shouting and he just fell down and started foaming at the mouth and then he was *dead*."

Bernadette had seen death, Louise knew. Many times. But this… this kind of death was something different. And even though Reverend Millings had been no friend of theirs, seeing that happen right in front of her had obviously affected Bernadette deeply.

Louise felt a certain amount of guilt that her first emotion was relief. No more fire and brimstone sermons directed their way from the church's pulpit would be one small weight off her shoulders, at least.

"Come on." She put her arm around Bernadette and helped her to her feet. "Let's get you upstairs."

Handing her sister over to Mrs Poole's motherly care, Louise headed back downstairs, wondering if she should go over to the vicarage. Mrs Millings would surely take to her bed and Ruth would… Louise had no idea what Ruth would do. But if Ruth needed a refuge outside her home, she'd come here. Best to stay downstairs with the door unlocked in case Ruth came, Louise decided, and settled herself behind the counter, reaching for a fresh sheet of paper.

She'd write to Marie. Reverend Millings' death was too exciting a piece of news not to share, and Marie had suffered as much abuse as any of them, or more, though she had been fortunate enough not to witness the most recent sermons. The tirade from the pulpit the Sunday after Marie ran off to Scotland to marry Renwick had almost shaken the stained glass from the church's windows.

Not only that, but Marie understood a little of what Louise was feeling. Far away as she was, she had written some very kind letters to Louise since Shaun had gone away to fight. Marie had suffered her own heartbreak when she thought Renwick wasn't coming back for her; she knew what Louise was enduring.

Thank goodness nobody came through the door, because if they had, they would have seen Louise smiling as she wrote the words, *"Brimstone has just dropped dead, right in front of 'Dette!"*

There was no immediate replacement for the deceased clergyman. As the next day was Sunday, they still headed to church, as did many from Hatfield, but there was nobody to lead the congregation. Even though gossip spread quickly, there were many who had no idea what had transpired the day before.

It was all a bit odd; the building was there, everything looked the same, but nobody was in charge. Bernadette said she'd visit Mrs Millings later that day. The woman would most likely still be in shock. Ruth would be with her mother, trying to console her. For a moment, Louise wondered whether the two of them might be relieved he was dead as well.

Cousin Joshua puffed himself up and took charge as the

church filled up. He walked to the altar and stood as if delivering a speech on behalf of the king. Louise rolled her eyes in anticipation of their cousin putting himself at the centre of town events.

It took longer than usual for people to take their seats, as chatter increased about why the town magistrate was standing up the front and not Reverend Millings.

"Dear people of Hatfield, I bring terrible news," Joshua said. He was trying to make his face look stern, but failed.

Bernadette whispered, "He looks constipated."

Louise tried not to laugh.

Thank goodness Joshua did not hear them. "Our beloved leader in faith," he intoned, "has passed suddenly. We do not know all the facts at this time, and no-doubt everybody is in shock. We shall have a period of official mourning and will not be able to resume services until the bishop sends us a replacement."

This brought a murmur of chatter as people wondered how long they'd be without a clergyman. Somebody nearby scoffed, "I'll not be going to the Catholics."

Joshua had delivered his news, but was not stepping down. "I urge all to treat this event with solemnity and lean on your faith. Now is not the time to engage in idle gossip." At which point he looked directly to Bernadette and Louise.

Louise rolled her eyes with exasperation. Joshua would do better to look to his own wife, if he didn't want idle gossip spread!

The town was agog with the terrible news that their community leader had died. Louise was so relieved Bernadette had not been on her own when it had happened, because the gossip Mrs Poole and Rosie shared was leaning towards some people suspecting Bernadette had done something to bring it on. A cruel rumour started by Phoebe, Louise suspected, though she had no proof.

The bishop sent a replacement curate to stand in temporarily, but he was a small man who spoke so quietly nobody ever learned his name, and certainly could not hear him even in the front pews of the church. No wonder he had no church of his own, Louise thought. Luckily Lord Ferndale continued their routine of having lunch at Ferndale Hall afterwards.

They were part way through a lovely meal when Miss Yates asked, "This business with the Reverend is most upsetting. How are you faring, Bernadette?"

"I'm recovering from the shock. As are Mrs Millings and Ruth."

"The poor dear," Miss Yates said, "Although, would it be very wrong of me to now think we have more chance of the parsonage land being used for the hospital?"

"And we will have a clergyman of sense, sooner rather than later!" Lord Ferndale said firmly. "The living is in my gift, after all. I shall be interviewing suitable candidates quite soon and I will be selecting someone without Reverend Millings' many character flaws, this time around!"

"Perhaps you should let me interview him too, brother," Miss Yates said.

Lord Ferndale opened his mouth, perhaps to dismiss the suggestion, but then stopped himself, looking thoughtful. "Do you know, Florence, that is an excellent suggestion. I should like to know the new man's *true* beliefs regarding women's capabilities, before I make any irrevocable decisions. Yes, you shall interview the candidates too... and perhaps we can suggest that they call into the bookshop and learn their views on young women in business and literature of what some might consider to be a frivolous nature, too."

"One problem solved, at least," Louise said, though she thought privately that it solved none of hers.

In the middle of June, as summer made itself felt, Benjamin Baxter returned to Hatfield for his term break and there was a fire that very night.

Louise wasted no time, once Rosie rushed into the shop and told her the news. She went straight to the livery stable, hired a horse and rode to Ferndale Hall.

"Benjamin Baxter's back," she said as the butler Mr Thorne showed her into the breakfast parlour.

"Oh, dear." Lord Ferndale looked up from his plate.

"And there's already been a fire."

"Of course there has."

"Was anyone hurt?" Miss Yates said anxiously.

"Not yet, but it's surely only a matter of time. With Mr Jackson and his men gone…" Louise shrugged, fighting against the pain those words caused her. She hadn't heard a word from Shaun, and the news was absolutely terrifying, with Napoleon having gathered a vast army to him and news of shocking battles and lives lost.

"I don't have anyone to appoint to watch him!" Lord Ferndale spread his hands helplessly. "Not to cover the entire district, anyway. Maybe just in town…"

A thought occurred to Louise. "What if he didn't have the horse?"

Lord Ferndale frowned. "Your cousin's horse?"

"Joshua barely ever rides it anyway," Louise paced,

trying to think things through. "What if… the horse was… stolen?"

"I am not risking any of my men for horse thievery, and you are certainly not to do it yourself!" Lord Ferndale said sharply. "Your cousin could have you transported, if you were caught!"

She certainly did not want that, and she would not endanger any of Lord Ferndale's men, either. "Well, what if for some reason the horse couldn't be ridden?" An idea came to her. "The farrier!"

"Mr Hollick?" Miss Yates said. "What about him?"

"He's a good man, and he and Cousin Joshua are not friends. His wife is very fond of Bernadette after 'Dette helped her through childbed fever. I'm sure he'd help."

"Temporary lameness," Lord Ferndale guessed. "Well, that's clever, Louise. Very well. I shall write you a note to take to Mr Hollick requesting his assistance."

"And perhaps we shall confine Benjamin's activities to the town where he is more likely to be caught!" Louise felt almost giddy with hope.

Miss Yates nodded in fervent agreement. "And do not forget, dear, to be very sure to point out to everyone that the return of the arsonist means it could not *possibly* have been Mr Jackson, too."

Louise froze. She hadn't even thought of that, but of course! A moment later, she drooped a little. "What good is it to clear his name, if he doesn't ever come back?" she said bitterly.

"Now, now, dear, you are not to think like that." Miss Yates took her hand and drew her to a seat at the table. "Mr Thorne, do bring Louise some tea, and a plate of toast. You're to sit down and eat some breakfast while Arthur writes that note for Mr Hollick." She shot Lord Ferndale a pointed look.

"Indeed, I shall get to that at once." Lord Ferndale abandoned his half-eaten breakfast and made for his study.

Half an hour later, Louise was on the horse again riding back to Hatfield, and as soon as she arrived back in town she went to Mr Hollick the farrier, who listened thoughtfully to what she had to say, read Lord Ferndale's note and then tossed it into his forge.

"Best there's no evidence that ever existed," he rumbled, a twinkle in his eye. "Leave it to me, Miss Louise. I'll get it done while the Baxters are eating their dinner... always have it precisely at six, they do. That horse'll be lame if the boy tries to ride it anywhere tonight." He tapped his hammer meaningfully against his palm. "And if he tries to light any fires around here... well, folks'll be watching."

She felt a lot better by the time she got back to the bookshop, though as she opened the door Bernadette looked up where she was trying to comfort a sobbing Brutus and said; "Where have you *been*?"

"Ferndale Hall." Louise took in the huge bruise on Brutus' face and clenched her fists with silent fury. "Is that courtesy of your brother?"

"He's meaner than ever," Brutus sniffled. "Can I stay here, please? Please don't make me go home..."

"You can have Marie's room." Louise made a snap decision. "Has Dr Williams seen him yet, Bernadette?"

"No, I can handle this, it's only bruising."

"It may well be, but I should like Dr Williams to see it all the same. As a witness," Louise elaborated when Bernadette gave her a curious look. "So that when I tell Cousin Joshua that Brutus is not going back to that house while Benjamin is there, we have someone with some authority to back us up."

"I'll take him straight across to see the doctor now." Bernadette took Brutus' hand.

"I can really stay?" Brutus asked Louise.

"You really can. But you might have to be brave and come in front of the town council with me and show them your injury, and explain that your brother did it, if your father demands you back. Do you think you can do that?" Louise asked him.

"Yes. I can do that." Brutus jutted his jaw, before wincing and putting his free hand to his cheek.

"Off you go to Dr Williams. Mrs Poole," Louisa called up the stairs. "Could you and Rosie come down for a moment, please?"

Mrs Poole and Rosie came down, looking at her curiously. Louise put her hands on her hips. "I am *done* sitting back and letting Cousin Joshua and Phoebe spread their slander to all and sundry without fighting back," she said. "So. I need you two."

Rosie grinned, catching on quickly. "What do you need people to know, Miss Louise?"

"Three things." Louise held up a finger. "First of all, that since the arsonist is apparently back, and that Mr Jackson is still bravely fighting in France, *obviously* he was not the culprit."

Mrs Poole nodded approvingly. "Oh, indeed. And Mr and Mrs Baxter will owe him an apology, when he returns."

"What's the other two things?" Rosie asked eagerly.

"The second is that Brutus Baxter will be living here with us until his older brother leaves for school again. You haven't seen him yet, but Bernadette has just had to take him to the doctor because Benjamin gave him a dreadful bruise on his face. I shouldn't wonder if his cheekbone is fractured." Louise wasn't even exaggerating.

Mrs Poole and Rosie both looked horrified. "The poor wee lad!" Mrs Poole cried.

"Exactly! I want everyone in town to know his parents don't care a jot… tell them that Joshua would let Benjamin beat him to death and not step in. Well, I won't have it."

"Good for you, Miss Louise," Rosie said. "And the third thing?"

Louise took a deep breath. She might be making a mistake… but she might be saving lives. She would not have deaths on her conscience. "Be careful how you phrase this. But let it not go unnoticed that the very day Benjamin Baxter returned to town is when the fires began again."

Mrs Poole gave a little shriek. "Louise! You don't think…"

"Yes. I do think it. And Mr Jackson suspected him too, before he had to leave. He fits the build of the man both Mr Jackson and Mr Stratforth almost caught setting fires, and he had the means. And the motive. Every building burned belonged to someone he - or Joshua - disliked."

"Saints preserve us!" Rosie, who was Catholic, crossed herself. "And his father the magistrate!"

"Precisely," Louise said grimly. "He will need to be literally caught in the act. He must be watched."

"I'll fetch my hat," Mrs Poole said. "You leave this to us, Miss Louise. Everyone sensible in Hatfield will know before nightfall what's been going on, you have my word!"

Louise smiled tightly as the maid and housekeeper hurried off. "I wish you were here, Shaun," she whispered to the empty bookshop. "But since you're not… I shall take care of myself, and everyone else too."

For a moment, she could almost hear his voice, smell the woodsy scent of him when he stood close to her. *"I have not the slightest doubt that even if you had nobody at all to help you out, you'd pull through, Louise Baxter,"* he'd said to her once. *"You're really quite remarkable, you know."*

"You'd be proud of me, I think," she said aloud, before squaring her shoulders and marching behind the counter to take her usual seat. Because no matter what, Baxter's Fine Books was still going to be open for business. Today, and every day, if she had anything to say about it.

CHAPTER 22
An Unexpected Proposal

A little to Louise's surprise, Joshua and Phoebe didn't come looking for Brutus. They didn't even seem to notice that he was no longer sleeping or eating at their house. Or perhaps they were too busy trying to keep a lid on the rumours beginning to spread around Hatfield about Benjamin; the one time Louise saw Phoebe in the street, Phoebe appeared to be desperately trying to make some point to her friend Mrs Wellworth, who stood with arms folded, looking as though she didn't believe what Phoebe was saying. Louise smiled and went into the printer's before Phoebe could spot her.

Brutus was much happier living with them, and having his smiling face around was a small bright spot in increasingly grim times. The news from France was more dreadful by the day, and on the twenty-second of June, Bernadette hid the newspaper behind her back when Louise reached for it.

"'Dette…" she didn't want to know, but she had to look. The previous day's news had been bad enough, with reports of a dreadful battle at a crossroads somewhere, but from the look on Bernadette's face, this was much worse.

Slowly, Bernadette pulled the newspaper out and placed it on the counter. She stood beside Louise as she read, hand on her shoulder in a gesture of silent support.

The account of the battle of Waterloo, as it was being called, was a dry dispatch written by Wellington himself.

"They won the battle," Louise murmured, as she reached the bottom of the article. "But what does 'our loss was great' mean? And the Quarter-Master General was killed…" She did not like that particular snippet. While she had not the slightest idea where Shaun might have been deployed, she knew he had been a quartermaster. Had he been with the general when the fatal cannonball hit?

"It was a decisive victory, I think," Bernadette said hesitantly. "The French are in full retreat."

A sound reached Louise's ears, and she realised it was a cheer; someone in the inn yard next door, perhaps being told the news.

"They'll be celebrating at the Midsummer Assembly tonight," Mrs Poole declared, marching in and dusting off her skirts. Looking at Louise's expression, her cheer slipped a little. "Do you feel able to come, my dear?"

"I don't think I feel like dancing," Louise said, looking down at the newssheet again. *'Our loss was great.'* The words seemed to be mocking her. *What about my loss?* she wanted to scream. *What about Shaun?*

"I'll stay with you," Bernadette said, but Louise shook her head firmly.

"You will not. You're going to go and hold your head up high and dance with Dr Williams, and make sure everyone knows you're not afraid to show your face. If people ask where I am, tell them I'm staying home because I don't want Brutus to be alone."

"Very well," Bernadette acquiesced, though she also unaccountably blushed a little. Louise didn't press her as to why. Bernadette had her own troubles; Phoebe and Joshua were trying to blame Reverend Millings' death on her, as though that were even possible. There were multiple witnesses who could attest that the vicar had always flatly refused even the suggestion of Bernadette's assistance. It was important that Bernadette go to the assembly and show that she had nothing to hide.

Louise sat with Brutus instead and played a card game with him after supper, listening to the music spilling in through the open kitchen window. Thinking about when she had danced with Shaun at the Midwinter Assembly, the way she had felt light and graceful in his arms for the first time in her life.

"It's your turn, Louise," Brutus said, and she startled, looking down at the cards in her hand.

"I'm so sorry. I was woolgathering."

He looked at her with wise eyes. "You miss Mr Jackson very much, don't you?"

"Very much," she said, her throat tight.

"He'll come back," Brutus said, with the unshakeable confidence of a twelve-year-old boy. "And then the two of you will get married. Can I come and live with you, when you do?"

She forced a smile. "Of course. I'll tell Mr Jackson to make sure there's a room for you, when he buys us a house."

A beautiful little fantasy, with decreasingly likely odds of ever becoming reality. When their card game was finished,

Louise sighed and shooed Brutus off to bed and sat alone, listening to the music.

Bernadette found her sitting there in the dark, the candle having gone out, when she came back in.

"Lou!" Bernadette startled, hand to her chest. "I didn't see you there! Why no candle?"

"It went out. I was listening to the music." It was still playing; Bernadette had obviously tired and come home before the end of the assembly.

"You should have come." Bernadette relit the candle and put the tea-kettle on the banked stove. "Mr Stratforth asked after you."

It took a moment for Louise to recall who Bernadette meant. "Oh. The farmer?"

"Yes, he seemed very disappointed you weren't there."

Louise shrugged, uncaring.

Bernadette poured hot water into the teapot and sat down opposite her. They looked at each other for a moment, and then Bernadette said "What are we going to do, Lou?" very quietly.

She knew what her sister meant. The deadline to get the paperwork the Chancery Court had requested was only a few days away now, and they had nothing to send. What would happen next, neither of them knew.

"I don't know." Louise reached out, took Bernadette's hand and held it tightly. "But I do know I'm not going to stop fighting. No matter what."

Bernadette puffed out a breath, then nodded, squeezing back. "No matter what."

Louise opened the bookshop the following morning and was just scraping up Crafty's usual leavings - having another litter of kittens had not slowed down the cat's murderous rampage any - when an unexpected visitor walked into the shop.

"Hullo, Miss Louise," Ruth Millings said timidly.

"Ruth!" Louise dropped the ash pan and shot to her feet. "Dear girl! How are you?" She hadn't seen the girl since her father's shocking death, almost four weeks ago now.

Ruth looked as pale as she always did, and as thin, but less... beaten, somehow. She stood a little taller and straighter, a brightness in her eyes Louise had never seen before. She accepted the impulsive hug Louise dished out.

"Well, black doesn't suit you," Louise said honestly, and Ruth actually smiled.

"I've not much choice."

"Sit down and tell me what's happening. How is your mother?"

Ruth thought about that for a moment before saying "Better."

Louise didn't press any further, although she wondered what exactly Ruth meant by that. Recovering from her grief? Less beaten-down and terrified?

"Well, it's nice to see you," Louise said diplomatically instead. "Dare I ask if you are considering coming back to help us?"

"I want to come back. It's good to get out of the house!" Ruth lifted her chin. "And... we need the money. Paid to me, now."

Louise hadn't considered the Millings' living situation, but of course the vicarage must go to the new parson, when he arrived. She was sure Lord Ferndale was not about to order Ruth and her mother out immediately, but they must find somewhere to live, and their income would be gone.

"What is your situation?" Louise asked forthrightly.

"Mama has a small jointure. Enough to rent us a little cottage and have a maid of all work, but not much more. If I could be paid my wages here, that would be enough to be sure of food on our table."

Ruth's confidence had certainly blossomed, Louise thought. She nodded. "Of course, that is more than fair! I was never easy about being required to put your wages into the collection plate at all. In fact, there is a week's worth of wages for the last week you worked before your father passed, that was never put in. Let me pay you that now."

Ruth looked pleased, and put the coins in her pocket before collecting the duster and setting about the shelves as though she had never been away.

It was good to have her back, Louise thought with a little smile as she returned to dealing with the mouse remains.

It was not half an hour later when another visitor entered the bookshop, this time a slim young man Louise estimated to be only a few years older than herself. He had a nice smile and a clergyman's collar, which caused her eyes to widen.

"The famous Baxter's Fine Books!" he said, with an engaging smile. "I knew I must come in at once, to meet Lady Renwick's sisters."

Louise blinked, startled. "You know Marie?"

"Indeed! I do beg your pardon." He had already doffed his hat, now he made her a very polite bow. "Mr John Charles, at your service. You must be Miss Louise; Lady Renwick made such good descriptions of you all, I feel that I know you already!"

Mr Charles! Louise put two and two together. The former

tutor for Renwick's sons, who Marie said was completing his seminary studies at Cambridge. Clearly he had done so - and Renwick had sent him here?

"Are you here to be our temporary vicar?" she asked, seeing Ruth peering out from behind the shelves, eyes wide.

"Indeed; Lord Renwick has commended me to Lord Ferndale, who was good enough to invite me to come, and to pay for a room at the Red Lion for a month while we see if I should suit the parish." He grinned, enthusiastically engaging. "I am quite delighted with it already."

Louise thought he seemed a very nice young man. She looked at Ruth, asking with a silent twitch of her eyebrow if she would like to be introduced, but Ruth shook her head and drew back behind the shelves. Very well, Louise would not press her. "And have you met Lord Ferndale, yet?"

"No, but the innkeeper advised I may procure a horse at the livery stable and furnished me with a map to Ferndale Hall." He brandished a piece of paper. "I shall be off directly, but I could not pass up the chance to see the famous bookshop and meet you. Is Miss Bernadette here? I should like to pay my respects to her, too."

"She is out, I'm afraid, but I'm sure she will be pleased to meet you at your convenience. Why don't you join us for dinner this evening?" Louise suggested.

"That is most kind!" Mr Charles beamed at her. "I am honoured, and delighted to accept."

"Well, he seemed nice," Louise said, once the cheerful young man had bowed and departed.

"Hmph," Ruth said, from behind the shelves.

"I'm sure you needn't see too much of him if you don't want to."

Ruth didn't reply to that, and Louise smiled, returning to

her work. But no sooner had she begun making out a list of books to order from the London printer than the door opened again, and she sighed and looked up, mustering a smile for the incoming customer.

"Oh, Mr Stratforth! Good morning."

The tall dairy farmer came to stand before the counter, turning his hat around in his hands. He was wearing his Sunday best suit, Louise noticed, and suddenly began to feel vaguely uneasy.

"I missed seeing you at the assembly yestereve, Miss Baxter," he said.

"Oh," was all she could think of to say.

"I had something particular I wished to ask you."

Oh no.

Please don't! she wanted to shriek, but he was already barrelling on.

"I already spoke to your cousin Mr Baxter who gave his permission proper like, but a'course I need to ask you. We talked about what I have to offer, at the last assembly …"

No, you talked and I tried to ignore you, Louise thought in irritation. He'd never bothered to ask for her input or opinion.

"And so, if you could see your way clear… I'd very much like if you were to say yes, and marry me." Mr Stratforth ran down at last, and stood looking at her expectantly. He was still twisting his hat in his hands, though, and didn't look in the least bit confident, which made Louise feel rather more sorry for him than she otherwise might.

Asking Joshua for my hand before he asks me, indeed! And Joshua said yes! She gritted her teeth, taking a moment. It wouldn't do to take out her fury with her cousin on this inof-

CATHERINE BILSON & EBONY OATEN

fensive man, whose only true flaw was that he wasn't Shaun Jackson.

"I'm honoured," Louise said slowly, choosing her words with care, "but…"

"But I ain't your first choice." He looked at her rather kindly.

"Well…" She truly didn't know what to say.

"If he comes back, I'm sure you'll be happy with him. But if he doesn't… I think maybe you could be happy with me. I'm willing to wait for you to make up your mind."

"You're a good man, Mr Stratforth," she said, deciding to be honest with him. "I do need some time. Thank you for the offer. I… will think on it."

It was the best she could manage, and he didn't seem to take any offence, wishing her a good day before putting his hat back on and leaving again. Louise sat a little stunned, wondering what she should do. What if Shaun never came back? Could she be happy with a man like Mr Stratforth? She tried to imagine it, and couldn't. The simple fact that Joshua apparently thought she should marry him made her instinctively recoil.

Mr Charles' first sermon was a breath of fresh air in Hatfield, all about loving thy neighbour, and Louise could feel a change in the atmosphere of the whole town afterwards. There had been no more fires since everyone started watching Benjamin Baxter, and his sulky, rage-filled expression at church brought a satisfied smile to Louise's face. "Stay close," she murmured to Brutus, though, not wanting him to get close enough for Benjamin to target him. "Ruth,

234

too." Ruth and her mother had come to church and were sitting in the Ferndale pew too, at Miss Yates' urging.

Mr Charles came to Ferndale Hall with them afterwards and a pleasant time was had by all. Still, Louise found herself unable to really enjoy the afternoon, her thoughts far away, with Shaun or her father, neither of whom had been heard of in far too long.

The lists of the dead began to appear in the newspapers on Monday, and every day that week Louise steeled herself to read through them. Shaun's name was not there, though, and she allowed herself a tiny glimmer of hope, even while she reminded herself that there were many who were not able to be identified.

She did find the tragic news of Hugh and John Fox having fallen at Quatre Bras, however, and was briefly overwhelmed with terror. They were with Shaun; had he fallen beside them? She scoured the lists once again, but could not find him, or Sobriety Jones.

"Stop," Bernadette said gently as Louise turned the page back and started from the top of the list a fourth time. "Lou. He's not there."

"There'll be more names tomorrow," Louise said, letting Bernadette take the paper from her.

"I know. But let us believe him alive and safe, for now, just as we believe Father is alive and safe."

Louise wasn't sure how much longer she could keep believing, especially when the following week brought more bad news. Since they missed the Chancery Court's deadline, the Court sent them a new letter advising that the Court would make a decision on trusteeship of their father's estate, and guardianship over their persons, at a hearing on the first of September. While they were permitted to attend, they must have a legal representative appointed if they wished someone to speak for them.

"I'll write to Marie again," Louise said, her hands shaking as she held the letter. "Renwick said his man is instructed to help us, but it would be so much better if he was here."

"The court might listen to an earl, you mean?" Bernadette asked.

"Exactly. He said he would be coming in the middle of September to bring the boys back to Eton, but I think it would be much better if he could be here for the hearing."

Bernadette nodded in agreement, and Louise sat down to write to Marie again. She wasn't sure there was any point in writing to Estelle; it was unlikely that the letter would arrive in Ireland in time for even Mr Yates to make his way home without Estelle, if he would even leave her. And there was no point in panicking Estelle during her pregnancy. No, a letter to Marie begging Renwick to come was all Louise could think of.

"I do wish you were here, Shaun," she whispered as she sealed the letter and wrote the direction on the front. "You'd have thumped Joshua's head and told him to leave us alone!" She half-smiled even as she said it, knowing such an action would have been of no use. Somehow, though, she was convinced Shaun would have thought of something, some plan to make Joshua back down.

"Where are you?" she murmured, sitting back down behind the counter after going to the post counter at the Red Lion to send the letter. Examining the fresh newspaper she'd just collected, she found much shorter lists of the dead and articles about the Coalition army being almost upon Paris.

With the French forces entirely broken, victory seemed certain.

A few soldiers had already returned home, all with minor injuries. Louise had rushed to see every man reported back, but not a single one of them could recall having seen Shaun anywhere. She could have wept with frustration.

"Why can't men just write letters?" She barely restrained herself from banging her fist on the counter. "First Father, and now you!"

She wasn't being fair, but emotion wasn't always rational, and it was the not knowing that was the worst. It was a dreadful kind of limbo, fearing the worst but holding always to a thin thread of hope.

"Just come home," she said quietly at last, setting the newspaper aside and resting her chin on her hands, careless of the black newsprint on her hands leaving smudges on her face. "Just… come home."

CHAPTER 23

Homecoming

Almost four months after leaving Hatfield, Shaun Jackson arrived back in town late one evening. Driving a small, second-hand coach he'd bought in London along with the two horses pulling it, after getting thoroughly fed up with the inadequate transportation he'd been able to get for Riot Jones with his broken leg, he pulled into the yard at the Red Lion and jumped down from the driver's seat.

"Mr Jackson!" Coming forward to take the horses, Mr Thomas gaped at him. "Well, I never! Aren't you a sight for sore eyes!"

Shaun smiled, clasping the burly ostler's hand. "It's good to be home, Mr Thomas! Can you take care of the horses and find somewhere to put the coach? It's mine."

"Of course, of course!"

"And I'm not alone." Shaun opened the coach door to reveal Riot, trying to scowl but failing miserably, all too obviously happy to be back.

"Riot Jones!" Mr Thomas looked at the Welshman's

splinted leg, propped amidst a stack of cushions on the seat. "Ah. . I see the need for the coach."

"And the reason I've been so delayed. Couldn't leave him." Though every day had been painful, Shaun wouldn't abandon the Welshman who'd followed him into hell and back. He owed Riot too much for that. They would go home together, or not at all.

"Let's get you upstairs to a comfortable bed, eh?" Shaun said to Riot, who shook his head.

"Sod off, silly bugger. Thomas here can help me. You go." He nodded to the building next door, where Shaun's heart yearned to be. "You got me here safe, didn't you? Job done. She's waiting."

He could see light in the upstairs windows above the bookshop, and though propriety said he should probably wait until morning, Shaun had waited quite long enough. With a grateful smile at Riot, he turned on his heel and ran around the corner of the building, to the front door of the bookshop.

He was about to create quite a din, half the town would probably be coming to see what was going on, but he didn't care.

"Louise!" he roared, banging on the bookshop door. "LOUISE!"

There was silence for a moment, and then above his head, a window opened.

"Who's making that racket?" Mrs Poole said irritably.

"It's me, Mrs Poole." He grinned up at her, seeing her expression change in an instant from annoyance to delight. "Is she here?"

"Of course, of course… Brutus, run downstairs and let him in!"

He had only a moment to wonder why Brutus was there so late at night, when the door crashed open, and it wasn't the young boy standing there staring at him, it was her. His beloved.

His Louise.

"Shaun," she whispered, her face pale with shock. "Shaun? Is it really you?"

He didn't answer her, not with words anyway. Instead he did what he'd dreamed of every hour since he left her; he stepped forward, took her in his arms and kissed her until neither of them had any breath left.

"Will you marry me?" he asked when he lifted his head at last.

"What? I… Shaun, where have you *been*?"

"France," he said. "Well, Belgium mostly, but also France. Did you not get my letters?"

"Not a single one!" she cried, and he realised she was really quite overwrought, swaying where she stood. Pulling her closer against him, he hugged her tightly.

"I should never have left," he said into her hair. "Realised it as soon as I was on the ship, but there was no way to turn around and come back, I had to see it through. But it's over now, I promise, and I'm not leaving again. Will you marry me?"

She was clinging to him now, her whole body shaking, and he realised to his horror that she was crying, great wracking sobs. She was in no fit state to answer him.

"You're back, then," a voice said dryly behind him, and he looked around to see Dr Williams had arrived, presumably having come out of Mrs Bell's after hearing Shaun shouting and banging on the bookshop door. "Dear me, Miss

Louise looks a little overwrought. Why don't you bring her into my consulting room?"

Probably the only place they could have a passably respectable private conversation this late at night, Shaun thought, and nodded gratefully. Dr Williams accompanied them to show them into the consulting room, and then made himself scarce. Through the window, Shaun saw the doctor go across the street to the bookshop and inside, presumably to tell Bernadette and Mrs Poole where Louise had gone.

She was still crying, though as Shaun led her over to sit on the small couch, she stopped and reached up, framing his face in her hands.

"It really is you!"

"It really is me," he said.

"I needed you!"

Something was wrong, more than just his prolonged, and, to her, unexplained absence. Shaun took Louise's hands in his. "Is it your father?" he asked gently. Matthew Baxter's even longer absence had been weighing on him for a long time; perhaps the bad news had finally come.

Louise shook her head, then nodded, then shook it again. "Oh, I don't even know where to start!"

"Tell me," he said. "Tell me everything."

Once she began, the words seemed to spill out faster and faster, until he could barely make sense of them. He heard enough, though. Reverend Millings dead... of poison? And Phoebe Baxter, that horrible woman, trying to claim Bernadette had something to do with it? And then Joshua Baxter going to the Chancery Court... Shaun's outrage grew.

"How *dare* he," he said, through gritted teeth.

"And then Benjamin came back..."

Shaun stiffened. "Fires?" he asked, suddenly terrified.

"Only one." She smiled, a little victorious, though tears still ran down her cheeks. "I set Mrs Poole and Rosie on him. On the whole town, spreading gossip... that the fires stopped when he went away and came back as soon as he returned. The farrier made Joshua's horse lame so Benjamin couldn't go far afield, and everyone in Hatfield has been watching him like a hawk."

"I bet he's hating that," Shaun murmured.

"But Brutus had to come live with us, because Benjamin beat him so badly."

"The poor little lad!"

Louise seemed to have calmed now, and just sat, clinging to his hand so tightly Shaun thought she might never let go. His right hand, fortunately; the fingers of his left were still splinted together, which had made driving the coach an uncomfortable business.

She spotted the bandage then and reached out, crying, "What happened?"

"I don't even know," he admitted. "Waterloo was... chaos. At the end, Riot had a broken leg and I had two broken fingers."

"Riot's alive?"

"And home with me," Shaun confirmed. "We lost the Fox brothers, though."

"I saw their names, in the lists."

He could only imagine how she must have felt, reading those lists. Looking for his name, undoubtedly. Lifting her hand to his lips, he kissed her fingers.

"Marry me. Joshua won't have any power over you, then."

"Yes." She said it so simply, he didn't understand for a

moment. When he just blinked at her, she laughed, threw her arms around his neck, and said loudly "YES!"

He had to send her home to bed, eventually, and took a room in the Red Lion even though Dr Williams offered his old room back. Shaun shook his head. "I'm going to be a married man. I need my own house."

"Well, congratulations." Dr Williams looked a little wistfully across at the bookshop. "Miss Louise is a fine woman. Both the Baxter sisters are."

"You've changed your tune about Bernadette," Shaun said, amused, and was still more entertained when Dr Williams blushed. Was the good doctor sweet on Bernadette? What an interesting match that would be! It was too late to ask any more questions, though, and Shaun made his way to a bed at the Red Lion and the first good night's sleep he'd had in many months.

The following morning was Saturday, and Shaun was woken early by a knock on his door. Pulling his trousers on, he opened it to find Louise standing there, a grin on her face. She looked him up and down, smiled even more widely and said;

"Do get dressed, dearest. We need to go and see the vicar. I'm not waiting another Sunday; the first banns can be called tomorrow!"

He laughed, reaching for his clothes. "I quite agree! Tell me, who exactly is the vicar now?"

"Oh." She leaned against the doorframe, watching quite shamelessly as he put his shirt on. "It's Mr Charles, who's a lovely young man from Cumbria - Renwick sent him. Lord

Ferndale seems to have taken to him, too, I'm sure he will give him the living when his trial period is over."

"Must be a nice change, after Old Brimstone." He sat on the edge of the bed to pull on his boots, before tying a very shoddy knot in his neckcloth and shrugging on his coat. "And will he mind us knocking on his door so early?"

"He's already out and about, I just saw him coming back from his morning walk. Come on."

Shaun had no objection at all to Louise's plans, and they went to see the young vicar together. Mr Charles congratulated them heartily and said he would happily add their names to the list of banns he was calling on the morrow - several returned soldiers had decided to make sure of their sweethearts and he had quite a rash of upcoming weddings to conduct.

Shaun spent the rest of the day happily becoming reacquainted with the town and his friends; he thought about riding out to see Lord Ferndale but decided that since he would see him in church in the morning, that would be soon enough.

On Sunday morning, Lord Ferndale was quite overcome to see him returned safe and embraced him like a long-lost son, which made Shaun feel rather choked up. He gladly accepted his regular invitation to sit in the Ferndale pew, which meant he could share Louise's prayer book and hymnal and gaze at her during the service. Dr Williams appeared to have been adopted too, he noted, seeing the doctor standing beside Bernadette. Something was definitely going on there, and Shaun made a note to quiz the doctor at some point when he had the opportunity.

Mr Charles beamed happily around the church as he

began to call the banns; Shaun recognised the names of several people he knew. At last, it was their turn.

"I publish the banns of marriage between Shaun Jackson of this parish and Louise Baxter of this parish. If any of you know cause or just impediment why these persons should not be joined together in Holy Matrimony, you are to declare it. This is for the first time of asking."

Shaun smiled down at Louise as Mr Charles read their banns, and she smiled back at him, her face full of joy.

And then everything came crashing down as Joshua Baxter stood up, three pews behind them, and said "I object!" in a loud voice.

The church erupted in shocked gasps and whispers. Mr Charles did not seem to know where to put himself; Shaun supposed this was not something he had ever expected to happen.

"I... what is your objection, sir?" Mr Charles said finally.

"Louise Baxter is not of legal age. As her closest available male relative, she requires my permission to marry." Joshua smiled smugly. "And I do not give it."

"I'm going to kill him."

Shaun had thought the words, but it was Louise who said them, loud and clear. A fresh wave of gasps rolled through the church, and Joshua cried out; "You heard her threaten me! She's a madwoman, belongs in Bedlam!"

"Sit down," Lord Ferndale said sharply as Shaun began to rise to his feet, his fists clenching. "Jackson. Leave this to me."

"Sir!" Shaun could not possibly stand by and let this happen.

Lord Ferndale gave him a glare, and stood up, his cane rapping sharply on the floor.

"Silence, if you please," he said, and the whispers stopped. Looking at Joshua, Lord Ferndale said, "This is neither the time nor the place for your petty nonsense, Baxter. Now, get out of this house of God until you can learn some Christian kindness and generosity."

Shaun's jaw dropped open. He had never, until that moment, heard Lord Ferndale so much as say an unkind word about anyone; the old baron was the soul of politeness even in the face of extreme provocation.

Joshua Baxter seemed shocked too, staring at Lord Ferndale in silence. At least until Lord Ferndale looked at Shaun and said "Mr Baxter appears to be hard of hearing, Mr Jackson. Would you escort him outside for me, please?"

"Gladly!" Shaun said, getting to his feet. "Perhaps I might give him some education on the topic of manners while we are outside, my lord?" He would very much like to beat some manners into Joshua Baxter!

Phoebe Baxter jumped to her feet, pale-faced, and pulled on Joshua's arm. The two of them made their way out without meeting the eyes of a single soul, Benjamin trailing behind them with venomous glares back over his shoulder. Every eye was on Lord Ferndale, standing at the front of the church.

"Thank you, Mr Charles, and I do apologise for the interruption. Please carry on," Lord Ferndale said, retaking his seat. Glancing at Shaun, he winked.

Shaun appreciated the old baron's intervention, but he was also quite sure that Mr Charles would not be able to conduct the wedding ceremony unless Joshua Baxter relented. Louise was not twenty-one until October, and he did not want to wait that long to marry her.

"We could go to Gretna Green," he suggested, as they all

sat down to luncheon at Ferndale Hall after church. "Your sister Marie did, with Renwick."

"We can't," Louise said despairingly. "We wouldn't get there and back in time for the Chancery Court hearing. And I couldn't leave Bernadette all alone anyway, not with Cousin Joshua being so dreadful, and with Benjamin in town just looking for an opportunity to be awful in some way."

"She wouldn't be alone," Dr Williams protested, flushing a little when Shaun raised an eyebrow at him.

"We wouldn't be back in time. We can't," Louise repeated, and Shaun sighed, accepting that she was right.

"I suppose we can wait until you turn twenty-one, then," he said, a little glumly.

"Well, perhaps not. If we win our petition at Chancery Court, I'll be their legal guardian," Lord Ferndale pointed out cheerily. "And you'll certainly have my blessing!"

"I:," Louise muttered grimly.

Shaun reached for her hand, under cover of the table-cloth, and squeezed it. "We're going to get married," he promised her quietly. "Sooner, rather than later."

She smiled back at him and squeezed his hand, but he could see the doubt and fear clouding her eyes. Honestly, he could just wring Joshua Baxter's neck!

Life in Hatfield resumed very much as it had before he left, which seemed strange to Shaun, after everything he'd been through. With Lord Ferndale's blessing, he hired a few more returned soldiers and began nightly patrols again, which allowed the good people of Hatfield to relax a little and stop being quite so vigilant over watching Benjamin Baxter. The boy was clearly simmering with rage and frustration, a powder keg just waiting to explode. He was spotted several times climbing out of his window at night and wandering the town, but with Joshua's horse still lame, Benjamin was limited to where his own two feet would carry him, and he was inherently lazy. A few piles of rubbish were found aflame in alleys, but no property had yet been targeted, Benjamin obviously too afraid of being caught.

"Bore da." Shaun looked up from his contemplation of his plate of breakfast in the Red Lion's dining room to see Riot hobbling over to join him. Walking with the aid of a crutch Dr Williams had built for him, Riot was starting to get around quite well, though he still wasn't up to resuming patrols. Not that Shaun had any intention of allowing him to do so.

"Good morning, Riot." Shaun returned the Welshman's greeting, waved to catch Mrs Haye's attention and asked her to bring some more breakfast over. Riot settled into the seat opposite him with a grin.

"It is, that. Good to be out of my room. Getting sick of those four walls."

"As to that, you look almost ready to travel," Shaun noted. "Perhaps next week?"

"And where would I be going?" Riot looked startled.

"Home, of course! I should have sent you home to Wrecsam long ago, man. Time you got back to your family."

Riot shook his head. "No, not me. I'll be staying, I think."

"What? Why?"

"Still haven't caught the arsonist in the act, have we?" Riot looked down at the table, a little grin coming to his face. "Eh, listen to me, I'm as bad as you were, making up excuses. Truth is, there's a woman, isn't there?"

"Is there indeed!" Shaun sat back, rather enjoying himself. He'd put up with a good deal of teasing from Riot over Louise. "And who might that be?"

"For an observant man, you can't see what's right under your nose. Or maybe it's just that when Miss Louise is in the room, you can't see anything but her!"

And there was the teasing again, right on cue. Shaun scowled, and Riot chuckled.

"It's Rosie."

"Rosie!" Suddenly, several things made sense. Riot had always been eager to keep an eye on the bookshop, and Shaun had spotted him talking with the maid several times, but hadn't put two and two together. "And does she return your affections?"

"Aye." The little smile stayed on Riot's face. "Came to see me, she did, when we got home. We agreed, when I'm back on my feet, and I've got a steady job, we'll look for a little cottage and speak to Mr Charles to call the banns for us."

"Well, I'm very happy for you," Shaun said sincerely. "And about that job. Lord Ferndale's been talking to me about setting up a regular police force. There's no crime in Hatfield these days with the nightly patrols; he wants it to be permanent and has asked me to manage things. I could do with a good sergeant to help me out."

"Policeman, is it!" Riot offered his hand, but then paused and drew it back. "And will we be under the direction of the magistrate?"

"Joshua Baxter? Absolutely not." Shaun grinned. "Lord Ferndale has already petitioned the Lord Chancellor to have Baxter stripped of his warrant, and he had the support of a majority of the town council, who put their names to the petition. Turns out Ferndale was at university with the Lord Chancellor, back in the dark ages."

"And who'll get the job?" Riot asked.

"You're looking at him. The petition suggests me as a qualified and willing replacement, about to marry a local woman and settle here permanently."

"Well in that case, count me in." Riot held out his hand again, and Shaun shook it.

After finishing breakfast, Shaun made his way next door for his favourite part of the morning routine. Louise had just unlocked the bookshop door and smiled when she saw him, turning her face up for a most satisfying kiss.

Brutus, cleaning up Crafty's leavings behind the counter, made a small gagging noise, which they both ignored. Shaun cuffed the top of Brutus' head gently as the lad scurried past him with the ash pan.

"You'll change your mind when the right girl comes along, lad."

Brutus made a scoffing noise, but the grin he flashed Shaun was full of respect, almost hero-worship. He was a good little lad, and Shaun was very glad he was out of that house, where his parents ignored him and his older brother tormented him.

Ruth was the next arrival, flashing a shy smile at Shaun. And there was another change; although the lass was still on the shy side, before she could hardly even stand to look at him. Her father's death was probably the best thing that had ever happened to Ruth, shocking as that might seem.

"Ugh." Ruth froze near the counter, nose wrinkling. "What's that *smell*?"

"Oh, sorry. I brought down some fresh glue for Brutus and I to work with… oh."

Ruth clutched at her stomach, put a hand over her mouth, and rushed back outside.

"Turned her stomach, poor lass," Shaun said sympathetically. "It is a mite early in the day for a smell that strong."

"She's never noticed it before!" Louise shook her head, putting a lid on the pot. "Take it back upstairs, would you, Brutus? If it's making Ruth feel sick, it might drive customers away. We'll do the gluing upstairs."

"I'm sure Bernadette will love that," Shaun said dryly.

"I'll put it in my room, I don't mind the smell," Brutus said cheerfully, taking the pot and scurrying off.

For a brief moment, Shaun and Louise were alone again, and he wasted no time in stealing another kiss. She laughed, putting her arms around his neck and kissing him back, and he held her close against him, trying to think of a way he could bully Joshua into withdrawing his objection to their wedding, because waiting another three months to marry this beautiful, clever, wonderful woman was just not something that felt possible right now.

CHAPTER 24
Boiling Point

At church on Sunday, Mr Charles called the banns for a second time. Joshua and Phoebe hadn't come to the service this time, perhaps fearful of being shamed by Lord Ferndale again before the whole congregation. And while Mr Charles had agreed to continue to call the banns, he regretfully told Shaun and Louise that he could not legally perform a wedding ceremony while the question of her guardian's consent was undecided.

"I'll work on that," Shaun said. "You call the banns… and by the time they're done, things might be different."

It was a beautiful, warm summer day. They spent a most pleasant afternoon at Ferndale Hall, returning home afterwards in the Ferndale carriage, and Shaun and Louise stood talking outside the bookshop while Brutus ran down the road to talk with another boy his own age who was playing with a dog on the green.

"Shaun!" Louise grabbed at his hand suddenly, her happy expression changing to one of alarm. "It's Benjamin, look!"

Shaun spun around, to see Benjamin walking up to Brutus and the other boy.

"Go inside," he said to Louise, before setting off at a run to intercept. He couldn't hear what Benjamin was saying, but he could see the boy's stance, shoulders squared and fists braced.

Brutus didn't seem afraid of his brother, standing bravely straight. Perhaps he saw Shaun coming at a dead run, because as he got close enough to hear them, Brutus said;

"And what are you going to do about it?"

Benjamin took a swing, Brutus dodged, and Shaun arrived before Benjamin could swing again.

"Oh, no you don't, sonny," he said, stepping in between the two brothers.

"This is none of your business!" Benjamin snarled at him.

"It's always my business when someone's being a bully."

"Why don't you just go back to where you came from!" Benjamin yelled, red in the face and furious.

Shaun took a step closer. "That's not happening, lad. This is my home, now. I'm staying. For *ever*," he emphasised. "And while I'm here? You'll not be bullying anyone."

Benjamin gritted his teeth and clenched his fists, and for a moment Shaun thought the boy might be foolish enough to throw a punch.

"You watch your back," Benjamin said nastily after a moment, taking a step back.

Shaun laughed, not in the least intimidated. "I'm not afraid of you, boy. Run along home now. Before I give you the thrashing you so richly deserve."

Benjamin hesitated, Shaun took another step forward, and the boy took to his heels.

Watching him run, Shaun was more certain than ever that

Benjamin was the man he'd chased outside the bookshop that night, the one who'd dropped the tinderbox. Fast and agile, his gait was unmistakable, as was his height and build. Shaun watched until the youth was out of sight, before he turned to discover that Louise had not gone into the bookshop as he had instructed, but had followed him and now stood watching, her arm around Brutus' thin shoulders.

Shaun smiled ruefully, going to join them. "Of course you didn't do as you were told. And you!" He wagged a finger at Brutus. "Didn't anyone teach you that poking a wasps' nest is a bad idea?"

"I knew you wouldn't let him hurt me," Brutus said, and Shaun shook his head.

"He could have laid you out with one punch before I got there, if it had connected. Stay away from him, Brutus."

"Yes, Mr Jackson," Brutus said penitently.

"Did you really think I was going to go inside and leave you to deal with that on your own?" Louise asked as Shaun took her hand and the three of them turned to make their way back to the bookshop, Brutus' friend and dog having already made themselves scarce.

"No." He grinned. "But I don't think my protective instincts are going to fade away any time soon, so I'm afraid you'll just have to live with them."

"And... you're not angry with me for disobeying?"

Shaun ruminated for a moment. "I think the only time I could be angry with you is if you put yourself in danger without warning me that you're going to do it first. So I can provide backup."

Her smile was like the sunrise, and she squeezed his hand tightly. "Thank you."

"You've done an excellent job of taking care of yourself thus far without me. You're an intelligent woman, my love. I trust you to know when you're out of your depth and to ask for help." She'd already demonstrated the ability to do so, having told him all about her appeal to Renwick for help with the Chancery Court.

Shaun joined the Baxter sisters for a light supper in the kitchen above the bookshop, prepared by Mrs Poole. Dr Williams joined them too, and afterwards they played a merry game of lottery tickets, pleasing Brutus who loved the game

As always, Shaun did not want the evening to end, but at last Mrs Poole pointedly told him and Dr Williams that it was time they were in their own beds. Louise walked them downstairs to let them out and lock up behind them, Shaun lingering for one heavenly but all-too-brief kiss.

"Have you found a house yet?" Dr Williams asked laughingly as they listened to Louise locking up the bookshop before walking away.

"Not yet." The one and only fire Benjamin had been able to set when he returned to Hatfield had been the house Shaun had been looking at before he went away, and it had burned to the ground. There was really nothing else suitable, and Shaun was beginning to wonder if he would need to build new. At least the doctor's cottage was almost finished now the men working on it had returned home. Glynn would be able to move there soon.

"Good night," he said to the doctor, and made his way to the inn. Riot was standing in the yard, leaning on his crutch, briefing the three men who would be patrolling town that evening. All of them offered respectful nods, but Shaun stood back and waited until Riot had finished and sent the men on their way.

"All good?" Shaun checked.

"Aye. Norbury's new, but the other two will show him the ropes." Riot sighed, tapped his crutch on the ground. "Can't wait until I can be rid of this bloody thing."

"Not long," Shaun consoled. "You're almost sound on that leg."

Riot looked a bit despondent. "Not sure I'll ever be as fast as I once was."

Shaun patted his shoulder. "Come on. I'll buy you a beer before I turn in."

"You'll put it on Lord Ferndale's account, you mean," Riot gibed.

"He's a generous employer," Shaun said with a grin.

"Eh, we've fallen on our feet here and no mistake," Riot said. "Twas a lucky day for me when I ran out of money to travel home here in Hatfield. Found a fine job, the girl of my dreams, and a good friend."

Riot had hit the nail squarely on the head there, Shaun thought as Mr Haye brought them two tankards with a cheerful smile. They raised them in a silent toast to each other, before enjoying the excellent brew always served at the Red Lion.

"Well, I'm for bed," Shaun said, when his jaw cracked in a yawn. Normally, he would take the first evening shift, but since today was Sunday and he hadn't been able to sleep in the afternoon, he and Riot would swap over. Riot would wake him sometime after midnight, and until then Riot would be out the front of the Red Lion on a bench placed there, where the patrollers would check in with him regularly… and where Riot could conveniently keep an eye on the bookshop.

Hours later, Riot woke him. Shaun sighed and dragged himself from the comfortable bed. When he was officially the magistrate, he wouldn't be doing night patrols, he decided. Though hopefully he'd have Benjamin Baxter in custody long before that, and they wouldn't need to be so vigilant.

The new man, Norbury, was waiting as Shaun reached the front of the inn. "Evening, sir," he said with a nervous little nod.

"Anything to report?" Shaun said, manfully swallowing another yawn.

"Well…"

"Out with it." Shaun's attention sharpened.

"I was just by the livery yard," Norbury pointed through the archway between the Red Lion and the bookshop, that led into the inn yard and then to the livery stables behind. "I did think I saw someone in the field behind, and then climbing over the wall."

"Which wall? Show me."

It was quite dark, with only a sliver of moon showing. Norbury was carrying a lantern, though, so they could see their way quite well.

"This wall, sir." Norbury stopped and pointed.

Shaun felt a sudden cold fear clutch at his heart. It was the wall that separated the bookshop's small back garden from the livery stable's side yard. Not an easy wall to climb, by any means, but for a tall, light youth… "Cover that lantern," he said sharply. Norbury put the lantern down and draped his coat over it.

"Give me a leg up," Shaun ordered tersely, and Norbery

obeyed, enabling Shaun to get his hands to the top of the wall and pull himself up.

For a moment, while his eyes adjusted to the darkness, he couldn't see anything. Then, faint movement caught his eye. Someone was climbing the ivy at the back of the building!

"I see you!" he shouted.

The figure froze.

"Come down from there!" Shaun roared. Looking down at Norbury on the other side of the wall, he added quietly, "Run around to the front of the bookshop, quickly, and start banging on the door and making a ruckus. We need to rouse them, and fast!"

Norbury set off at a dead run, and Shaun looked back at the dark figure who was clearly up to no good, just in time to see an arm swing wide.

"No!" Shaun shouted, but the crook wasn't listening. A window shattered and something was flung inside. Shaun was grimly sure he knew what, as he heard more glass breaking.

"Louise!" he yelled, as loudly as he could. "Wake up! LOUISE!"

The dark figure was scrambling sideways along the ivy like a damned spider, heading for the side of the building, before leaping down onto the wall and then into the inn yard.

"Oh, no you don't!" Shaun scrambled down off the wall and raced after them. "Benjamin Baxter!" he roared, quite sure he knew who he was chasing. "Stop right there!"

The lad froze for the briefest instant before taking off like a startled rabbit. Damn, he was fast; how was Shaun going to catch him? But as the boy reached the front of the Red

Lion, he tripped over something, and suddenly fell full-length on the cobblestones.

"And stay down, *cnaf*!" Riot Jones snapped, planting the end of his crutch on the back of the lad's neck.

"Well done, Riot!" Shaun caught up and bent down to yank back the hood over Benjamin's head, revealing the lad's furious face. "Well now," he said. "What do we have here?"

"Shaun?" he heard Louise's voice, but didn't look up.

"He broke a window and threw a hurricane lamp in."

"I know, it was right into my bedroom! I smothered it straight away." She came to his side, pulling her cloak tightly around her. "Oh, Benjamin," she said, looking at the boy on the ground. "What a mess."

"What do we do with him?" Riot asked.

"Nothing! My father's the magistrate!" Benjamin shouted. "You can't do anything to me!"

"Is that what you think, lad?" Shaun laughed. "You were caught in the act. Not even your father can save you from what's coming."

Fear dawned on Benjamin's face as Shaun reached down and yanked him to his feet. Others were coming out of the inn now, drawn by the shouting and noise, and there was a circle of furious faces looking back at the boy.

"You caught him, then?" Mr Haye said.

"Indeed. Climbed the back of the bookshop and broke a window to throw a hurricane lantern in. Pretty conclusive, I'd say."

Riot reached into Benjamin's pockets and pulled out a tinderbox. "Indeed, what's a boy of sixteen doing roaming the streets at two in the morning with this in his pocket?"

"String him up," someone said, and too many people made noises of agreement.

Louise gripped Shaun's arm, giving him a panicked look.

"That, we're not doing," he said loudly. "That's not justice. If someone could take a horse and ride for Ferndale Hall, though… ask Lord Ferndale to come at first light."

"And in the meantime, the coal cellar's got a lock on it and no other way out," Mr Thomas suggested sensibly.

"That'll do nicely." Shaun dragged Benjamin over by the scruff of his neck, half-hoping the lad would fight back, but he was limp and unresisting. Still confident his father would get him out of this, Shaun guessed. Well, the lad had another think coming.

"Should we get Mr Baxter?" Mr Haye asked.

"Absolutely not." Shaun grinned tightly. "Our good magistrate has insisted ever since patrols began that he wasn't to be bothered in the night by any criminals we might happen to catch. We'll obey his instructions and not fetch him until after he's breakfasted."

Laughter greeted this suggestion, and then willing hands were grasping hold of Benjamin and tossing him into the coal cellar.

"Go back to bed," Shaun told Louise quietly, putting an arm around her shoulders to hug her tight. "Or maybe, go and share with Bernadette for the night. I'll come and put a board over your broken window in the morning."

"All right." She reached up to kiss him, a smile on her lips. "You did it," she whispered. "You caught him."

"It's not over yet," he cautioned, but privately, he was feeling confident. He walked her back to the bookshop and waited until she had locked the door before returning to the coal cellar door, where Riot was standing guard with Norbury.

"You did well," Shaun told Norbury, who puffed up and looked proud of himself. "But now, I want you to go and get some sleep. In the morning you're going to need to be very clear about what exactly you saw, so get some rest and be ready to be questioned."

Norbury gulped - he was only a young lad himself, not more than twenty - but nodded bravely. "Aye, sir, I can do that."

"Off you go, then. Mr Jones and I will stand guard here."

"For sure I'm not risking anyone letting the little *cnaf* go," Riot said with a triumphant grin. "Not after so much effort to catch him!"

"He's lucky he doesn't have a broken ankle. Quick thinking, to trip him with your crutch!" Shaun congratulated.

"Fast as a rabbit, that one. You weren't going to catch him!"

Shaun acknowledged the truth of that, but he and Riot were both far too jubilant to gibe at each other. They leaned against the coal cellar door, grinning happily, until dawn came.

Mr Thomas had taken a horse to Ferndale Hall himself, and clearly roused Lord Ferndale at the crack of dawn, because the church clock was just striking seven when the Ferndale carriage rolled into the inn yard.

"Well, well." Lord Ferndale stepped down, all smiles. "I hear you've caught our miscreant, Jackson!"

"It was a team effort, sir," Shaun said, determined to give

credit where it was due. "He was spotted by young Mr Norbury, a new man, and Mr Jones here apprehended him by tripping him while he was making a run for it."

"Excellent! And he is secured in the coal-cellar, Mr Thomas told me?"

Shaun gestured to the heavy wooden door behind him. They'd not heard a peep out of Benjamin since locking him in, but Shaun trusted Mr Thomas; there was no way for Benjamin to make an escape.

"In that case, I think we might leave him here with Mr Jones and Mr Thomas to keep an eye on him, and you and I shall go and pay a call upon Joshua Baxter, what do you say?"

"With the greatest pleasure," Shaun said happily.

The Baxter's housekeeper looked astounded to see Shaun and Lord Ferndale at the door at such an early hour, but she admitted them to the breakfast-parlour, where Joshua and Phoebe were sitting together. A maid had their youngest, Barnaby, in her arms and removed him from the room.

"Good morning," Lord Ferndale said. "I'm afraid Mr Jackson and I come as the bearers of quite dreadful news."

Phoebe and Joshua looked at each other in apparent puzzlement before looking back at Lord Ferndale.

"The arsonist was apprehended last night," Lord Ferndale said.

"Well... that is *good* news, is it not?" Phoebe said with a silly little laugh.

"For Hatfield, certainly," Shaun agreed. "For your family, I regret not. We caught your son, Benjamin, in the act of smashing a window and setting fire to Baxter's Fine Books."

Both Joshua and Phoebe looked absolutely shocked, and Shaun realised they had either not heard the rumours about

Benjamin or had not believed them. Did they know their son at all?

"That is ridiculous!" Phoebe cried. "My darling boy! Of course not! Why, he is fast asleep upstairs, where he has been all night?"

"Is he?" Lord Ferndale said, his tone quite kind. "Would you care to go and check, Mrs Baxter?"

"Go and look, Phoebe," Joshua said, his voice strangled, and Shaun could see that the truth was beginning to sink in. Shaun and Lord Ferndale would not be here grave-faced at this hour of the morning with false information.

Phoebe, going pale, stood up and hurried past them. They waited silently while her feet pattered up the stairs, and then there was a distant shriek.

"I think you'd better come with us, Mr Baxter," Lord Ferndale said.

"I... this cannot be right," Joshua blustered, even as Phoebe came rushing back down. "You have... set Benjamin up somehow! Framed him!"

"The only person who has set him up is you," Shaun said coldly. "You have set him up to fail in life by coddling him beyond sense and spoiling him rotten."

Phoebe shrieked, and Joshua turned on her. "This is your fault, woman!"

"Casting blame everywhere but at yourself? How very like you," Lord Ferndale said, shaking his head slowly. "Mr Baxter. It is time to face the truth. Your son is a criminal, and your failure to even notice what he was doing could be considered aiding and abetting his crimes. Now, will you come with us to discuss what has to be done, or do I need to ask Mr Jackson to drag you?"

CHAPTER 25

Negotiations

L ouise was on tenterhooks waiting for Shaun and Lord Ferndale to return. She'd gone back to bed, going in with Bernadette as Shaun had suggested, but neither of them could sleep after the excitement and lay in bed talking quietly until dawn, wondering what was going to happen now that Benjamin had been caught in the act.

"Let's not open the bookshop today," Bernadette suggested sensibly. "Neither of us will be able to concentrate. I'll put a sign on the door and send Ruth home when she comes, or if she wants to stay maybe she can just sit and read. Keep Brutus company. I think we'd best keep him out of the way."

Louise agreed that was very sensible. Certainly there was no possibility that she could sit patiently behind the counter and carry on her usual business while wondering what was happening!

"I'm not going to wait around to find out what's going on," she said. "I'm going to ask if I can be involved in whatever decisions are made. We're victims here, after all. Benjamin literally tried to burn me in my bed."

Bernadette shuddered. "Do you think he knew it was your window?"

"I don't know." Louise wasn't even sure how he'd managed to climb the ivy that far. "Perhaps it was just the easiest one to reach."

"I'm going to start pulling that ivy down today! Brutus can help me, that will keep him busy. If Benjamin could climb it, someone else could too!"

Louise doubted that, but since pulling down the ivy was a harmless task that would help Bernadette feel a little happier and more useful, she said nothing.

Blessedly, Brutus and Mrs Poole had somehow slept through all the noise the previous night, their rooms being on the top floor. They listened open-mouthed, Mrs Poole giving occasional horrified little screams, as Louise explained over breakfast what had happened.

"What will happen to Benjamin?" Brutus asked with great interest as he spooned up his porridge. "Will he be transported to the colonies?"

It was an indictment of just how awful Benjamin had been that his younger brother had hope in his voice as he made the suggestion, Louise thought. "I don't know," she said honestly, "but I do know that Lord Ferndale and Mr Jackson will want to be sure he can't do anything like this again. And not even your father will be able to get him out of this mess scot-free, Brutus, don't worry about that." She smiled at him. "I'm going to see if I can find out what's happening, but I want you to stay here, all right? Bernadette has a job for you pulling down some ivy on the back wall."

"All right," Brutus said cheerfully enough, and returned his attention to his food.

Louise's stomach was churning too much to eat; she smiled an apology to Mrs Poole and abandoned her plate, making her way downstairs and next door to the Red Lion, where Mr Thomas and Riot Jones were still standing guard in front of the coal cellar door.

"You must have been up all night, isn't your leg aching?" she asked Riot. "You should get some rest. I'm sure we could find someone else to stand here."

The thin Welshman smiled at her. "Right kind of you, Miss Baxter, but I'll hold my post until Mr Jackson tells me otherwise."

"And where would he be?"

"Gone with Lord Ferndale to Mr Baxter's house." Riot nodded behind her. "Here they come now."

Lod Ferndale's carriage was indeed just rolling into the inn yard. Shaun was riding up with the driver, hopped down and opened the door to assist Lord Ferndale out first. Joshua then climbed out, face grim, and walked away, leaving Shaun to assist a sobbing Phoebe down.

"Oh, no," Louise muttered. "Why didn't they leave Phoebe at home?"

"Where is he?" Phoebe shrieked. "Where is my darling boy?"

Louise exchanged a frustrated glance with Shaun.

"She insisted on coming," Shaun said in a low voice as Louise went to him.

"Everybody inside," Lord Ferndale said, in a no-nonsense voice. "Ah, good morning, Mr Haye. I wonder if we might use the assembly room for an impromptu meeting? And if you could possibly send some runners out, I think it would be best if the town council convened in oh, say, two hours?"

Phoebe was wailing and sobbing, and Louise, feeling a little sorry for her - not that Phoebe really deserved it - put an arm around her shoulders.

"Brace up, Phoebe," she said, not unkindly. "Carrying on does nobody any good. Pull yourself together and you might get to have a say in what's going to happen."

"This is all your fault!" Phoebe shrieked at her.

"It's *my* fault that *your* son has burned down multiple buildings and *killed three people*?" Louise said incredulously, and the sharpness of her tone, the seriousness of her words, must have cut through Phoebe's shock and grief, because she stopped sobbing and stared at Louise wide-eyed.

"Phoebe, Benjamin is in serious trouble." Louise urged her towards the door to the inn. "You and Joshua need to stop pointing the finger of blame at other people and be prepared to beg for mercy."

All the fight seemed to go out of Phoebe then, and she walked where Louise directed, listlessly taking a seat at the table in the upstairs room. Joshua, too, seemed to have deflated, sitting down quietly and folding his hands in front of him.

Shaun came in with a young man Louise didn't know, and Riot Jones followed too. Lord Ferndale gestured for them to take seats at the table, and then Shaun held out a chair for Louise. She smiled thanks at him and sat down, pleased that nobody had suggested she shouldn't be here. As she'd told Bernadette, this was very much her business.

"Where is Benjamin?" Joshua asked in a quiet voice.

"Being held securely in the coal cellar downstairs," Shaun replied, "guarded by Mr Thomas and two of my men.

If required, we'll bring him up, but I think you should hear what happened first."

Joshua nodded, and Shaun pointed to the young man Louise didn't know. "Mr Norbury. If you'd please share what you saw in the early hours of this morning."

Mr Norbury flushed, coughed, and began a little haltingly to explain that he'd been on patrol when he thought he saw someone climbing the wall between the livery yard and the bookshop's back garden.

"I wasn't sure, though, so I fetched Mr Jackson and gave him a leg-up onto the wall, and he saw someone climbing the ivy. Mr Jackson told me to run around front to the door and bang and shout to wake the Baxters, so I was just doing that, and then I heard glass breaking."

Shaun took up the tale, and then Riot explained how he'd been unable to sleep for the heat and had come back downstairs before hearing shouting and seeing someone come running out through the archway onto the High Street, and tripping him up.

"And Mr Jackson pulled his hood back, and we all saw that it was Benjamin Baxter," Riot finished, and there was silence in the room.

"And Miss Baxter," Lord Ferndale said. "I understand it was your bedroom window that was smashed?"

"Yes… I woke up when I heard shouting, and then the glass broke and a lantern was thrown in through the window. It broke on the floor. I jumped up and smothered the flames with the blanket from my bed."

Phoebe began to cry again, but more quietly this time. Joshua made no move to comfort her. He just sat, staring at his hands.

"Mr Baxter," Lord Ferndale said, "did you have any suspicion that Benjamin was the arsonist?"

Joshua jumped, almost as though he was surprised to be asked, but he shook his head vehemently. "No, never! A few people came to me saying they'd heard rumours, but I thought… I thought…" He glanced quickly at Louise before looking down again.

"You thought I was spreading them in retaliation for you spreading rumours about us," Louise said, comprehension dawning.

"Did you purchase lanterns or tinderboxes for Benjamin?" Lord Ferndale asked.

"Absolutely not," Joshua paused, before saying slowly, almost as though the words were being dragged out of him, "but… he did have a generous allowance. I never queried what he spent his money on."

"And you never checked that he was in his bed at night?"

Louise found herself looking at Lord Ferndale with new admiration. He could have been a judge in court, asking incisive questions which cut straight to the heart of the matter. He was continuing now, asking Joshua why he thought Benjamin had chosen his targets for arson, making Joshua cringe, because the answer was obvious. Apart from the old schoolteacher Mr Flyte who had tried to teach Benjamin, and Dr Rasley who had reprimanded him publicly, every other person or property that had been targeted belonged to someone Joshua considered his enemy.

"Whether or not you aided and abetted his crimes," Lord Ferndale said finally, "it is your negligence in raising him and your vindictive attitudes that have created this disaster."

"I'll pay," Joshua muttered, still not looking up. "I'll pay for everything that was burned."

"How will you pay for three people's lives?" Lord Ferndale raised his voice at last. "Mr and Mrs Flyte, and Doctor Rasley? You cannot buy lives, Mr Baxter! That is not justice!"

Joshua screwed his eyes shut, while Phoebe cried quietly beside him. At last, Joshua said dully; "What do you suggest, my lord?"

Lord Ferndale steepled his fingers, and then he looked at Louise. "What do you think, Granddaughter?"

She blinked, a little startled. Shaun gave her an encouraging nod.

"Well," she said after a moment, "paying reparations for the property damage and to the families of the deceased is a good start, Cousin Joshua, and there is no question that must be done. But Benjamin cannot be free to begin wreaking havoc again. He will never stop. None of us could sleep safely in our beds at night."

"If the case is taken to Crown Court, he will be either hanged or transported," Lord Ferndale said gently. "Dependent on the whim of whatever judge is appointed."

Phoebe let out a low wail. "Oh no, oh please no, please, my lord!"

Louise had no desire to see a sixteen-year-old boy hanged no matter what he had done, and transportation, alone, to the far side of the world amongst hardened criminals would likely be just as much of a death sentence, if a more prolonged and painful one.

"What about emigration?" Shaun said.

"Emigration!" Joshua stared at him in shock.

"To the Americas," Shaun clarified. "Not just Benjamin. All of you, as a family. Even after paying reparations, if you sell your properties you will still be a very wealthy man, Mr Baxter. You could start a very fine life in the New World, away from everyone who knows what your son has done."

"Do you think you will still be welcome in Hatfield, after all this?" Louise pressed the point when Phoebe looked horrified at the idea. "Do you think your social circle will accept you back as though nothing has happened? It's all over town by now, what Benjamin has done."

"And certainly, this is the last straw for your continuing as magistrate," Lord Ferndale added to Joshua. "You must stand down at once."

The negotiations continued for another hour, but by the end of it, Joshua had agreed to all their demands. He and Phoebe would arrange emigration to the Americas and leave immediately with Benjamin and Barnaby; Brutus they agreed could remain with Louise and Joshua's interest in the bookshop was to be settled on Brutus, which would ensure their safety. Shaun bullied Joshua into settling fully half of what would remain of his estate on Brutus in trust, to be managed by Lord Ferndale, Shaun and Mr Yates until Brutus was of age. All of Joshua's other properties would be sold at the best prices which could be achieved, reparations paid for the fires, and monies sent on to Joshua and Phoebe wherever they settled.

"I advise you to keep a very tight leash on Benjamin," Lord Ferndale said sternly. "A military school, perhaps, and a warning to the headmaster about his tendencies. And if suspicious fires begin again... perhaps a hospital for the insane."

"And don't spoil Barnaby," Louise added to Phoebe as a parting remark. "I don't know how Brutus has turned out as decent as he has, but he is living proof you aren't total failures as parents. Don't fail Barnaby as you've failed Benjamin."

Phoebe shot her a look full of hate, but said nothing more, just turned away and leaned heavily on Joshua's arm.

"Make sure Benjamin isn't released until they are ready to leave town, please, Mr Jones," Lord Ferndale instructed Riot. "Get him food and water, but don't let him out of that cellar."

That would speed Phoebe's packing, Louise thought.

"Oh, and one last thing," Shaun said, just before Joshua and Phoebe left the room. "Before you leave town, Mr Baxter, please ensure you call on Mr Charles and advise him that you grant permission for Louise to marry me."

The noise which came out of Joshua was very like a growl, and the look he shot Shaun was full of rage, but he nodded grudgingly and left the room with Phoebe clinging to him. Riot excused himself and followed, taking Mr Norbury with him.

"Well." Lord Ferndale leaned back in his chair. "What an absolutely dreadful business."

Louise reached to take his hand. "Grandfather, you were remarkable! Cousin Joshua did not even have so much as an opportunity to argue."

"Catching the lad throwing a lantern through your bedroom window isn't the kind of thing that can be argued away," Shaun said dryly.

Footsteps on the stairs announced new arrivals, and Mr Haye tapped on the door. "The town council members are here, Lord Ferndale," he said. "Shall I send them in?"

"Indeed!" Lord Ferndale straightened in his chair. "And could I trouble you for some tea, my good man? And perhaps some biscuits, or even some toast? I didn't get to have breakfast…"

"That will not do at all! I shall go and see to having something brought up for you." Louise squeezed his hand, and leaned over to kiss his cheek. "Thank you, Grandfather, for everything."

"You are most welcome, dear girl." Lord Ferndale squeezed back.

As she left the room, walking past the council members assembling outside waiting to go in, Louise heard Lord Ferndale say to Shaun; "Best speak to Mr Charles, Jackson. The third banns will be called on Sunday; what do you say to Monday for the wedding?"

Louise almost danced down the stairs, a wide smile on her face.

Monday would suit her just fine.

Not everything could be resolved quite so easily, however. The Chancery Court would not dismiss the case before it just because Joshua was leaving the country; though he wrote letters at Lord Ferndale's direction withdrawing his request to be made trustee of Matthew's estate and guardian of Louise and Bernadette, the Court would still rule on the matter. Renwick had written back promising to come, and Lord Ferndale would stand up for them, but it was still possible the Court might grant the trusteeship and guardianship to some crony of theirs.

Which, of course, was why Shaun was so determined to marry Louise before that came to pass; her guardianship would then not be in question and she would be safe. She seemed more than happy at the idea, and a week later walked down the aisle on Lord Ferndale's arm with a joyous smile on her face.

Joshua had already left town with Phoebe, Barnaby and Benjamin, who had spent two nights in the coal cellar and seemed very subdued by the time he was finally dragged out and bundled into a travelling carriage. Irrationally afraid that Joshua would let him out, Shaun had ridden halfway to London watching the carriage before finally turning around and coming home.

Mr Charles conducted the ceremony, delighted to do so with both Joshua's verbal agreement and a signed document from him consenting to the wedding.

And for where Shaun and Louise would make their home? Well, with Joshua's departure, quite a number of properties had suddenly come on the market, but the one which best suited their needs was the house which had been Joshua's own. It was quite perfect, being large, a short walk from the bookshop, with a field behind for Shaun to keep his horse. There were plenty of bedrooms too, including of course the one Brutus had always called his own, although Brutus seemed quite keen on staying at the bookshop with Mrs Poole and Bernadette. Lord Ferndale decided on a fair price for the house, and Shaun paid it quite happily. They needed some new furniture, but that could be easily managed in time.

Lord Ferndale and Miss Yates threw them a beautiful wedding party at Ferndale Hall, at which Lord Ferndale surprised Shaun yet again by informing him that he must take at least two weeks off to spend with his new wife and that he should take Louise away for a holiday by the seaside.

"I have booked you in at the Grand Hotel in Eastbourne

for a week," Lord Ferndale said, a twinkle in his eye. "You both need a holiday, I think."

"But the bookshop!" Louise protested immediately.

"Well in hand," Lord Ferndale said firmly. "Bernadette tells me that young Ruth is doing very capably behind the counter these days, and Brutus is there too. I am sure they will manage admirably."

Shaun could see that Louise wanted to argue, wanted to insist that the bookshop was her responsibility, but she glanced at her sister, dancing just at that moment with Dr Williams, and looked thoughtful.

"A holiday by the sea does sound wonderful," he said, and she looked up at him and smiled.

"I've never seen the sea."

"Never?" he gaped.

"August is the perfect time to go to the seaside," Miss Yates enthused happily. "A little sea-bathing will be just the thing. Louise!"

"Very well," she acquiesced. "And we will be back in plenty of time for the Chancery Court hearing, of course."

She would not miss that for anything, and neither would he. It was too important to her that the bookshop must be kept running - perhaps in her mind, as long as the bookshop remained open, her father might yet come home - and that meant Shaun would do everything in his power to make it happen.

"Come dance with me again," he begged. She laughed and took his hand, and Shaun thought that he would never tire of dancing with her, his Louise, this beautiful tall, strong woman who was now his wife.

Bernadette's Dashing Doctor

Early March, 1815
Hatfield, Hertfordshire

Bernadette Baxter, the youngest and definitely the most helpful of the four Baxter daughters of Baxter's Fine Books in Hatfield, Hertfordshire, kept a close eye on the pot of bubbling honey and lemon mixture on the stove. She added a dozen whole cloves into the mix, careful to avoid getting her hand too close to the simmering liquid. Experience had taught her that the ensuing burn would hurt agonisingly if she made a mistake. The syrup smelled deliciously sweet as she stirred it three times one way, then three the reverse, breathing in the fragrant steam. The cloves would impart their pungent healing oils, but remain intact for her to tweezer out of the lozenges before they set.

The doorbell to the bookshop tinkled, and she heard her sister Louise give whoever had arrived directions to go to the kitchen.

Light footsteps pattered up the stairs, followed by a slim boy with a shock of scruffy brown hair.

"Oh good, Brutus, you're here!" Bernadette was delighted to see her young cousin - her favourite, but then there really was no competition in that regard - had arrived to assist.

"It smells much better than the binding glue Louise cooks up!" he said, face full of cheer.

"It's almost ready to pour. Would you like to do the

honours?" She lifted the pot off the stove carefully and placed it on the iron trivet on the kitchen table.

"Yes please!" he said, coming forward eagerly.

He was a fast learner and eager to please, always ready to lend a hand no matter how dirty or smelly a task they might assign him. More than that, Bernadette had become grateful to have Brutus accompanying her around town. He was young enough not to be threatening to the women she helped. He stayed out of the way, but most importantly, he helped her carry the produce home that her customers provided as payment. Sometimes her basket was so full of fruit, honey, meat or other items given to her by grateful patients she could barely lift it by herself.

Brutus was a meticulous sort of boy, and soon became adept at pouring the cooling mixture onto the wax paper under her directions. One by one he dolloped a teaspoon-sized amount onto each paper, then moved on as Bernadette followed along behind him with her tweezers, carefully picking out the whole cloves. Moments later, they had a bench full of individual sweets.

Bernadette gently waved one of her hand fans to keep them cooling. Once they set, it required only a quick twist to close the wax paper and the lozenges would be ready to take to Mr Lennox the apothecary.

"May I have one?" Brutus asked, opening his mouth and pointing to the back of it. "I think there's a tooth coming through at the back."

Bernadette brought him over to the window for better light and peered into his mouth. "The gum does look red. I'll make some clove tea."

He winced.

"Yes, I know it tastes awful," she agreed. "But it's the best thing to remove the pain."

"Can't I just have a lozzy?"

She tried not to roll her eyes. Young people took such liberties with language! She ignored the fact that she had barely seven years on Brutus, but then she had been raised in a well-educated household, whereas Brutus could not honestly be said to have been raised at all, considering he was ignored by his parents and bullied by his ghastly older brother. It was truly a surprise that Brutus was turning out as well as he was; she could overlook some casual informalities in his speech.

"Yes, for now." She glanced over the bench and picked up the most oddly-shaped one, handing it over to him. "I'll get the clove tea brewing and by the time we get back it will be nice and strong."

His shoulders slumped even as he popped the lozenge into his mouth. "Thanks," he mumbled around the sweet, and Bernadette smiled. Brutus had sweet manners, even if she suspected he wouldn't thank her after she made him gargle the pungent clove tea. He willingly helped her load up her basket and hefted in manfully, shaking his head when she checked if it was too heavy. She packed up a second, slightly lighter, basket for herself and they made their way downstairs.

They waved goodbye to Louise as they passed her at the counter and then the two of them made their way through Hatfield to Mr Lennox's business.

"Ahh, the Baxters! How wonderful to see you!" The apothecary always greeted them with a smile. He did not get to his feet, however, and remained sitting behind his counter. Try as she might, Bernadette had not been able to make any kind of medication that might help the dear man. He'd lost a leg below the knee during valiant service with the Navy years before, and now walked with a peg leg. He suffered constant pain in his lower back if he stood for more than a few moments, but flatly refused to take laudanum, saying with a dark look on his face, "that road leads nowhere I care to go," on more than one occasion when Bernadette suggested it might help.

They greeted his assistant, who everybody called "Young Devon," with a smile and a wave, but didn't interrupt as he dealt with several customers.

Mr Lennox's eyes gleamed at the sight of the basket, and he quickly reconciled the herbal sachets, lozenges and salves Bernadette laid out on the counter, and paid her.

Bernadette thanked him and said, "While I'm sad we lost Dr Rasley, I must confess, I've never been so busy."

"I concur," Mr Lennox said, reflecting a suitably sad expression. "Terrible loss for the town. But now I'm so busy, I need Young Devon here every day."

Bernadette leaned in and mentioned, quietly, "I set a broken wrist last week." She was quite proud of herself. The young boy who'd been tree climbing had fainted, but she was quite sure she had done a good job and he would heal with no troubles.

Mr Lennox chuckled. "Good for you. We never stop learning, do we?"

"That we do not!" She readily agreed. "It's a shame the nearest doctor is in St Albans - there are some people in town with ailments that truly do require a proper doctor's skills and they aren't able to travel to him."

"Dr Edmonds isn't fond of coming this far," Mr Lennox agreed. "We'll get a new one soon, I'm sure."

Dr Rasley had tragically perished in a suspicious fire just a few weeks earlier. A new doctor had been hired in London, supposedly, but hadn't arrived yet... perhaps he was waiting until the doctor's cottage had been rebuilt, Bernadette thought. And in the meantime, she, Mr Lennox and Hatfield's three midwives were very nearly run off their feet.

They parted on excellent terms and waved to Young Devon on the way out.

The rest of the morning Bernadette and Brutus were kept busy, walking from house to house to visit the women who needed help.

She kept track of each one in her notebook, but used her own special code for their names, just in case the book ever fell into the wrong hands. Like her Cousin Joshua's, or Reverend Millings'. They'd get a sermon to curl their ears if *he* ever found out the full scope of her activities.

The women paid Bernadette with produce or herbs they grew in their gardens. Sometimes eggs from their chickens, or best of all, honey from a nearby hive. The coming spring would bring out the meadow flowers and bees, once the weather warmed a little more.

Returning to the bookshop after several hours, Bernadette and Brutus deposited their baskets on the counter with a sigh of relief. The baskets were even heavier now than when they'd gone out!

Brutus said, "What a morning!"

"The clove tea will be well-steeped by now," Bernadette said with a grin.

"It doesn't hurt any more," he said quickly.

Louise chuckled and said, "Welcome home, both of you. Mrs Poole has made soup for lunch."

There was a fresh cob loaf of bread in one of their

baskets. It was delicious spread with freshly churned butter and eaten with Mrs Poole's thick parsnip-and-carrot soup. Bernadette ate hungrily, knowing she'd be busy again all afternoon. She had several more patients to visit.

The new doctor couldn't arrive soon enough, though she certainly hoped he'd be a little younger and have more up-to-date training than old Doctor Rasley, Lord rest his soul.

Wednesday was Bernadette's regular day to visit Lord Ferndale and Miss Yates at Ferndale Hall, which was almost ten miles from Hatfield. Although the visit took most of her day, she wouldn't miss it for anything, being extremely fond of the elderly brother and sister, who had been friends of her family for many years and were now relatives-by-marriage. The carriage arrived soon after breakfast to collect her. She waved to Mrs Bell as she climbed into it, just coming out of her house directly across the street from the bookshop. Mrs Bell was one of three midwives in Hatfield, who were all exceptionally busy at this time of year, what with it being about nine months after the various midsummer festivities.

She could call back in to see Mrs Bell on the way home and check if any of the women needed assistance, perhaps with herbs to help to bring in the mother's milk, treat mastitis or childbed infections.

It was lovely to see Lord Ferndale, who insisted that she must now call him 'grandfather' since her sister Estelle had married his grandson Felix, and Lord Ferndale's sister Miss Yates looking so well. Bernadette couldn't stop fretting about them during the cold winter months, but they'd come through the worst of it well. Ferndale Hall's butler Mr

Thorne and the housekeeper Mrs Sykes were grateful for the jar of clove tea, which Brutus hadn't used in the end.

In the glass house, the gardeners were happy to see her and helped with harvesting a few tubers of ginger that Bernadette had planted there a few months earlier. It was a temperamental plant and needed lots of warmth, which made it expensive and difficult to buy. But it was so good for expectant mothers in the early months for keeping their retching at bay.

"Grandfather, I can't thank you and the gardeners enough for growing the ginger. You're making people's lives so much better." She looked happily at the small basket of ginger root the gardener handed her. "It would cost a fortune to buy this much, and I would have to charge far more than most people could afford. Growing our own means I can help so many more people."

"I was thinking," Lord Ferndale said, "I know you usually make a tea or cordial with it, but what if you added the ginger to a lozenge? Would that make it easier for people who can't keep fluids down?"

Bernadette's eyes sprang wide. "That's brilliant! I should have thought of that! Oooh, I think I might call it 'Ferndale's Ginger Relief'."

"An excellent notion, my dear. Now do come inside, Florence will be waiting for us!" He patted her hand kindly and they went indoors for nuncheon.

<hr/>

Back in town later in the afternoon, Bernadette crossed the street to Mrs Bell's house before going back into the bookshop. The midwife looked weary, resting her feet on a footstool as she sipped on a cup of herbal tea. No doubt she'd been getting little sleep of late, with all the births in town. Babies always did seem to come at the most inconvenient times.

"Is there anything I can help with, Mrs Bell?" Bernadette asked.

"Aye, I saw Mrs Pennyrigg today." Mrs Bell sipped her tea and shook her head. "Mr Pennyrigg won't leave her alone, I'm afraid."

"But she has nine children already, and the eldest is barely ten!" Bernadette said, horrified.

"Aye." Mrs Bell eyed her over the rim of her teacup. "She's only just missed her courses, though."

"I'll call in and see her tomorrow," Bernadette said immediately. While it was not an infallible remedy, she had learned of a very particular combination of herbs from her mother, which when steeped into a strong tea and drunk at the correct early stage of one's first missed course, could prevent the pregnancy from progressing any further. Poor Mrs Pennyrigg needed a rest from being pregnant... and Bernadette would take a moment to tell Mr Pennyrigg to leave his wife be for a while too!

Every woman of marriageable age in Hatfield knew what Bernadette's herbs were capable of, and not one of them, not even her ghastly cousin Phoebe, would ever breathe a word about it in the hearing of a man. It was women's business and none of men's, and a woman who betrayed that code would likely find there was suddenly no midwife available if she should happen to need one.

"I've a tonic for you," Bernadette said then, digging in her satchel and handing Mrs Bell a bottle.

"For me?" The midwife looked surprised. "What ever for?"

"For when you get called out in the wee hours and are struggling to find the energy to get out of your warm bed." Bernadette smiled at her. "Might put a hop in your step."

Mrs Bell laughed, but she tucked the bottle away and thanked Bernadette. "You're a good lass, and no mistake."

Making her way back across the street, Bernadette turned her face up to the sky, enjoying the warm spring sunshine. It had been a miserable winter and a wet early spring; today's sunny sky was a pleasant change.

She re-entered the bookshop at the same time as the maid Rosie, who held the door open for her with a friendly smile. Rosie was shy around some people, but could be positively garrulous if she liked someone. She talked a good deal to Bernadette, who had found that Rosie was very well-informed in what people around town were getting up to. Between their housekeeper Mrs Poole, the midwives and Rosie, there wasn't much that happened in Hatfield that Bernadette didn't hear about sooner rather than later.

"Got some news for you, Miss Bernadette." Rosie beamed at her. "New doctor's here."

"In town?" Bernadette stooped to prevent Crafty, the bookshop cat, from dashing out through the open door.

"Arrived this morning, like. Took a room at the Red Lion, on Lord Ferndale's account, since his cottage ain't ready yet." Rosie nodded importantly, obviously pleased to have imparted interesting news.

"Well done, Rosie," Bernadette beamed with the fresh information. A doctor in town at last was so very welcome. There was Farmer Allom, whose shoulder was still not sitting properly after falling from a barn roof. Bernadette had studied diagrams in a medical text and knew the theory of what she attempted, but when she tried it in reality, she lacked the brute strength required to reset the shoulder properly in its socket.

She hoped the new doctor would not be too old and frail for the heavy work that would be required in a town as large as Hatfield.

She marched upstairs and bundled her fresh herbs to hang, then put away the ginger grown at Ferndale Hall, as well as several little treats Miss Yates had insisted she bring home. The lemon biscuits had been particularly excellent; Bernadette considered another one, but she'd had three earlier. She'd leave these for Louise, Brutus and Mrs Poole to enjoy, it was only fair.

Now, where was that list she'd nearly completed? A little more rummaging and she found it.

No time to waste, she skipped down the stairs, waving to Louise and Mr Jackson writing in the ledger behind the counter and headed to the Red Lion.

The landlord, Mr Haye, was delighted to see her and asked what she might need.

"I heard the new doctor has arrived. Which is his room?"

Mr Haye smiled broadly and said, "Aye, you're right! Top of the stairs, last on the right."

Just as she was about to take herself up the stairs she paused to quickly ask, "What's his name?

"He goes by Williams," Mr Haye said.

With that knowledge, Bernadette took to the stairs and arrived only slightly out of breath. What with rushing from house to house to help people, she was used to putting on the pace.

She knocked on the door and called out, "Doctor Williams? Are you there?"

There were footsteps, then the door opened a little. She had been hoping for a doctor younger than Rasley, but the face she saw appeared far too young to be a doctor at all. Perhaps this was the doctor's son. He might have brought him along?

"Hello?" The man was a little over middle height with dark hair and eyes, and skin that appeared to have a tan far too early in the year. As if he'd lately returned from sunnier climes, like Portugal or Spain.

"I'm looking for Dr Williams," she said. "I'm Bernadette Baxter from Baxter's Fine Books, which is just next door."

"I am Doctor Williams," the man said.

"But you can't be. You're only four and twenty if you're a day!"

"I can be, and I am. You're right about my age, though. Good guess." He opened the door a little wider and she could see past him into a comfortable room and a badly damaged open travelling cabinet with different sized drawers.

"Gosh, what a beautiful cabinet, but why is it so scuffed?"

He turned and looked back at it. Some sections were polished to a high gleam, but there were large chips of timber missing from the sides and two buckled belts held the whole cabinet together. "It got me through the war."

"Can't imagine you were in service very long?"

"Three years," he replied with a slow blink of those dark eyes that seemed to see through her. Then he added, "Three *very* long years."

Bernadette nodded and still couldn't quite fathom how

he could look so young. People who returned from war looked haggard and older than their years, in her experience! He must have signed up fresh out of the school room.

Still looking at that intriguing cabinet, she said, "We have a good number of skilled tradesmen in Hatfield, but they are busy with repairs after the ah…" she stopped herself. Dr Williams would know why. "Anyway, I brought a list of patients who I think you should see first."

She handed it over with a flourish, walking just over the threshold of his room, but standing near the open doorway.

Dr Williams looked at her in a slightly puzzled way and shook. "That's all very well, but I'm here under the auspices of Baron Ferndale, so I only take orders from him."

Bernadette puffed herself up to her full height, which really wasn't much, and said, "I'm Lord Ferndale's granddaughter, he asked me to provide you with this list."

Dr Williams tilted his head with suspicion. His voice was accusatory. "I understood he had only one grandson, who is currently in Ireland with his new bride."

Bernadette beamed at that. "Correct. The bride is my sister, Estelle Baxter, and now Lord Ferndale insists we all call him 'Grandfather'."

His confidence dimmed, shoulders slumping slightly.

She inwardly cheered her success. "The list. See to it."

"Now see here," he said.

"No, *you* see to the list." She put her hands on her hips and stared at him.

Really, this was a dreadful beginning! If the new doctor wasn't going to listen to her, how would he ever learn what the people of Hatfield needed?

About The Authors

Catherine Bilson and Ebony Oaten are long-time collaborators, creating bestselling multi-author Regency romance anthologies over many years.

At the 2024 Romance Writers of Australia conference in Adelaide, they were busy running the Indie Book Store when they came up with the idea for this series. A bookshop would feature strongly - they were living their fantasy of selling books to readers anyway.

Why not set an historical series in a bookshop itself? With sisters who each find love in a bustling town. Instantly they brainstormed complications and issues - what if their father raced off to France after Napoleon was exiled away on Elba, to gather rare books? The characters weren't to know Napoleon would escape only a few months later and wreak havoc on France!

Also, at this conference, Catherine won the RUBY - the Romantic Book of the Year award - for her novella *The Bride Said No*. This novella had started life in one of their collaborative anthologies, of course.

Ebony had also won the Ruby several years earlier, for one of her sweet romance novels, *The Girl and The Ghost*.

With their powers of romance combined, surely they could come up with something wonderful.

You can follow the authors by heading to their respective websites and joining their newsletters.

Catherine is here:
www.catherinebilson.com
Ebony is here:
www.ebonyoaten.com

ABOUT CATHERINE:

"I grew up in a 14th century manor house in North Wales and spent most of my youth making up stories about the people who might once have lived in it. I ran off and married a handsome Australian a few years later and now live with him and our two sons in the permanent sunshine of Queensland.

I write original Regency romance, Austen-inspired variations, and Pioneer American romance. I also write contemporary romance and romantic suspense under the pen name Caitlyn Lynch."

ABOUT EBONY:

Ebony is from Melbourne, Australia and used to be a journalist at several suburban newspapers across the city. Then she turned her hand to writing romance and hasn't looked back. She married a Welsh 'boyo' and they are raising their son in Melbourne, where it can be stinking hot one day, pouring with rain the next.

The Bookshop Belles

NOVELS:

Estelle's Ardent Admirer

Marie's Merry Gentleman

Louise's Christmas Champion

Bernadette's Dashing Doctor

EXCLUSIVE BONUS NOVELLA FOR SUBSCRIBERS:

Matthew's Willing Widow

www.ingramcontent.com/pod-product-compliance
Lightning Source LLC
Chambersburg PA
CBHW030613170726
48283CB00002B/582